DAN

BURN

Born in 1970, Dan Smith lives and works in the North East of England where he has a wife and two children to keep him on his toes. He was the winner of a Northern Promise Award for writing in 2005. Burn Out is his first novel, but you can bet it's not gonna be his last.

For Jim, The Globe-trotting plumber!

BURN OUT

First published 2006

ISBN 978-1-4116-8785-1

Copyright © Dan Smith 2006

The right of Dan Smith to be identified as the author of this work has been asserted by him in accordance with the Copyright, Designs and Patents Act 1988.

All rights reserved. No part of this publication may be reproduced, stored in or introduced into a retrieval system, or transmitted, in any form, or by any means (electronic, mechanical, photocopying, recording or otherwise) without the prior written permission of the publisher. Any person who does any unauthorized act in relation to this publication may be liable to criminal prosecution and civil claims for damages.

All characters in this publication are fictitious and any resemblance to real persons, living or dead, is purely coincidental.

DAN SMITH

*For Divya.
She reads my words
and scratches her head when
they make no sense.*

BURN OUT

Dan Smith

BURN OUT

BURN OUT

DAN SMITH

THIS COULD HAPPEN IN ANY CITY. YOURS, MINE; THEY'RE ALL THE SAME.

BURN OUT

SUNDAY 19TH DECEMBER

BURN OUT

JACK

The air in the car was thick with the stink of smoke and sweat and blood and fear.

I thought for a while and said, 'Okay, so this guy walks into a bar, right...'

'Oh, come on Jack.' He was interrupting me before I'd even started.

I looked at Sean from the corner of my eye. 'What? What's wrong?'

'Well, it's not very original is it?'

'Eh?'

'I mean, how many jokes start out like that? *So this guy walks into a bar*. Anyway, is it a bar or is it a pub? When you say 'bar', it makes me think of something American. You know, like 'Cheers' or something. But if you say '*pub*', then it's more...well, it's more English, isn't it? You know, makes you think of cold nights, pints of beer, pork scratchings and chicken in a basket. That kind of thing. I mean, who the fuck eats pork scratchings anyway?' Sean was rattling now, excited that we were on our way and wound-up about what we were going to do. Any normal person would've been exhausted after what he'd been through, but he was probably thinking that the fun wasn't over just yet.

I shook my head to clear the dust and chase away my brother's comments. 'Whatever,' I said. 'It doesn't really matter.' Christ, I felt as if I'd have to scrape out the inside of my skull with a spoon to remove the fuzz that had built up in there over the past few days.

'Matters to me, Jack.'

I took a deep breath. 'Okay, which d'you prefer? *Pub* or *Bar*?' In the past twenty-four hours I'd been tied up, beaten up and shouted at. I'd been tricked, kicked and humiliated. I'd been threatened and I'd been lied to. I was more tired than I'd ever been in my life and by all rights I should've been dead. And the driving conditions were murder so I reckon I'd had just about as much as I could take.

'Pub,' he said. 'And there's no need to get arsey.'

'All right, Sean. Fine. It's a pub. And I'm not getting arsey.'

'Good.' Sean touched his lips with his right hand, ignoring the tremble, and allowed smoke to trail around his nose and about his forehead.

'Good.' I risked closing my eyes for just a second. I wanted to look away from the road altogether, squeeze my eyelids shut and wish everything gone. I wanted to say 'there's no place like home', click my heels three times and wake up in Kansas. I wanted to be anywhere but here.

I raised a hand and rubbed my face before starting again. Sean liked a good joke and it was usually the best way to calm him down. 'Right. So this crocodile walks into a bar, sorry, **pub**, and goes up to the barman...'

'Hang on a minute. Why's the guy suddenly a crocodile?'

'Hm?'

'Why is the *guy* suddenly a cro-co-dile?'

'Because I changed the joke, Sean.'

'Why? Why would you do that? Right in the middle, I mean. Why would you change the joke right in the fuckin' middle? You trying to confuse me?'

I turned my face away from him as another car overtook us with a swish of rubber on wet tarmac. Then I looked back so that Sean could hear me. 'No, I'm not trying to confuse you. You said it wasn't very original so I changed it.'

'Yeah, but that doesn't mean I don't want to hear it. I mean, what else is there to do?'

'Look, do you want me to tell this joke or not?' I felt my voice tighten, the seconds were running out and I was just about to hit zero.

'Yeah. Sure. All right. Go on,' Sean settling back again.

I took a breath. 'Right. So this *crocodile* walks into a *pub*. It's a traditional...English... *pub*. Pork scratchings, dark beer, chicken in a fuckin' basket...'

'Yeah, yeah, all right.'

'So. The crocodile goes up to the barman and orders a pint of lager. Not dark beer, not diet Pepsi and not bitter fuckin' lemon. He orders lager, all right? Lager. And the barman says... 'Why the long face?''

For a second, just a fraction, all I heard was the radio and the road, then Sean's saying, 'Right. Then what?'

'Hm?'

He's turning in his seat. 'Well, then what happens?'

Keeping my eyes on the road. 'What d'you mean *'then what happens?'* That's it, Sean. That's the joke.'

'*'Why the long face?'*? Is that funny? I don't get it.'

'It's a crocodile, Sean.'

'You're winding me up.'

'It's a crocodile. It has a long... oh, forget it. I give up.'

'No. I won't forget it. You haven't finished the joke. Either that or you're taking the piss. What happens next?'

'Fuck, I wish you were someone else,' I banged my fist on the steering wheel.

I felt his eyes on me for a while and then Sean slipped further down his seat saying, 'Yeah. Yeah, me too.'

I took my eyes off the road and looked at my brother. Motorway lighting pulsed into the car and an orange glow was cast across Sean's tired face. Black, orange. Black, orange. Black, orange. The light made him look drawn and unusual. His cheeks were sallow and pulled tight against his skull so that his face looked like an x-ray picture as it repeatedly shone and then faded. And when the headlights of an oncoming truck stared directly into the windscreen, I could see that Sean's eyes looked dry and dead, the bruises shining gray like mould on an orange.

I looked back at the road and forced myself to concentrate. Looking through the thin fog and snow was like looking through cataracts so I focused on what I could see of the white lines to give myself a point of reference. But the lines became one, even at low speed, and I watched them being eaten by the bonnet of the car.

Long nights in a hotel kitchen washing the dishes of the rich had paid for that car. Hours up to the elbows in scalding water; reddened hands and aching feet. Scraping and scrubbing and cleaning. And then days on the cold factory floor, twisting and cutting for less than minimum wage. Punctured fingers on the production line. Shit, a lot of toil and trouble had paid for that car, it was my pride and joy, *mine*, I'd earned it - worked for years to scrape together enough money to buy it, fix it up, put some sound in it. And now it was all gone, carried away by a gunshot on the wind.

We'd have to dump it. I'd seen enough TV shows and films to know that cars pick up evidence. Scratches, dents, tiny flecks of paint, pieces of fabric, hair, bone, brains and blood. These things stick to the inside of a car as sure as iron filings stick to a magnet. These things get everywhere - under your fingernails, behind your ears, in your mouth, your clothes. You watch a film, any film, and you know this. You see experts in paper suits and paper shoes carrying clear plastic bags. They pick up stuff. They find DNA. They catch killers.

I took a cigarette from the open packet on the dash and sniffed it before putting it between my lips. I watched the coloured reflection of the pack in the windscreen as the wipers repeatedly washed it away, like they were trying to rub out a stubborn stain.

My mouth was dry and the filter stuck to my bottom lip. I clicked open the dented gold Zippo which lay beside the packet and touched the flame to the tip of the cigarette. The first drag is always the best and I felt myself relax a little, just a little. A pleasant buzz numbed my brain for a second, but that was all. I took the cigarette from my mouth and a small piece of skin came away from my lip where it had been stuck. I winced and touched it with my tongue, the taste of blood bringing a memory.

As soon as I could, I'd report the car stolen. The police would find it burned out down by the quarry - nothing unusual about that - it wouldn't be the first car to be torched down there and I was pretty sure it wouldn't be the last. It would be painful, but on the whole, ditching the car would be easy. Get out, pour on petrol, open Zippo, avoid fire. It should be easy. It was the other thing that was going to be the problem. Moving the body.

Once again I looked over at my brother. My brother, Sean. He looked wired, sure, but normal enough, tapping his fingers on the dash, in time with the monotonous teeny-bop trash which rattled on the radio, but I could tell he was *this* far away from tipping right over.

Heavy baggage hung under his bloodshot eyes and he was smoking even more than usual. The muscles bulged and pumped along his jaw-line as he ground his teeth, and the only time he stopped grinding was when he took a long drag on the stubby cigarette which was jammed into the first knuckle of his right hand. His body just soaked up that nicotine like an old oily rag. I used to joke that if Sean had his lungs squeezed out, there'd be enough tar in there to make us rich.

'Have you any fucking idea what you've just done?' I didn't really want to talk about it, but I couldn't help myself. Like scratching an itch when you know you shouldn't. My voice was low and hoarse and I kept it as quiet as possible. I'd done a lot of talking over the past few hours and my throat felt like it had been scraped down with the flat edge of a razor blade.

Sean didn't reply, though, he just carried on drumming his fingers, smoking his cigarette, dropping ash, and nodding his head up and down. The glowing end of the cigarette was gently finding its way towards his yellowed fingers and I was sure that it must be hot on his knuckles, but Sean made no attempt to move it.

'Did you hear what I just said?' I raised my voice this time.

'Yeah, yeah, I heard.'

'So?'

'So what? What do you want me to say? Yes. Yes, of course, I know what I just did.' He snapped his head around to look at me. 'Anyway, it was a crap joke. I liked the one about the duck better.'

'Fuck the joke. What about Magda?'

'What about her? You saw what she was gonna do, I had to do something. Anyway, I didn't like her much.'

'You didn't like her much? Jesus Christ Sean, you didn't like her much? Jesus.' I stared at the road and tried not to think about the blood.

Sean stopped nodding to the beat from the radio and a smile cracked his sunken features. Chirpy music continued to waft into the car and surround us. 'It'll look good won't it?' he said.

'What will?'

'When it all goes up. The fire, I mean. When we burn her up. Course, when they find her, it'll be your car she's in.' He's staring at me now. '*Yours*.'

I was still for a moment, feeling his eyes on me. 'Doesn't matter,' I said. 'They'll have it down as stolen. Probably never find it, anyway.'

'But if they do, they'll tell him. You hadn't thought of that, had you? They'll tell Montoya.'

I searched my brother's eyes. Shit, it was going to be a long night.

SATURDAY 18TH DECEMBER

BURN OUT

SEAN

I stopped at the end of a trail of dying footprints and listened. I could hear a motor running, chugging away out there somewhere, and cocked my head to see where the sound was coming from but couldn't. It didn't bother me, though; just hearing it was enough, so I spread my arms and leaned back to look up into the sky while behind me, the giant gray door slid and clattered along its runners. I didn't flinch, I'd heard it a hundred times before, I just closed my eyes against the falling snow and widened my mouth into a grin. No more gray walls, no more gray doors, no more gray fences or faces. No more razor wire, it was all behind me now. I stuck my tongue out and caught a flake on it, like a fucking kid, my first taste of freedom for a long while, but it tasted of nothing in particular, just spit and water.

The shoulders of my dark jacket were quickly covered and my hair turned white. My feet were cold in unsuitable shoes, my cheeks reddened, the tops of my ears began to sting and the tip of my nose started to burn like hell. The air was mean and it pinched my skin tight like it was a couple of sizes too small for my head but I ignored all those things and stayed like that for a while. Face up, arms out, just trying to feel good about myself, trying to feel *clean*. Didn't work, though, just wasn't me.

'Bollocks to this.' I was bored of the feeling of the cold air on my face. I thought it would be different, expected it to feel pure, fresh, new. I thought it would make me feel free, but nothing had changed, everything was still the same, I was still me. Maybe I'd had too long to think about what it would be like, and everyone knows things are never as good as you think they're going to be.

Behind me the door finally banged shut, muffled voices, a loud buzzer and then everything was quiet except for the sound I'd heard before. The car chugging away, closer now. I leveled my head and looked across to the other side of the empty road. There was a sky blue car parked up and the motor was still running, puking gray fumes out into the snowfall. The side windows were covered in thick condensation and I strained to see the driver but couldn't make out anything more than a faint shadow. I took a step closer and stooped for a better look, hands on my knees, having a feeling about that car and knowing that when the window went down, I'd be looking at Jack.

Sure enough, the rubber seal at the top of the window cracked and the glass jerked down into the door, an inch at a time. The driver was leaning across the seat, working at the old fashioned handle and I'm thinking for Christ's sake, the car doesn't even have electric. I thought everyone had electric these days. When he was done he turned his face up towards me. We breathed steam and looked at each other through the snow, neither of us smiling. I knew he'd come. He was as predictable as ever.

'Well, what you waiting for?' Jack said. 'Get in.'

I didn't need to be asked twice - I was starting to freeze my tits off out there on the pavement and the car looked warm. I held my coat shut with one hand and jogged across the road without looking. My leather-soled shoes were worse than useless on the ice and I skidded a couple of times but managed to stay upright. Falling flat on my arse wouldn't have looked good, not cool at all, so I slowed to a walk. Once there, I pulled open the passenger door and dumped myself onto the black fabric seat, bringing with me a rush of winter and the fresh smell of outside. Without turning to look at my brother, I stamped my feet onto the newspaper in the foot well and slammed the door. All I could smell now was the pine air freshener which hung from the rear view mirror. One of those little green cards shaped like a tree.

I rubbed my hands together. They were dry and smooth and felt like they belonged to somebody else. 'It's good to see you, bro,' I said looking down at my fingers.

'Good to see you too, Sean. How you feeling?'

''Bout as good as you might think, I s'pose.'

'Yeah,' he said. 'Yeah. You know, it really *is* good to see you, Sean.'

'Yeah, it's good to be out. You don't ever want to be in there.'

Jack told me he didn't have any plans to go inside, said he wasn't ever going to get put away, and he was right. Jack wouldn't ever see the inside of the hole I'd just stayed in.

My hands were a strange colour of red and blue despite the warmth inside the car so I held them tight together, to keep them from shivering. It looked too much like I was praying so I tried rubbing some life back into them but that didn't make any difference and I gave up, ramming them under my jacket and into my armpits.

'Jesus, it's cold. Couldn't you have organised the weather?' I said.

'There's some gloves in there if you want them,' Jack pointed to the dash in front of me.

This time I looked him right in the eye. 'In the glove compartment?'

'Uh-huh,' said Jack. 'Where else?'

'You've got gloves…' I said, '…in the glove compartment?'

'Yeah, why not?'

'Not chewing gum or maps or parking tickets or…I don't know, maybe a gun?'

'No.'

'You got *gloves*?'

'Yeah.'

'In the glove compartment?'

Jack smiled. He knew I thought he was as straight cut as the purest cocaine - he was the god of everything normal and sensible as far as my world was concerned. I mean, who the hell keeps *gloves* in the glove compartment? My brother Jack, that's who.

I laughed out loud. It was a good laugh, and Jack laughed along with me. He knew that I'd never be like him, but I reckon he loved to be with me all the same, people do, I can make them feel good. And maybe he thought that with a gram of luck and a kilo of hard work he might be able to clean me up a little.

'So, we going to see this new flat of yours, then?' I said, pulling on the gloves. They were navy blue woolen jobs, a little frayed around the edges, but they'd do just fine.

Jack crunched the gears and pulled away from the curb. He said yeah, we were going to his flat. It was a big deal for him, this place, he'd worked hard for it.

'Is it warm?' I said.

'Course.'

'I hope so, Jack, 'cause I'm used to it warm. Shit, I'm used to it fuckin' *tropical.* They keep it hot in there, you know. Reckon it's so you can't be arsed to do anything but sleep. Keep you out of trouble, if you know what I mean.'

'The heating's on,' he said. 'I got some takeaway in the oven, a few cans in the fridge and a couple of packs of cigarettes. Thought we could chill out tonight.'

'Regular little housewife.'

He told me to piss off. 'I just thought you could do with the time, that's all. You know, decide what you're going to do.'

I shook my head. 'No, I was thinking I might hook up with a few old friends and go clubbing. After I get clean, that is.' I needed to wash that place off me.

'You sure that's a good idea? I mean, maybe you should just chill for a bit? You know, take stock.'

'Take stock? You fuckin' kidding? No offence Jack but I don't want to play mumsy tonight. I've had too long to take stock, it's the last thing I want to do. No, I'm thirty-one, not *ninety*-one.'

'But...'

'Uh-uh. No buts, man. Not tonight. I *need* to get out.'

'All right, all right,' he backed off. 'I guess it's been a while. But you'll need to think about it, you know. What you're gonna do.'

'What're you? My fuckin' parole officer?'

He said he was just concerned, that's all, he's my brother for Christ's sake, he's just concerned.

'Yeah, yeah,' I said. 'Well don't be. I've already got a few ideas.'

He asked what kind of ideas.

'Oh, give me a break, Jack.'

'Legal, I hope.'

'Why don't you come too. Tonight, I mean. It'll be fun. We'll hook up with Hornrim and Cleaver. Maybe even Goat.'

'Goat's dead, Sean.' He said it almost like he was pleased to give me the bad news - like he was getting his own back for not wanting to hang out with him, all serious on my first night out.

'Dead? Shit. I bet he went out shooting.'

'No, Sean, he wasn't Butch Cassidy, you know.'

'How then?'

'He took some bad stuff not long after you went in', Jack told me, saying his heart gave up, just popped in his chest like a balloon. Dead. 'No glory in that is there, Sean?'

'What kind of stuff?' I asked.

'Dunno, does it matter? Mind you, it must've been bad. They say there was blood coming out of every hole in his body when they took him in. His mouth, his nose, his ears. I heard he was bleeding from his eyes and his arse, Sean, his *arse* if you can imagine that.' Jack looked at me. 'No glory in that is there?'

I shook my head and screwed up my nose. 'Jesus! I *knew* that fucker would come to a sticky end.'

'Is that all you can say?' Jack keeping his eyes on the road.

'I never liked him. Got any smokes?'

Jack held his breath for a few seconds before taking a packet of Regal from his jacket pocket and throwing them onto my lap. He shook his head, saying, 'Give me one, too,' and he pushed the car lighter in to heat it up.

I handed my brother a cigarette and stretched my legs enough to pull a dented gold Zippo from the hip pocket of my jeans. I flicked the top and spun the wheel, pushing the flame in my brother's direction. He leaned forward slightly to light up just as the car lighter popped out.

He said cheers and blew out the first drag of blue smoke.

When I'd lit my own, I snapped the lighter shut and rolled it across my knuckles like a magician does with a coin. Something I learned inside when there was nothing else to do except maybe read. 'Like it?' I asked my brother.

'The lighter? Sure. Where d'you get it?' Jack flicking his eyes my way.

'I bought it in duty free on the way out, where the fuck d'ya *think* I got it?'

'Okay, what I meant was what did you *do* to get it. You didn't have it when you went in.'

'It's yours,' I said putting it on the dash alongside the packet of cigarettes. 'A present from inside.'

Jack didn't say thanks, he just wound down his window enough to let out some of the smoke.

'We'll call Cleaver then,' I said getting back to it.

'He's dead too, Sean.'

'What?'

The way he told it, Cleaver got mixed up with some local mafia wannabes, right scruffy types, and ended up getting taken out by a couple of big guys, called themselves Sledge and Hammer. The Sledgehammer, if you can believe that. Beat him up a bit, then turned him around and popped him straight through the back of the head. No mercy, no messing, no more Cleaver.

'Fuck!' I smoked in silence for a while, thinking about old times, how things had moved on. 'How about Hornrim? Somebody *must*a killed him by now.'

'Nope. Alive,' said Jack.

'How about that, eh? Hornrim's alive. I'll give him a call.'

The truth of it was that I really didn't give a shit for any of those guys. I didn't care if they lived or died bleeding from their arses, except that they were people I could hang with. I wanted to go out that night, live a little if I could, and I needed some company. Jack wouldn't have been any good - just a couple of beers and he's done for the night.

'Tell me a joke, Jack. You always told a good joke.'

He smiled and told me the one about the talking duck.

After an hour of banter and jokes, we were driving into the centre of Newcastle, Jack steering us into the car park over the road from his block of flats. We went through the underpass on foot. It was dark and smelly, but it wasn't any worse than where I'd just been. He used a swipe card to get into the lobby, if that's the right word for the graffiti covered dump at the bottom of the stairwell, and we tried to hold our breath all the way up in the lift because someone had puked in the corner.

Once we were in the flat, I flopped onto the sofa and lit another cigarette, smoking and chilling while Jack made coffee. I couldn't see an ashtray anywhere in the living room and I reckoned that maybe Jack didn't usually smoke in there, but he'd make an exception for me. When the ash was about to fall off, I leaned forward and tapped it on the edge of a half-full Diet Coke can that was on a coaster on the second hand coffee table. I stayed as I was, sitting on the edge of the sofa with my forearms resting on my knees, and looked around. I had to admit, the place was pretty comfy - a hell of a lot better than some of the shit-holes I'd stayed in over the years. I mean, you wouldn't have wanted to spend too much time in the stairwell or the lifts, but the flat was good.

The wood-chip walls were plain white and looked like they'd been touched up recently. They were bright and clean and the room still smelled of paint. The light bulb hanging from the ceiling had been covered with a round paper lampshade about the size of a football and the carpet was green. It was faded and worn in places around the doors, but it was okay. The sofa was hidden by a badly fitting cover that matched the colour of the carpet and worked hard to disguise the old wreck underneath. It slipped off when you sat down and left bits of dark green fluff all over the floor. Two armchairs were hidden in the same way, they weren't much but he'd done a good job with them. There were cushions too. In fact, there were fuckin' cushions everywhere, and that made me think.

At the far end of the room, to my left as I sat, Jack had set up a place with a table and four chairs - somewhere to eat. The table looked like it was made from cheap wood, but had been spruced up with a couple of silver coloured candlesticks with half-melted white candles jammed in the top. Probably got them in the charity shop, that's my Jack. To my right, beside the door which led into the small kitchen, there was a shoulder-high bookshelf which matched the table and chairs. There was a load of paperbacks on the shelves but I only recognised one or two of the names printed down the side. I hadn't read any of them but I might have seen the films. Beside them, was a stack of CDs, some good and some crap. I wondered when it was that my brother started listening to Celine Dion and then got to thinking that maybe the CDs weren't all his. Christ, I *hoped* they weren't all his.

Most importantly, though, the flat was warm. I like it warm.

I stood up and went to the window. We were on the sixth floor and the view was good, even if the sight wasn't. Most cities look pretty much the same from above; roads, lights, dirty buildings, shops, people. Crap. Nothing good there. It was nearly dark outside now and I could see my ghost in the window. I dragged on the cigarette and blew the smoke at my reflection. 'Nice place,' I called through to the kitchen.

'Thanks,' Jack said over the sound of the kettle boiling.

'Too neat for a single guy, though. Unless you've gone the other way, that is. You know, kicking with the left foot and all that.'

Jack called through telling me exactly how far I could fuck off, then the kettle clicked off and I heard mugs clink together.

I reckoned that Jack had a woman, I knew he wasn't into guys. Anyway, the flat carried a woman's touch, all that fresh paint, the flowers in the vase on the windowsill, the books, the cover on the sofa. All those cushions. Oh yeah, and the Celine Dion CD. 'What d'you do?' I shouted through. 'Ship her out for a while so the ex-con can come to stay?' The other thing was the smell. The whole place smelled of vanilla – probably coming from the beige plastic mushroom sitting under the coffee table. It was strong, too strong for my tastes, but it smelled better than Deeks and my nine by twelve.

'What?' He was still moving about in the kitchen.

'Keep your brother hidden away. Don't want people to know,' I said.

'What are you talking about, Sean?'

'Or maybe she just stays *some* nights, eh?'

'Whatever you say.'

I moved away from the window and bent down to pick up the book which was on the floor beside the sofa. It was blue and had a picture of a long-nosed fish on the front. 'Since when did you read?' I said.

'I always read.' A teaspoon tinkled in a mug.

'Yeah, maybe, but not this shite. 'The old Man and the Sea'? What the fuck's that? Sounds crap.'

'You wouldn't be interested,' he called.

I'd never heard of it but I flicked the pages and felt the breeze against my face. As it fanned, I noticed handwriting so I ran my thumb across it again. I stopped at the third or fourth page and opened it out so that I could read the inscription. '*Happy Birthday, Jack. I hope you like the book. Lots of love, M. XXX.*'

I knew it. A woman. I might not read books, but I'm not fucking stupid.

I had to admit, Jack seemed to be sorted. Full-time work, dinky little flat, all neat and tidy; woman in tow. He was so different from me that I could hardly believe we'd come from the same sack of walnuts. For Christ's sake, the guy had even *bought* a car. I couldn't believe it when he told me it wasn't stolen. I'd never paid for anything I didn't have to - if I wanted a car, I just used someone else's and then torched it in an empty car park somewhere.

'There's a good film on tonight and I've got beer in the fridge.' Jack coming through from the kitchen. 'How does that sound?'

Well, you got to love him for trying but I told him not tonight bro', I didn't feel like playing housey tonight, and then I asked him where he kept the 'phone.

'In the hall,' he said. 'Help yourself,' but I was already on my way.

JACK

Same old Sean. Same old straight to the point, no beating about the bush Sean. I was hoping to keep him in on that first night, maybe talk about what was next, but after just a few minutes with him in the car I knew it was pointless. He was the kind of person who couldn't be persuaded once he'd decided on something - been like that as long as I could remember – so I took it easy, told him a few jokes. Even so, all the way back to my flat, he was going on about how long he'd been inside and how he needed at least one night to have some fun, get his head together and all that. I wasn't sure if he was trying to persuade me or himself. And when we got back to the flat, he hardly even sat down before he was asking for the phone. He stayed in the hallway, watching me through the open door as he dialed.

It rang for a while before someone picked it up, and then Sean was straight into it saying, 'Hornrim? Hornrim, is that you?'

They talked for a while, swearing and insulting each other, the way guys like them do, and then Sean was asking him what he was up to tonight.

'I thought we could meet up for a drink and then go to a nightclub or something? I'm all choked up and need somewhere to let off. Why don't you come round here later on?'

Sean looked over at me and asked what our address was. It sounded strange, him saying it like that. *Our* address. Up until now it had always been *my* address. I didn't like the idea of Hornrim coming round to my place, knowing where I lived, I wanted to keep those people as far away from me as possible, but I did it for Sean. I told him what it was, slowly so that he could relay it back to Hornrim.

When he was finished, Sean put the phone down and came through to where I was sitting. I sighed and put my coffee mug back on the coaster saying, 'You're definitely going out, then?'

'Yep.' He dropped down beside me on the sofa.

'Well, take it easy won't you?'

'Okay, Mum.'

MAGDALENA

The automatic doors slipped shut behind me, cutting the blast of cold air from the snowy evening outside. I immediately felt the warmth which dropped from the heaters overhead, so I stayed where I was, just for a moment, waiting for the chill to pass from my face. Then I stepped off the wet mat and started across the marbled floor of the Monterez. I headed straight for the stairs, knowing not to take the lifts.

My heels clacked on the hard surface, but it was barely audible over the sounds which filled the place. Guests checking in, people meeting, bellhops pushing trolleys, Christmas music drifting, lift doors opening and closing. Everything was exactly as I expected it to be and I immediately felt enclosed and safe, like all the bad things had been left behind, sliced off when those doors slid shut on my tail.

There was a strong smell of fresh coffee and pastries in the air and it made me think about buying a drink, but it would have to be something stronger than coffee. I looked at my watch, thinking 'well, it *is* after six pm', so I changed course and went towards the lobby bar, looking for a quiet table out of the way. It was much warmer in there, a little smoky, and there was the faint sound of a piano tinkling somewhere just beyond reach. It wasn't crowded but the few men who were in the bar noticed me when I walked in, even those who were not drinking alone. Most gave me a second look. I liked the attention, always thought there's no point in looking good if you don't want anyone to notice you.

'Vodka and tonic,' I said to the waiter who came over. 'Absolut, if you've got it. Ice and a slice. Lime, not lemon.'

He smiled graciously, the way they always do in those places, and put a round paper mat and a small napkin on the table in front of me. He added a bowl of multicoloured nuts that looked far too strange to eat, saying, 'Certainly madam,' and his gaze lingered over me for a second or two more than it needed to. 'Would there be anything else?'

'No there wouldn't. Thank you.'

As I watched him walk away, I took a silver case from my bag and removed a menthol cigarette. I lit it and blew out a pale cloud while turning my hand to inspect my nails. The white filter looked good against the blood red varnish.

I had been sitting with both feet flat on the floor, as if I hadn't quite decided whether or not I was going to stay, but once I'd ordered I felt a little more relaxed so I sat back and looked about. The bar area was cut off from the main lobby by smoked glass walls which reached from floor to ceiling, and it was filled with plants which made it more cosy. They were probably fake but I didn't care enough to reach out and touch one to find out. The seats, arranged in twos and fours, didn't seem in any particular order other than that they made space for a small stage at one end. Only the nearest seats would be able to see the stage, though, because everything was broken up by mirrored pillars.

I looked at myself in the pillar opposite my seat and thought how my make-up was on the heavy side. I'd done it that way to cover the bruises on my cheek. Other than that, my mouth was a little too pinched, my eyebrows a little too high, my nose a little too long and my ears a little too big. I'd had a few nips and tucks here and there, nothing too major, and I was nearly there, but not quite.

The waiter's reflection appeared beside mine and he bent at the waist to place my drink on the round paper mat. 'Madam,' he said.

I thanked him without looking at him.

'Shall I put it on the bill, madam?'

'No.' I laid a note on the table, thinking how Tony had told me not to sign anything, not to talk to anyone. No names, no room number. 'Keep the change.'

I squeezed the slice of lime against the inside of the glass with the cocktail stirrer and looked out across the lobby. And that's when I noticed him, the funny little man.

He wasn't actually looking at me now, he was standing by reception with his back to me, talking to the concierge, but he *had* been looking at me just a second ago. He turned away just as I glanced up from my drink and I wondered if maybe I was being paranoid, that maybe he was just another lecherous man hoping to get a glimpse of my legs.

Or maybe he was an associate of Rubeno's.

It was a possibility. There was no doubt that Rubeno would send someone after me. I didn't think for a second that he'd give up the box without a fight, that's why I'd been moving from one hotel to the next, but I didn't think they'd be on to me so fast.

I took another sip from my drink and dragged on my cigarette, but didn't take my eyes off him. He wasn't tall, five foot five maybe, not much taller than I was, and he was wearing a strange leather cap that was still wet from the snow outside. His little round spectacles made him look like a mole. Or maybe a rat that was trying to look like a mole.

I stirred my drink and squeezed the lime again as I tried to think if I'd seen him before. His face seemed somehow familiar. Maybe I'd seen him at 'Noir' or perhaps in the town, I just couldn't think.

He nodded at the concierge and turned around. This time he looked straight at me, not at my legs, but at my face and then he shifted his eyes. It was so quick I hardly noticed, but he definitely looked straight at me. And what made me suspicious was that he'd looked at my face, nothing else, and there weren't many men who did that.

He didn't look at me again as he crossed the lobby, but I knew he had to be following me because I'd been told what to look for, the signs people make without knowing it. And this man was almost making a *point* of not looking at me.

He came directly into the bar and sat down with his back to me, ten feet away, where he could watch me in the mirror. His eyes flicked up and met mine for a second time and then I was sure. He *was* following me. There was no doubt about it. I thought for a moment and drained my glass. Then I sat forward and signaled the waiter to come over.

DEEKS

Damn it. She'd spotted me. She must have done, she couldn't have missed it. She looked up and I turned away. It was obvious, too damn obvious. This whole business was getting me nervous and I was starting to make mistakes because I was too busy trying *not* to make them. If this went on any longer, I'd have that tick back in my eye and I'd start to lose my hair again.

I'd only just started checking the hotels and it was completely by chance that I'd found her so quickly. I'd come into the Monterez, hoping to have a nose around and there she was, clear as day, strutting through the doors and crossing the lobby like she owned the place. Straight into the bar, she was, throwing her fur coat over the arm of the chair and sitting there with her legs crossed, that black dress lifting high enough to flash off those thighs. Low cut on the neckline and high cut on the leg-line. She didn't try to pull it down like women normally do, though, like they're wishing they hadn't worn something so short. No, she let it stay right where it was, showing everyone how fine she was. The high-heels looked good on her, too, nice and shiny on the end of those long legs and I reckoned she'd be wearing stockings – black ones, the kind that stay up on their own. Nothing else under there, mind you. Maybe a bit of perfume, a little damp squirt of number five around the top, but that's all.

I reminded myself what I was there for, and switched my focus. I knew I'd have to play this one carefully now that I'd found her, so I hung back out of sight, thinking that Sawn-off would be a happy man when he heard that I'd found her so quickly. If things panned out in the right way, there might be a little bonus in it for me.

I went over to the concierge's desk, asked a question and pretended to listen to the old man's drivel about room rates and special offers, but all the time I had my eye on her, sipping her drink in the bar. And that's when she sussed me. She looked up, just a glance, and her eyes swept right across mine. I turned away, back to the old man, but I knew she'd seen me. I'd have to do something to put her mind at rest, so I nodded to the concierge, and then turned to face out into the lobby. Magda was still watching me through the smoky glass so I made eye contact with her, briefly, letting her think I was eyeing her up. If I acted like a guest, maybe she'd drop her guard and let it go.

Seeing her sip her drink like that, all relaxed, made me want something myself. I didn't usually get so worked up, not on a straight follow job, but this one was different. There was a lot at stake, and a drink might have helped to calm my nerves. My heart was starting to pound, I could feel the sweat forming on my brow, and that bloody tick was itching to come back so god knows I needed *some*thing. When I was inside, the shrink told me to think about running water if I felt the jitters coming back, so I tried thinking about rivers and streams, but that took me to taps and urinals and then all that running water just made me need to piss. I gave up and crossed the lobby, feeling more nervous than I should've for a job like this. It was just a follow job, that's all, just a follow job for Christ's sake.

I wandered into the glassed off area, not in a hurry, and ordered a Perrier at the bar, deciding that the alcohol was a bad idea. Once I had the drink, I took a seat in plain view, like I had nothing to hide. I sat with my back to her, but I could still see her in the reflective surface of the pillar I was facing. I let our eyes meet again, a quick flash so she'd think I was eyeing her up, and then I looked away.

I must've done the right thing, because finally she seemed to settle back, probably thinking she was paranoid and needed to get a grip. She raised her drink and drained it in one go, like she was trying to calm her nerves, then attracted the waiter's attention, calling him over. She said a couple of words, maybe ordering a second drink, and then he walked away with her empty glass. She carried on smoking her cigarette, exhaling it upwards like she was the queen of bloody Sheba, but she wasn't looking in my direction anymore. She'd switched her attention to the waiter, probably checking him out, dirty bitch.

Eventually she crushed her cigarette into the ashtray, moved as if to straighten her dress and... shit, my view was blocked. I was so busy watching her, I hadn't noticed the waiter. He stepped between me and the mirror, all black suit, bow tie and smarm, saying, 'From an admirer, Sir,' and putting a cocktail glass on the table. It was huge, with fruit hanging off it and umbrellas sticking up from it, looking like Carmen Miranda's head.

'Admirer?'

'Yes sir.'

'What admirer?' Then it clicked into place. The intrusion had caught me off guard, I'd made another mistake. It took me about five seconds to realise that it was a ruse, but that was all she needed. I put out one hand to push the waiter aside while leaning round to look at the mirror.

She was gone. Shit. Damn her to hell.

I whipped around in my seat just in time to see her disappear into the stairwell. She was carrying the fur coat and moving quickly.

I pushed the waiter away from me saying, 'Get the fuck out of my way' and caught my knees on the underside of the table as I stood up. The cocktail glass slid off, emptying the contents down the waiter's trousers and the glass shattered on the floor. I ignored it, leaving the bar and hurrying across the lobby. I dodged a brass trolley of bags, clipping the bellhop and pushing him to the floor, then I pulled open the door and stepped into the stairwell, but Magdalena was long gone. It seemed that she wasn't just smart, she was fast too.

I looked up and around, leaning over to see as far up as I could but she wasn't there. A door banged but there was no way of telling which floor it was on. It was a good move her not taking the lift, knowing I wouldn't be able to see what floor she got out on. The hotel had maybe ten floors and she could've sneaked out into anyone of them. All she had to do now was lay low for a while, wait until the coast was clear and then off to her room, if she even had one.

I took off my specs and polished them with a handkerchief as I went back into the lobby.

*

The young blonde at reception smiled as I approached. Her badge told me that she was called Helen and I liked the look of her. She had naïve blue eyes and the buttons on her blouse were drawn tight.

'Hello, sir. How can I help you?'

'I was wondering if I might leave a message for a friend of mine,' I said. I smiled as much as I could but I wasn't happy. I could feel sweat on my brow and I dabbed it with the hanky I was still holding.

'Is he a guest at the hotel, sir?' She had a distasteful look on her face now and she lifted her nose like there was a spot of turd on her top lip. I changed my mind about liking the look of her and said 'Yes, she is.'

'No problem at all, sir. Do you have the message?'

'I'll have to write it down.'

She handed me a piece of notepaper and an envelope, and I used one of the pens on the counter to scribble a few words before putting the note inside the envelope and sealing it. I wrote 'Magdalena Montoya' on the front.

Helen took the envelope, scanning the front and saying, 'Do you know what room she's in, sir?'

'Afraid not.'

I watched her fingers on the keyboard as I waited for her to find the room number on the computer. She had pretty hands, good manicured nails, long fingers, and I tried hard not to think about what they'd look like touching me. I thought about my plan instead. Once she'd found the room number, I'd see which of the pigeonholes behind reception she put the message into. That would give me the room number I wanted.

She was tapping for a while before she looked up at me saying, 'I'm sorry, sir, we don't have a guest under that name.'

I bit my lip. 'Are you sure you got the spelling right? She's definitely staying in this hotel.'

'Yes, I think so. M-O-N-T-O-Y-A? No, I'm sorry, there's no one under that name,' she confirmed. 'I've checked it twice now, Sir.'

'Perhaps she's using her maiden name. Ruiz. Try that. R-U-I-Z.' I took off my specs and dabbed at my brow again. My left eye was just begging to twitch, I could feel it pulling all the way down my cheek.

'I'm sorry, sir, there's no one under that name either.'

That bitch Magda had outdone me at every turn. She couldn't have set it all up on her own, she wouldn't have known how to run from someone like me, she wasn't clued up enough. She was just a bloody housewife, for God's sake, she must've been getting advice from someone.

'Check again,' I said. '*Please*. Check again.'

'But, sir, I've already...'

'Fucking check it again.'

She turned back to the computer, her fingers working hard, her face flushed red.

'It *has* to be one of those names. Check them both again.'

She looked up. 'I'm afraid they're really not on the computer, Sir.'

I was about to suggest that I help her stick the computer somewhere dark and painful when a hand grabbed my shoulder and a voice said 'If you'd like to follow me, Sir.'

I turned around, face to face with hotel security. The guy was wearing a chocolate brown uniform and probably wished he was a plod but never made it through the physical. Standing beside him was the cocktail drenched waiter.

'I'm afraid I'm going to have to ask you to leave,' he said. 'Now.'

Damn, damn, *damn*.

BURN OUT

RUBENO 'SAWN-OFF' MONTOYA

I leaned back in the expensive leather swivel chair and linked my fingers behind my head thinking - damn, I'm good; you'd have to get up early in the morning to get one over on Sawn-off Montoya. People had tried to trick me before, but it was different this time. I was older and wiser and it was all a little closer to home. That bitch Magdalena thought she could fool me and take off with the box, but I'd clocked her faster than she could drop her knickers for whichever dead man it was she'd been screwing. And Deeks had phoned through in record time.

'D'you want us to hurt her?' asked Sledge, standing in front of my desk. His voice was deep and raw, like he might've had carpet tacks and broken glass for lunch, and his head was shaved as bald as a balloon.

'No,' I told him. 'Just give her a scare.'

She'd been screwing around behind my back, but I didn't want to hurt her. Maybe I was getting too old for this shit. Anybody else, they only get one chance and then all ties are cut; one screw up and they're lying face down in wet soil with a hole punched through the back of their sorry head, but this was different, this was Magdalena. I mean, I wouldn't exactly describe it as love, nothing like that – not in the way that maybe a man *usually* loves his wife, anyway. Not like 'Honey I'm home'... 'What's for dinner?'... and all that crap. More in the sense of ownership, like a man cares for his dog. You take your dog for walks, you feed him, you give him somewhere to live, you pet him, you do stuff, you're together, you have an understanding. He shits on the carpet you don't take him outside and cut his throat. No, you rub his nose in it, give him a kick and then he's out of the house. Same thing with Magdalena, but there were two important things to take care of first. Important thing number one was my reputation. I couldn't let her ruin that, so I had to be seen to do something - it just wouldn't be good for me to sit around on my arse while she screwed about. But the second thing was even more important. The box. I couldn't let her take the box and get away with it.

'You sure? Just a scare?' That hoarse voice breaking into my thoughts again.

'Yeah I'm sure.'

'We could hurt her just a little bit. Nothing too serious. No extra charge. Maybe just break...'

'What, you got a problem with your hearing?' I started to stand up but stopped myself and relaxed back into the chair, thinking there's no point in taking it out on Sledge.

'No. No problem with my hearing,' he was saying. 'You just leave it to us. We'll sort it out.'

I expected him to leave, but he didn't. Instead he shifted his body weight from one foot to the other and then back again, looking like a kid who's about to piss his pants. 'What?' I said. 'Is there a problem?'

'Just a small one,' he said. 'With my bank manager.' He turned his hands out and shrugged his oversized shoulders. They were the kind of steroid induced shoulders that start somewhere just underneath the ears, where you'd normally expect to see a neck.

I pulled the swivel chair forwards and opened a drawer in the right hand side of my desk. It was a large mahogany job, the sort I'd always dreamed of owning, expensive and important; always impressed people when they came into my office. A man like me should always be seen behind a big desk if he wants to be taken seriously. I took out a wedge of cash as thick as a telephone directory from the drawer and fanned the corner with my thumb. Some used, some crisp, but all of it good and spendable, the smell lifting up to me as I flicked through it. Money isn't everything, they say, it just buys everything.

I dropped it between a pile of letters and the large marble cigarette lighter that Magda had bought me last Christmas. It looked rich but had stopped working a long time ago. 'Take it,' I said.

Sledge made a move for the cash but I beat him to it, covering it with one hand. 'You won't fuck this up,' I told him.

He looked at me for a moment but didn't speak.

I took away my hand and nodded. 'Okay, it's yours.'

Sledge picked it up, split it in half, and slipped it into his inside pockets saying something like, 'I won't count it.' He adjusted the line of his black suit and turned to leave the office. His frame filled the doorway and he moved slightly to one side to make his exit easier. His back was to the desk when I spoke again.

'And don't forget those pictures,' I said. 'Wilby's coming in tonight.'

'Got the camera already, Gov,' he said, making me wince inside like I do every time they call me 'Gov'. Makes me sound like a fucking bricklayer.

After that, the overbuilt bouncer took his meaty hands and his bald, villainous head out of my presence and quietly closed the door behind him.

I stood up and went to the large window which covered one wall of the office. I twisted the rod to open the silver Venetian blinds and looked out into the club. Sledge was moving down the neon lit stairs which led from the office. He moved with surprising ease and agility for a man of his size and age. His brother, Hammer - who could almost have been his twin - was waiting at the bottom. They spoke for a moment, nodding and looking serious, and then crossed the upstairs dance floor to the bar where the rest of the security guys were waiting for their instructions.

I watched as earpieces were twiddled into cauliflower ears, voice mikes were attached to thick necks and lapels were smoothed down over barrel chests. I had the bouncers out in force every Saturday, because with five dance floors and seven bars in 'Noir', that's a lot of dancers and a lot of drinkers. In my experience, a lot of people means the need for a lot of security, and peace of mind didn't come much better than Austin and Howard Taylor. Sledge and Hammer. Sledgehammer Security.

I closed the blinds and went back to my desk, picking up the heavy crystal glass which had about two inches of Jack Daniels in the bottom. The fumes made my eyes water and the liquid burned my throat but there's no point in drinking if it's too smooth, you want it to slap you, remind you who you are.

I sat down and replaced the tumbler on the desktop, watching the crystal, thinking about Magda, wondering who she'd dropped her knickers for. I hoped, for his sake, that it had been worth screwing my wife. Christ, I'd even named a nightclub after the bed-hopping bitch. The betrayal was bad – shit, the betrayal was squeezing my insides like a rusty vice - but that wasn't the whole of it. After all, once she was gone, she was gone, nothing I could do about it even if I really wanted to. But she'd taken the box, and after everything I'd gone through to get hold of it in the first place, *that* was the real twister.

I sipped the bourbon again and held it in my mouth for a while, keeping it behind my teeth and breathing in over it. I sucked the fumes straight to my head and pictured her leaning into that car, puckering up for whoever had been inside.

She wasn't beautiful when I met her. She had one of those faces that looked like she'd been sucking on a lemon for too long - pursed lips and raised eyebrows – but surgery and collagen injections had sorted that out. That was her idea not mine. It was her body that had caught my eye that first time; curves like Sophia Loren and tits like Marilyn Monroe, I used to tell her. She had the kind of figure that could make men weak and she knew how to work it. I loved it when people checked her out, thinking I wasn't watching.

I gave her the money and lifestyle she wanted, and in return she looked after the house, arranged parties. She looked good for my associates and I took care of business. We worked for each other, but she could be a righteous pain in the arse saying, 'Ruby, I thought we might have a soiree at the weekend.' A fucking *soiree*, if you can believe that. Jesus.

'Don't call me Ruby, honey,' I'd say. 'It doesn't suit the image.' She always called me 'Ruby' or sometimes, even worse, she called me 'Benny'. *Benny*, for fuck's sake. I mean, Benny sounds like a fat old dog or an ice-cream seller, and 'Ruby' made me sound like a hairdresser. What Magdalena didn't understand was that a man's name is important. 'Mr. Montoya' is okay for the respectable guests in the club - the politicians and the TV stars - but a guy called Sawn-off, now he'll eat your heart and smile while he wipes the blood off his chin. A guy called Sawn-off means business. Anyway, I earned the name, why the fuck shouldn't I use it?

SLEDGE

'Right, you lot, listen up,' I said, looking around at my people who were gathered by the bar. I knew that Mr Montoya would be watching from the window in his office, so I wanted everything to be just right.

We were standing at the edge of the upstairs dance floor, in the area that was reserved for lighter, quieter music. It was a favourite of the more mature nightclub guest and you needed special membership to get in. Most people who came up here were VIPs - Mr Montoya's special guests - and, of course, the people who wanted to be seen with them. Mr Montoya said he wanted there to be something for everyone in 'Noir' so he'd set the place up a bit different from your average club. Something for everyone. Four floors of fun. There was the quiet, exclusive bit upstairs, where we were now, and at the other end of the scale there was the basement level which was all set up for the lap-dance fan, with its feast of gyrating titties and fleshy arses. Thirty quid and one of the girls would take you to a quiet area for a personal jiggle. No touching, though, otherwise things could get nasty.

The first and second floor areas played the latest dance music, but that wasn't for me, all that electronic fast-beat shit screwing my head up. I tried to keep out of there as much as I could, let the younger guys work them, only going down every now and then to see how things were going. They were geared for the young at heart, the ones who wave their hands in the air and spin about like they're out of their heads. No drugs allowed, mind you, not as long as my people were running the door.

'We want a quiet night tonight, boys,' I looked at them in turn, making eye contact with each of them, letting them know who was in charge. 'No rough stuff.' I paused. 'Unless totally necessary, that is.' It raised a few smiles and lightened the mood, but they knew where they stood.

'We've got a few special guests coming in later tonight,' I went on. 'So I want everyone on their best behaviour.' As I was talking I could feel the bulk of the cash that Mr. Montoya had given me weighing down my jacket so I fastened the buttons and smoothed it over. I wasn't an easy nut to crack, but it was better if nobody knew that the money was there.

'And remember the rules,' I said as Hammer came up alongside me. 'No tie - no entry. No collar - no entry. No money - no entry. No drunks, no druggies, no jeans, no sneakers and no t-shirts.'

'Aye, and no fuckin' monsters,' Hammer said with a smile that made him look like a six foot four, sixteen and a half stone baby. He rubbed his hand over the top of his head and looked down at the dark blue carpet. When he looked up again, his smile had gone. 'Let's keep it smooth,' he said. His voice was low and everyone listened. 'You all know the score. No trouble. Especially not inside. Anything needs to be sorted, take it outside, but be nice. *Always* be nice.'

'Okay,' I said. 'Here's how we'll start. Pete, I want you take first shift on the door. Dave, you go with him.'

They nodded.

'And remember to smile, Dave. We don't want to scare anyone away, do we? We're security, remember, not bouncers. We're professional...'

'...and we care,' said the Hammer, batting his eyelids.

I let my brother take over and finish with the instructions while I took one of the guys, Simon, to one side saying that I had a special job for him to do. Something for Mr. Montoya that involved a politician, a camera, and a dancing girl. As we talked, staff began to drift in and dim lights came on behind the bar. Bottles of spirits lit up and blue and green neon strips which ran around the room jumped into life and chased each other about the walls. Things were starting to pick up and within just a few blinks the place was full of sound. Voices whispered, then mumbled and then grew louder as others joined in. Refrigerators hummed and glasses clinked as the staff lined them up on the black marble bar top. Soon the place would be full of people, drinking and dancing and having a good time, and we all had to be ready for them.

When I was done telling Simon what I needed him to do, I gave him the digital camera - one of those dinky, matchbox sized jobs - and told him to watch the door to the upper area. That's where I needed him to stay. Once the guests arrived, he could bring the girls up and get close to Wilby, just like Mr. Montoya wanted.

After that, I turned back to the others, hearing one of them saying, 'Why don't we let anyone in without a tie on?' It was the new boy, Joe, mouthing off to Hammer. We were testing him out for his first week in Noir, took him on because he was supposed to be some kind of kung-fu expert with a cool head and fast hands. We thought these martial arts guys were supposed to be all discipline and steel balls, but it was starting to look like he had an attitude on him. The week had started out okay, he was nice and quiet, did like he was told, but then his mouth opened up and he had trouble making it stop.

''Cause *Mr. Montoya* says so,' Hammer looked straight at Joe, laid back but mean, like he could have snapped the kid's neck and wouldn't have shed a tear over it. 'House rules, kiddo.'

Joe leaned back against the bar saying, 'The other clubs don't give a toss if you're wearing a tie or not. They just want your money. What makes this guy Sawn-off so special?'

Hammer stayed quiet, probably thinking how to deal with the kid. He'd be wondering whether or not to smack him and I could see the other guys shaking their heads, thinking the kid's going to get a pasting.

'Anyway, you can't move to dance music in a tie,' said Joe.

'Do I look like I give a fuck?' said the Hammer.

'We...'

'Look,' I stepped in. '*Mr. Montoya* likes his customers to wear a tie, so we make sure they wear a tie. This is a particular *kind* of club - not some pokey shit-hole for students and head-bangers. We have a wide selection of the finest Italian silk ties behind the desk at the front. Special guests may borrow one, non-special guests can pay for the privilege. That's all there is to it.'

'Aye, so shut the fuck up about the tie, all right,' Hammer pointing a meaty finger.

'Okay.' Joe shrugged and pursed his lips. He might've thought about pressing it, but for once he kept his mouth shut. Maybe he needed the job.

We finished giving out the instructions and dismissed our people to their posts before starting out on the final check through the club. I cast my eyes around the room again, this time looking for anything that didn't seem right. I took everything in, checking each member of staff getting ready for the night ahead, knowing that you have to be keen, notice every small detail. Nothing was out of the ordinary, though. Cleaning, polishing, preparing, chatting – just the usual stuff.

Satisfied, I turned back to Hammer but he'd moved away and pulled Joe to the far side to have a word. Hammer didn't look so happy, not liking the kid giving him cheek in front of the others, and I could see that his right fist was balled, the knuckles going white.

I was on my way over to calm things down when I caught sight of Deeks on his way up to see Mr. Montoya. He was wearing that flat leather cap pulled low over his brow and a pair of small, round, wire-framed glasses perched on the end of his nose. It looked like someone or something had ruffled his feathers, him being all jittery and nervous looking like that. A little sweaty, too, making me wonder what the sleazy little southerner was up to. Then I remembered the job tomorrow night. Deeks must've been doing some digging - probably following Mrs. Montoya, maybe even rummaging through a few bins, trying to find Mr. Montoya's box so Hammer and I could do our stuff.

He nodded his head at me, by way of acknowledging that I was there and then he slinked up the stairs like the vermin he is. I watched him slide into Mr. Montoya's office and then turned my attention back to Hammer.

'...it's *Mr. Montoya* to you,' he was saying when I came into earshot. Joe didn't look intimidated, but he seemed to have lost a little of his attitude. My brother was almost twice his size and looked as if no amount of kung-fu kicking was going to take him down.

'But everyone calls him sawn-off,' Joe replied.

'Not in here they don't,' I butted in.

'Bu...'

'How d'you think it's gonna look to the guests if we call him 'Sawn-off'?' I said. 'We get all sorts in here, you know. Actors, politicians, judges. Some of them are real high up, personal friends of Mr. Montoya, and we don't want to embarrass anybody, now do we?' I stood close to Joe and looked down at him as I spoke, me on one side, Hammer on the other.

'All right, all right,' he said, 'but why's he called 'Sawn-off'? I heard it's 'cause he's a short-arse and has to wear stack heels; is that right?'

I couldn't help smiling at that one. I mean, I'd heard a lot of people guess at the reasons for Mr. Montoya's nickname, but I'd never heard that one. The kid was a cheeky little fucker and he didn't know when to shut up, but you had to love his turn of phrase. I relaxed a little and lost the look, but Hammer still wasn't impressed.

'Stay right there,' I said to the kid. Then I took my brother's elbow and we walked away from Joe. 'Why don't you finish up the rounds downstairs and I'll set our little friend straight.' I said it quietly, keeping my voice low, so as Joe wouldn't hear.

'You gonna give him the push? Maybe we should just drop him now.'

'No,' I said. 'Give him a chance. I'll sort it.'

'What you gonna tell him?' My brother's breath smelled of the mint tic-tacs he sucked to blast out the ugly stink of coffee breath.

'The Sawn-off story,' I said. We told it to all the new guys.

'You sure? You're gonna keep him on for the night?'

'Yeah.'

He thought about that, his face blanking over and then shrugged, 'Okay.'

I turned back to Joe saying, 'Sit down,' and indicated the corner booth. The material that covered the seats was the same blue colour as the carpet, making them almost invisible. It wouldn't be practical anywhere other than a nightclub, but they were cosy in the dark. When the lights were low and the music was playing, those blend-in seats were more than perfect for a politician who's taking his fancy bit out on the town. Down to Noir for a few drinks and a grope in the dark before racing home for a bit of what the tabloids would like to know about. But that wasn't what I had in mind for Joe.

'Drink?' I said.

'Sure. I'll have a beer.'

I shook my head and looked at him. Stupid kid didn't know anything. Had a lot to learn. 'We don't drink when we're working,' I said. 'Tea, coffee, water - that's fine. Nothing else. Alcohol clouds our judgment, gives us red mist, and that's something we can't afford in our profession.' I leaned over and pointed a finger at him. 'If you drink and you hurt someone bad, then I'm the one pays for it. That's how it works, see. You fuck up, I pay for it. D'you understand?'

'Yeah.'

I put my hands down on the table. 'Good. So, first rule; no alcohol. Second rule; smile for the camera.'

Joe sat back in the comfortable booth, one of those people who always wants to say the last thing. 'I'm hardly going to get drunk on one beer,' he said, folding his arms and sniffing hard so that his face lifted on one side.

I'd seen the same pose a hundred times before from a hundred different people. He thought he was as hard as nine inch nails from Newcastle and that he didn't need to listen to a word I said. 'I don't care if you don't get drunk on *twenty* one beers,' I told him. 'If I catch you drinking on the job, you're out, simple as that.'

Joe sighed heavily and rolled his eyes up to one side. 'All right,' he said. 'I'll go without.'

I smiled and rested my elbows on the table like I was going to tell him a secret. 'There's something else you need to get clear.'

'Yeah?'

'Yeah. See, in here, Mr. Montoya is top. And that means he gets your respect. If you call Mr. Montoya anything *other* than Mr. Montoya, then you're disrespecting the man. And believe me, when you've heard what I'm gonna tell you, you won't want to disrespect him where he might hear you. Outside of here, you call him what the fuck you like, but in Noir he's Mr. Montoya. Okay?'

He shrugged.

'Good.' I called over one of the barmen and asked him to bring a couple of glasses of cold water. The barman smiled and nodded, and when he was gone, I looked Joe in the eye. 'You see that, kid? I know how to be polite when I need to, turn on the charm. What you need to understand is that there's always a line, and that there's a time to toe the line and there's a time to step over it. It's important you learn the difference 'cause you never know who you're going to piss off. I want to help you learn about that line, so I'm gonna tell you a story,' I said. 'And I want you to listen good.'

'Okay,' he said and unfolded his arms. 'I like stories.'

*

'A few years back, before you were even a squirt of juice in your dad's sorry sack, this quay was so run down, it was *bad*. I mean, they've cleared it up now, built all these fancy restaurants and clubs that you kids like so much, but years ago it was a shit hole. Boats came in, bars filled up and it was rough as hell. I can promise you wouldn't have wanted to bring your sweetheart down here, they'd have eaten a guy like you right up. Swallowed you whole and shit you out in bits.

Over where Magdalena's is now, there was a whole load of warehouses - one of them owned by none other than the friendly Mr Montoya himself. The guy you call Sawn-off. He's mellowed out a lot now, nice suits and diamond smile, but back then he was a real fuckin' hard-case, bad as you like. Ran a few rackets, bit of booze, fags, violence; usual sort of stuff. Anyway, one of the things he was into was a bit of sharking. Money lending. Lend it out at twenty-five percent a week straight, collect big time. Sweet if you can keep it under control and make sure the payments come in. Course, the only way to do that is by offering a little incentive where it's needed, and that's where me and the Hammer came in.'

'You mean you broke people's legs for him?' Joe sitting forward, interrupting me full flow.

'Why is it you people always think it's going to be legs?' I said. 'No, kid, not legs. We broke all kinds of things; used all kinds of stuff.'

'Like what?'

'That line I told you about before? The one I'm helping you with? Well, you're getting close to it right about now. You want to hear this or not?'

Joe crossed his arms again and sat back like he was sulking. 'Sure.'

'Then shut up and let me talk.' I waited for the comment but when nothing came I carried on. 'So, anyway, Mr. Montoya wasn't altogether bad, not rotten all the way through like some I've known. I mean, he didn't lend the money out to people who he knew could never pay it back. Kind of noble in that way - old school, if you like. Let's say, for instance, you and your girl wanted to get a flat, maybe a car, and needed a bit of the folding stuff. If you'd gone to Mr. Montoya, he would've sent you packing, wouldn't have given you a penny. Bad for business, you see, nothing coming your way. I mean, think about it. If you can't pay up, you're no good to him. Besides, he wouldn't want to hurt you unless he had to, so he'd never put you in that position.'

'Sounds like a pussy to me,' said Joe, trying to make out like he'd heard it all before - been there done that - but he was hooked, I could tell. Everyone's a sucker for a good yarn.

I eyed him for a second and sipped the iced water which the barman left on the table. Joe still had that look on his face, the one that Hammer had wanted to scrub off for him, but I knew it wasn't deep. Just under the surface, Joe was still a kid. He couldn't have been any older than twenty-one and probably felt like he had to put on a hard act if he wanted to be taken serious. I used to be a bit like that myself and it hadn't done me any harm in the long run. I mean, look at me now.

'He wasn't a pussy,' I said. 'He had good sense and he made a mint. It was like he was printing his own money.'

'So, he's a rich pussy.' He shrugged his shoulders again, making me think about stamping them down, but instead I took a deep breath and told him 'Well, maybe he is a pussy. And maybe he isn't. Tell you what, why don't you let me finish the story, then you can decide for yourself.'

'I thi...'

'That means shut the fuck up and listen.' Keeping calm, looking him right in the eye.

Joe clamped his teeth together hard, the muscles jumping out of his jaw on either side, but he kept quiet.

'Okay. So, one day this guy comes down to the quay and visits Mr. Montoya in his warehouse. Turns up in a flashy Jag, expensive leather coat, gold Rolex, shiny shoes - you know the score. The guy says he needs to borrow some money, tells Mr. Montoya he's in business, won't say what, and that he's had a temporary cash flow problem. Needs seven hundred and fifty grand to see him through the week. Cash. He's happy to pay the twenty-five percent 'cause he's got some deal in the offing and he knows the money's coming in soon enough. Says he'll have it repaid within a couple a weeks. Mr. Montoya thinks about it for a while and then says it's a lot of notes, but he'll see what he can do. Takes the guy's address and number, tells him he'll think about it, check him out, and get in touch the next day. When the bloke's gone, Mr. Montoya gets on the phone to make some calls, do a little bit of asking around to find out who Mr. Gold Rolex is. A few of the local players, people Mr. Montoya trusts, vouch for the man, saying they know who he is and that he's good for the cash. So, feeling pretty sure of it all, Mr. Montoya calls in a few favours. He doesn't have enough ready money to cover the loan that the guy wants so he has to borrow some himself. It's not something he'd normally do, but everyone's vouched for Gold Rolex and the money's safe as houses. Next day, everything's sorted and Mr. Montoya calls the guy up to arrange a meet over lunch in town. He takes the briefcase of folding stuff with him and hands it over to Mr. Gold Rolex. Job done.

Only it's not job done, is it? It's Mr. Montoya who's been done. A week goes by and Mr. Montoya doesn't hear from our friend. The interest payment doesn't appear when it's supposed to appear, so he calls him up, but the line's disconnected. Operator says the disconnection was requested. Next, he goes round to the address, but shop's shut and nobody's home. It's bogus, made up. So, Mr. Montoya, who's not a happy bunny right now, gets onto his pet, a sleazy little shite called Deeks, and sets him on the case to hunt down our mystery borrower. It doesn't take long for Deeks to get the hook on what's going on and he runs straight back to the boss.

Well, it turns out that a few of the local players thought Mr. Montoya was getting a little too successful for his own good, and decided to take a couple of steps to put him out of business. The people he called in the favours from? They were working against him the whole time. Used one of their own guys to pose as a rich borrower, hoping to take all of Mr. Montoya's money *and* leave him in debt to them - push him right out of the loop, soak up his business and have a good reason to pop him. It was a fit up.

Course, Mr. Montoya is a little bit upset by the whole thing and that's where me and the Hammer come in, 'cause Deeks finds out exactly where this Mr. Gold Rolex is staying and puts Mr. Montoya on to him. In turn, Mr. Montoya puts *us* onto him, so we go around and ask very nicely for the money to show up in the next five seconds or else. Only it doesn't, does it? Well, we weren't as patient then as we are now - must be something to do with getting old, I suppose - so we offer to break something. We were thinking maybe a couple of fingers but Mr. Rolex doesn't like our offer a whole lot and decides to turn us down. Things get pretty nasty pretty quick and... well, you know how these things work; someone got hurt. Ended up we took the suitcase of cash and called an ambulance on the way out.

What we *didn't* know, or what Deeks and Mr. Montoya didn't tell us, was that Mr. Gold Rolex - the one who was now in hospital with a blood clot in his brain and his neck in a brace - was Johnny Hart's old dad. Now, Johnny Hart was the *man* back in those days and he didn't take too kindly to his old dad getting the squeeze put on him like that. Well, everyone knew that for me and the Hammer it wasn't personal, it's only ever business, so Johnny went straight to the man who hired us - Mr. Montoya. Course, he could've just hired us himself and we'd have done the dirty for him back in those days, but no, he wanted to *taste* revenge not just hear about it on the local news. He wanted to feel it up close and personal, that's the way these guys are, so he gathered a few of his boys.

Somehow, Mr. Montoya knew he was coming. Don't ask me how he knew, 'cause I haven't got a clue, but he was always well informed. Maybe his find-out worm told him; who knows. Anyway, next thing you know, me and the Hammer get a call from Mr. Montoya saying he's got a couple a bodies in the office need tidying up and throwing away, could we come round and help? He's always up front with the cash so we pop round to see him - do a bit of cleaning.

When we get there, he's sitting behind this desk made out of old wooden crates, all rough and splintery. There's papers all over the floor, like he's just brushed everything off the top, and he's got such a look on his face. Like fuckin' thunder, he is. The door's open and the desk is facing it so he can see straight down the stairs from his office up on there on the mezzanine floor.

'Come in boys,' he says when he sees our heads appear up the steps, but when we get in there, there's no sign of any bodies to clean up. There's just him, behind this desk with papers all over the floor and this long line of red plastic things across the front like toy soldiers. I only realised what they were when I got up close. So anyway, I says to him 'where's the bodies?' and I'll never forget his answer. 'They're on their way,' he says. And he tells us to sit on the couch by the far window. We didn't want to argue - he had a look that said something bad was coming off. He had the red mist, like I told you about before, we could see it in his eyes clouding everything. Besides, the gun on the desk was enough for me. A shotgun. Not like one of them new ones, though, the over and unders. No, this one had the barrels side by side, like the kind that pig used to carry in the Bugs Bunny cartoons, except this one wouldn't have been much good for hunting rabbits. Not unless you were standing right on top of the little bastards, that is. You see, he'd taken the length off the barrels, cut them off with a hacksaw, I suppose. So there he was, one hand glued to the butt of that piece and his eyes glued to the door, looking down those stairs. His other hand was resting on the desk, ready to pick up the red plastic cartridges that were lined up along the front in a neat row.

It was about an hour before we heard them coming up the stairs, and in all that time, none of us spoke a word, didn't even dare clear our throats.

I was watching the open door, Hammer was too, but we couldn't see what Mr. Montoya could see. We were too far away, but he was in just the right spot to catch anyone creeping about. Eventually, those steps creaked so quiet that it might've been a mouse coming up them, but we all heard it, and Mr. Montoya lifted that sawn-off, nice and easy, so it was pointing straight at the door. He stayed like that for a second, setting himself steady, getting his bead, and then he loosed both barrels. Bang, bang; just like that. I'll tell you what, it was fuckin' loud in that empty room, and the smell of gunpowder and the gray smoke was everywhere. But he didn't stop. Shit, I've never seen anyone's hands move so fast. He reloaded that sawn-off and fired again. Over and over and over again, he was like a fuckin' demon, and you'd swear that no human could move that quick. The cartridges from the first shots were still falling to the ground when he fired the second two barrels, then he popped it open, pinged the empties and shoved in a couple more before I could blink. Fuck, he was fast. And he kept on firing for what felt like hours.

Me and Hammer, we tried to be cool. Didn't flinch, didn't move a muscle. Didn't even cover our ears, but I still heard ringing the next day...and the day after that. I'm surprised my fuckin' eardrums didn't bleed.'

My throat was dry from all that talking, so I stopped and took a sip of iced water, the cubes clinking together. I watched Joe over the top of the glass and it looked like he was taken in. He was quiet now, no cocky look anymore. I took another sip, slowly, waiting to see if he'd pipe up again, letting that mouth of his run away with him, but he stayed where he was. He wanted the rest, so I put the glass down and carried on.

'So anyway, when Mr. Montoya was done shooting, he sat back, laid the sawn-off on the table and took a silver flask out of his inside pocket. He pulled on it, swallowed and then turned to look at us. 'There's your bodies,' he says, 'five hundred for each one you clear.' Just like that, all chilly, like he was talking about taking out the rubbish, and all around him there was a gray haze in the air and the floor was littered with those red cartridges.

We cleared up six bodies from the bottom of those stairs - each one with his head and face all fucked up. I tell you, man, there was brains and blood and skull and shit all over that place like you wouldn't believe. It was fuckin' everywhere. And scattered with the bodies - including poor old Johnny Hart himself - we found three sawn-offs, a couple of snubs and an automatic, but not one of them had been fired. They hadn't managed to get off *one* shot, if you believe that.

We loaded up the bodies in a van, all wrapped up in plastic and then called Mr. Montoya down to count them so he'd know how much to pay us. He thanked us and said he'd give us *seven* hundred a piece, that's two more than he'd promised us to start with, and he went up to office right there and then to take the cash out of his safe - probably came out of the stuff we'd got back for him a couple of days before.

When we were ready to leave, he looked me right in the eye. 'Before you boys go,' he says to us, nice as pie, 'bring Johnny Hart's body up here. I want to cut out his heart and send it to his old dad when he gets better.'

*

'Fuck me, that's harsh,' he said eventually. 'That the truth?' Joe's hand was clamped firmly around his glass of cold water and the condensation was dribbling around his fingers. His cocky look was gone and now he was just an excited kid.

I half laughed. 'No. It's a lie. I'm rackin' your slide. What do *you* think?'

He considered for a moment and then shook his head. 'Naa. No way, man. It's a yarn. You're making it up.'

'Whatever you want to think,' I said, never taking my eyes off him. 'But you look at his face when you see him, and I mean really look, and then *you* tell *me* if he's the kind of guy you want to disrespect in his own club.' I stood up and put my hand on Joe's shoulder. 'Story time's over, kid. I think we'll try you out on the main door later on, but for now, go down and join Fraser in the titty bar. I know you're getting to like it in there.'

He pushed himself out of the seat, some of the cockiness coming back already, but as he left, I noticed Joe's head turn towards the stairs which led up to Mr. Montoya's office.

SEAN

Jack had finished clearing the takeaway cartons when I came out of the bathroom, but the place still smelled of curry.

'Feels good to have a decent shower,' I said walking into the living room. I was rubbing my hair dry with one of Jack's cheap Sunday-market towels. Other than that I was stark bollock naked.

Jack put his book down and looked back over the sofa. 'Cover yourself up, Sean.'

I peered down at myself and then back at Jack. 'What's the matter with you? Worried I'll show you up?'

'Show me up to who?' he looked about. 'I don't see anyone else here.'

'I dunno, maybe the mysterious 'M' might turn up and see the younger brother's got more to offer than the older,' I said raising my eyebrows. 'She might fancy a change; you know, something with a better action.' I pumped my hips a couple of times.

'You been reading through my stuff?'

'Maybe.'

'Well don't.'

I told him he shouldn't leave it lying around then. Anything was fair game now that we were living together.

'Fair game?' he said. 'Don't give me that. It's still my flat, remember.'

'Don't panic, I'll be out of your hair before you know it. Get rid of the con and then you can ship your girl back in. Wouldn't want you to be missing out on any action.' I pumped my hips again.

'Oh, just get changed, Sean. 'I don't know how much longer I can look at you like that without feeling sick.'

I smiled and went into the spare room, leaving Jack to drink beer on his own for a while. Maybe he'd find something to tidy up if he got bored waiting for me. I opened a few boxes, pulling out some of my old stuff and thinking that I needed to find a place of my own. Jack's spare room was beginning to feel even smaller than the cell I'd shared with Deeks.

*

The people you meet inside aren't always nice - I guess maybe that's why they're banged up – but you get to know what's what pretty quick, and as soon as I laid eyes on Deeks, I had him pegged for a scrawny little grease.

I'd been in and out of places all my life. The first time inside was young offenders when I was sixteen. Three and a half months in a cell next to my mates from the outside, it was like joining a party. Most days were spent in association or education, so it was easy time, me feeling like a big man going in there, knowing who everyone was. We passed the hours comparing notes, bragging about what we'd done. The worse you'd been, the more respect you got, so we made stuff up. By the time I was eighteen, though, I didn't need to make it up anymore.

Jack, he knuckled down and worked, tried to pass some exams while I was out robbing houses and selling wraps of speed to the local kids. If they split us up, sent us to different homes, we always managed to see each other, but mostly they kept us together when I was outside. As we grew older, though, we saw less of each other. Jack keeping straight, finding work, trying to climb the ladder. He had a couple of exams, not much, but he thought they might open a few doors for him. Me, I found other ways to open doors, but this last time I was inside, a couple of things made me think something needed to change.

The local Category B was a shite-hole. The opposite end of the scale from the cosy places I been in as a kid. It was one of those ancient prisons with a great hall in the middle, and wings spreading out from it. Ones, twos, threes, the levels went up high, the paint flaking on the walls, the railings bent and rocking in their fixings. The nets stretching between the upper floors were sagging and full of splits. Five hundred cons and a hundred and fifty screws. Sometimes there were just four of them out in the yard with maybe a hundred of us walking around. If we'd said 'no' when they told us association was up, there wouldn't have been anything they could do about it. I guess we could've had a riot in there, if it wasn't for the bang-up. Twenty, twenty-two hours a day sitting in a cell that's twelve by nine. Shit, that gives you a lot of time to think. It's not hard time, though, not the minutes anyway; it's the hours, the days, the weeks, the months. The fucking years. Course, if you earned a few privileges, got employment in the workshops or washing the floors, you might spend time off the landings, but that shit wasn't for me.

On remand, they stick you in a local because it's close to the court. Take away your aftershave in case you drink it, your wind up radio in case you make a bomb out of it, and, get this, no bananas in case you smoke them. Never met anyone who tried to smoke a banana or even smuggle one in, but I did hear about a guy who brought a knife in. Stuck it up his arse, is what I heard, but I reckon you'd have to be mad to do a thing like that. Part of the processing when you first go in, they photograph and strip-search you. Make you squat down, so that anything you stuck up there will fall out, so I reckon if you wanted something to stay put, you'd have to jam it pretty far up. People did it though, took all sorts of stuff inside, and once you were behind those walls, it was a seller's market. You could get almost anything you wanted if you knew the right people - stuff to smoke, stuff to shoot, stuff to snort - but you often saw greenhorns sweating and shaking with bleeding noses because they didn't know the right people. For guys like that, prison does good cold turkey.

Anyway, remand prisoners are taken over to the court on the escort bus. Packed in and shipped over. And that's when you get a really good look at the other cons. Sitting there, suited up, wondering what's going to happen to them. Some, they rattle. They sweat buckets, because they're green and they think doing time is all about getting buggered and bashed from the second they step onto those landings. Others, they're just blank, they don't care, they know that once you're in, you're in, you settle down, it's easy. But then there are the old hands. The guys who look like they should be collecting their pensions.

That last time I was on that bus, I was sitting opposite some old guy, watching his face, creased and craggy like someone had crumpled it up like a piece of paper. He was probably up on burglary or whatever, I don't know, maybe even murder, but he was ancient like he should've been in a home, shaking and sipping tea. His nose and cheeks were covered in tiny veins and his small eyes were watery and empty. His loose lips were thin and pale. A few wisps of grey were greased back on his head. He was almost *too* old to be a criminal, should've called it a day by now, but he'd probably been in and out all his life, judging by the calm look on his face. I guess by then he had nothing going for him. Nothing on the outside to keep him there.

Three years for beating a guy to a pulp usually gets you sent out to one of the nice new dispersal prisons, but as it turned out there were too many of us cons, so when the bus took me back, the screws put me through the process right there in the local. Took away my clothes and gave me the standard uniform. Blue striped shirt, grey sweatshirt, blue jeans, maroon jumper. 'What, no bathrobe and slippers?' I asked the screw.

'You've come too far over the bridge for that, son,' he said with a kind of smile. 'This isn't the fucking Hilton, you know.'

'Overcrowding' is what they told me in my reception interview, the officer giving me my booklet and smiling, calling me 'Mr.' Presley, like it was going to choke him every time he said it. That's why I had to stay local, he said, because there was nowhere else for me to go right now. If something came up, maybe they'd move me on, but for now they were going to put me up onto the first floor landing. After that, they gave me and a couple of other guys the induction; the video with the woman's voice telling us about the well-stocked canteen, all soothing and friendly like we were taking a holiday flight to Spain. What the video didn't tell us was that the new canteen was the old Death Cell, converted after they got rid of hanging, and that when we were out in the yard, we'd still be able see the old 'topping-shed'. I reckon they were waiting for the day when they could reopen for business.

Once the induction was done they took me and my bedroll up to see my new pad. I didn't know if I was going to be alone or sharing, so it was just the luck of the draw that they stuck me in with Deeks.

The screw unlocked the cell and showed me in, like he was a hotel porter showing me into some luxury penthouse. He stepped to one side and put out a hand to guide me in. Then he said 'Home sweet home,' and pulled the door closed behind me.

Most of the room was taken up by the iron bunk, the pale blue paint cracked and peeling on its frame, the legs concreted into the floor. There was a mattress rolled across the bottom section, the sheets were tidy, the blanket tucked neatly around the mattress. Down on the ground, beside one leg of the bed frame, there was a pair of glasses, small and round. On the wall, the fixed cupboard was open and I could see a couple of bits and bobs in there. Electric razor, soap, toothpaste, toothbrush, that kind of thing. There was a maroon jumper over the chair, same as the one I was carrying.

The smell was warm and strong, just like it would have been in all the pads on the landing. Sweat, shit, rot, all fighting for space in the small cell, nowhere to go except for the tiny barred window just below the ceiling. You could barely even see daylight through it.

In the corner, there was a steel toilet and basin. I couldn't see it, because a sheet had been rigged up to hide it from view, but I knew it was there because all the cells had them. They'd been put in when they abolished slopping out a few years back. Old timers talked about the days of buckets, saying we were being spoiled with proper facilities. They said we were getting soft, but lots of the guys in the cells put up some kind of screen to hide the toilet, it gave them a little bit of privacy. It was something the screws didn't like too much, but they were okay as long as it wasn't too high.

My first sight of Deeks was when his head popped up from behind the sheet. He looked at me and I looked at him. Fading bruises, grey and yellow around his cheek. His nose purple, his lip fatter than it was supposed to be. He smiled and shifted his eyes nervously. 'Don't like to shit in front of people I don't know,' he said with some kind of London accent, and I heard him taking paper out of a box, getting ready to wipe. 'Not nice.'

His head disappeared from view again, wiping sounds, and then he stood up and held out his hand. He was short and thin, his frame bony and unnatural.

'Deeks,' he said. 'Jeremy Deeks.'

I put my roll up on the top bunk and ignored him, letting him stand there with his hand out. I set up my bed so that my pillow was at the opposite end of the room from the toilet and then I climbed on and turned to face the wall.

I slept until seven when one of the screws unlocked the door for supper, so I had half an hour in the canteen and then got my head down again. I woke up once that night, but only because Deeks was shuffling and grunting in his bunk. I tried not to listen to him seeing to business.

*

The first morning in with Deeks, I didn't wake up until the screw opened the door at nine-thirty for association. Deeks was already eating his breakfast, sitting on the chair, facing the wall and tucking into the cereal and milk they gave us the day before at teatime. Couldn't eat it myself, it was always too stale by then. All that hot air and stink getting onto it since the day before.

I sat up and took a cigarette from the packet under my pillow, lighting up and taking a deep drag before Deeks turned around saying, 'I'd appreciate it if you wouldn't smoke.' He had milk on the corner of his mouth.

'Yeah?' I took another drag. 'Don't see any 'No Smoking' signs in here.'

Deeks went back to his cereal and took another mouthful, making sucking and crunching noises at the same time. I thought maybe he'd turn around again, but he didn't. ''Bout the only fucking place in the world you *can* still smoke,' I said.

When he'd finished eating, Deeks went behind the sheet to brush his teeth. He was at it for a long time, brushing like he was trying to scrub them off. Eventually he gargled and spat. After that he washed his face, and smoothed water over his hair, patting it down like anybody was going to give a shit what he looked like.

When I was done smoking, I dropped down from the bunk and picked up my towel.

'Good luck,' said Deeks looking over. I nodded and left the cell.

Association was like a lottery. You could take a shower, use the phone, go out into the yard or just hang about. There was a pool table and a telly in the centre, a prison shop for cigarettes and chocolate, but you only had an hour and a half. Once that time was up, it was back to your cell for bang-up. The reason why Deeks had wished me luck was because five hundred cons were unlocked at the same time. Sure, there were a lot of tough guys, people off their faces on drugs, guys looking for a fight, but that wasn't the problem. The problem was that everyone wanted to make the most of the time they had. And that meant queuing. Queuing for the showers, queuing for the phones, queuing for the shop. Some cons wanted to do everything in one session, but it was impossible. Me, I hate queuing, but at least I didn't have the phone to worry about – no one to call – and I had plenty of burn back in the cell so I didn't need the shop just yet. For me it was the shower. I wanted to feel just a little bit clean.

It took me about an hour to get to the showers. They'd converted them from a big communal job into nice little private cubicles, ten of them, just big enough to stand in with your shoulders touching the greasy white tiles. The water wasn't very hot but it was okay so, as long as you didn't mind the pubes blocking the drains, and the plastic curtain sticking to your arse, they weren't too bad. You couldn't ever get too comfortable, though, because after a couple of minutes, people started to get edgy out in the queue.

When I got back to the pad, Deeks was sitting on his bunk, leaning forward with his forearms on his knees. He kept his head down when I walked in, but I could see that his lip was fat again and that one eye was closing up. It looked like someone had freshened-up yesterday's fading bruises so I asked him 'What the fuck happened to you?'

'Nothing.'

'Painful kind of nothing. It happen a lot?'

He nodded.

'You in here for sex stuff?' I said. I'd thought it as soon as I saw him, but he shook his head hard saying, 'No. Fuck that.'

'So what then?'

He told me fraud, but I didn't ask what, I wasn't really interested. I was thinking how pathetic he looked, small and sorry for himself, probably not knowing how to keep his head down, do his time. I don't know why, but he made me think of those old guys on the bus again, the ones who looked like they'd die in a shite-hole like this. 'Someone's on your case,' I said.

'Cook.' He looked up at me.

I knew who he meant straight away. I'd been on remand for weeks, and I'd seen Cook around the place, throwing his weight about. 'You've got to hit him back, Deeks. It's what I'd do.'

He gave me a funny kind of smile like it was out of the question. 'Easier said than done.'

I shrugged to show him I didn't care either way but told him that if he didn't do something, he'd never get rid of Cook. 'He'll keep coming at you.'

'I know.'

I lit a cigarette and blew the smoke right at him. 'Make an application, then. Cry VP. See if you can't get moved out onto the block.'

'I already did.'

SEAN

Days passed, long and boring, just me and Deeks in the nine by twelve. The routine set in. Me smoking and lying awake thinking about those old guys in and out of the cage all their lives. Him cleaning his teeth, washing his face, tugging one off every night, and getting kicked about by Cook.

I didn't like him much, normally wouldn't waste my breath on a guy like Deeks, but when you're locked up with someone for that many hours a day, you can't avoid him. Some guys, they get so that it's like they're married the way they carry on. Me, I never liked my pad mates, especially when they want you to read their poetry or something, but Deeks wasn't like that, he was just oily. Even so, sometimes when the doors were open, we used to stand outside the cell, leaning over the balcony and looking down at the centre. There wasn't much to see other than cons getting on with doing their time. Guys milling about, playing cards, pool, reading at tables. Older blokes propped up in high backed chairs watching telly. A couple of them had their patches, yellow on the blue shirt, and Deeks asked what they were.

'Singles them out as cons who've tried to escape,' I told him. 'Stupid old buggers don't look like they're going anywhere now, though, do they?' I turned to look at Deeks, but his attention had shifted, so I followed his gaze and spotted Cook waiting in the shower queue. He was still some way out of the locker room and it didn't surprise me that he was standing in line just like everybody else. 'Look at that.' I said. 'A real tough guy would be at the front by now. You just have to stand up to him, you know.'

Deeks turned to me, his glasses crooked. 'It's not my style.'

'So do something that *is* your style. Take a shit in his bed when he's in the shower. Piss in his cup. Whatever it takes.'

Deeks laughed at that. A funny little hissing sound, his shoulders hitching up and down. 'That's my style?'

'I reckon.'

'So what's *your* style then? You'd just go down there and hit him?'

I nodded.

'It's as easy as that?'

'Sure it is. Just play it cool, wait for the right moment, walk right up to them and, bam.' I opened the Zippo, remembering the guy I took it from, and snapped it shut again. 'Smack them and they go down.' I looked at my pad mate and nodded again. 'Yeah, Deeks, it's as easy as that.' The Zippo's original owner had gone down hard.

'You think you could do something like that for me?'

'You want me to give you a hiding?'

'Not me. Cook.'

I told him I knew what he meant, did he think I was stupid. 'No way,' I said. 'I'm not doing your dirty work for you. Guys get ADA for shit like that.'

He gave me a look like he didn't have a clue what I'd meant so I said 'Additional Days Awarded,' and he nodded and turned away, like he knew it was final, but he mentioned it again that night when the lights were down and the landings were quiet. It was late; the radios were off, the privilege tellies were off, the jangle of keys was less frequent. It was about the time that I'd normally hear Deeks seeing to himself, but this time he started talking.

'What you in for?' he asked, his voice coming out of the dark at me in a kind of whisper.

'What do you care?'

'Must've been bad to end up in here.'

'They padded out my sentence.'

'So what would it take?' he said. 'For you to get Cook off my back, I mean.'

'Forget it Deeks. Do your business and go to sleep.'

'I'm serious,' he said.

I lit a cigarette, the flame from the Zippo jumping into the darkness, and smoked it in my bunk, lying on my back, listening to the tobacco and the paper burning.

'How about cigarettes?' he asked.

'I've got cigarettes.'

'I could buy you more.'

'Deeks, I know where you keep your money. If I wanted it, I'd just take it.'

'What then? What would it take?'

'It's not going to happen, Deeks. Go to sleep.'

He tried a few more times after that, once or twice a week for a couple of months, but he knew I wasn't going to do anything for him. I think it just became a habit, part of our ritual. I'd get back to the pad after a shower, Deeks would be black and blue, maybe his eye had closed up again, and he'd ask me to help him out. I'd say no. Then he'd ask me again, once the lights were down and I was smoking my cigarette. I always said no.

*

It's another world inside a place like that and it's easy to lose track of the days. They kind of merge into each other, but it must've been at least five months into our stretch together when Deeks pulled a fast one on me.

I was in the shower, as I was every morning around that time, when I heard the curtain being whipped away behind me. Before I had time to wash the soap from my face and turn around, I felt a hand on my back and I was pushed forwards against the tiles. I hit my chest on the single tap that stuck out of the wall, slipped in the porcelain trough, and then dropped to the floor of the cubicle. When I looked up, I saw Cook filling the entrance. He was fully clothed and red in the face like he'd come through in a hurry. Behind him, the queue was restless, some of the cons thinking he was pushing in, others probably hoping they were up for seeing a fight.

'That little cockney shite, Deeks, tells me you're going to sort me out for him.' He crossed his arms and puffed himself up as big as he could.

'What?' I stood up and moved towards him so that the water was falling down my back and not over my face.

'Says he's your boy.'

I had to laugh at that, him sounding like he'd seen too many films.

'Says you're going to look after him.'

I've been in a lot of fights and they've all been scrappy. Arms flailing, pushing, shoving, grabbing, they don't look good. Not like they do in films. There's no precision punching or fancy footwork, and this one wasn't any different. I saw Cook's fist coming a mile away, but being stuck in the cubicle made things hard for me, so I couldn't do much to avoid it. His fist connected square onto my cheekbone, missing my nose by just an inch, and his knuckles made a slapping noise against my wet skin but it probably hurt his hand more than it hurt my face. The punch wasn't hard enough to put me down, so I did the only thing I could think of. Me being naked and exposed like that, it seemed like the only fair thing to do. I kicked him in the balls, good and hard. He dropped straight away, his hands going down between his legs but I lost my footing so we both fell backwards together, him grabbing his balls, me grabbing my arse. The other cons had a good laugh, but I was the first one up so I gave Cook a few more kicks to make sure he stayed down.

I went through to the changing room and dressed in a hurry, breathing heavily and not caring that I was still wet. A cloud had come over me and I couldn't think of anything other than Deeks. Scrawny little grease had some nerve putting me on the spot like that. Deserved a good hiding for setting me up. Must've taken me for a fucking idiot. I left my towel where it was and headed for the stairs, still buttoning my shirt. I found him sitting on his bunk, as usual, wincing at the new bruises on his face.

'What the *fuck* did you think you were playing at?' I banged the door back against the wall and went straight to him, grabbing him by the scruff of his shirt and pulling him to his feet. Deeks didn't say anything, didn't even look at me, so I gave him a shake. 'He came at me in the shower, Deeks. In the fucking *shower*.'

'I had to do something,' he said looking up.

I pushed him hard against the bunk. 'So now *I* have to keep looking over my shoulder? Is that it?'

'You told me to do it my way. I ...'

'And you thought it would be easier to live with *me* on your case? Well you made a big fucking mistake, Deeks, 'cause I already told you I won't do your dirty work for you.' I pulled him away from the iron bed frame, spun him around and pushed him behind the sheet which hid the toilet. I forced him down onto the steel bowl and put my fingers around his throat. 'You really fucked up, Deeks.' I cocked my free arm back, nice and slow so that he could see me tighten my fingers, squeezing them into a fist. I wanted him to see it coming. I wanted him to see every kick, every punch. What I was going to do to him was worse than Cook could ever dream up. I was going break his nose, his fingers, his toes. I was going to push my thumbs into his eyes.

'Everything all right in here?' It was Barnsley. He was ex-Army or something and sounded like a drill instructor. 'There's rumours about you two ladies already.' Deeks and I both looked up, our heads well over the sheet.

I let go of Deeks, pushing him back against the toilet. 'Yeah well, you shouldn't listen to rumours, should you?' I stepped away and stared at Barnsley.

'You looking for a few additional days, Presley?'

I backed away even more and paused for a second before climbing onto my bunk. Barnsley stayed in the doorway, hands behind his back, flexing his toes up and down. 'Anything you want to say Deeks?' That voice filling the cell. 'You think Presley needs something extra?'

Deeks straightened his collar without looking at him. He kept his eyes down.

Barnsley stayed for a moment, letting the question hang and then he shrugged saying, 'I'll see you ladies later, then,' and walked away. His prison issue Doc Martins squeaked a little on the painted concrete floor of the landing.

When the screw was gone, Deeks sat down on the chair and ran his hands over his face. 'I shouldn't have said anything. To Cook, I mean.'

I lit a cigarette and looked down at him. 'You're fuckin' right about that.'

*

The next couple of days after the thing with Cook, I glared at Deeks and he edged around me in the cell looking scared. Every time I laid eyes on him, I wanted to tear him to pieces, but I kept thinking about Barnsley and his extra days. And that made me think about the old guy on the escort bus, so I told myself that maybe what Deeks did wasn't so bad after all. He was looking after himself, doing it his way like I told him to, and nobody had been hurt other than Cook. It took me a while before I could look at him without wanting to kill him, but I didn't want Deeks to think he was off the hook. I wanted him scared.

He twitched more than usual and jumped every time I climbed down from the bunk. He moved about a lot at night too, probably couldn't sleep with me lying just a few inches above him. He tried not to make eye contact and didn't say a word, but other than that we went on doing our thing. Not much changed except that he didn't get any fresh cuts and bruises. Not for a while, anyway.

Then one day he came in and dropped a couple of packs of Regal on the chair, so I asked him 'You taking up smoking?'

'They're for you.'

'You trying to buy me off?'

'Can I?'

'No.'

'How about money? '

'I already told you Deeks. If I want your money I'll take it.'

He picked up the cigarettes, tossed them onto my bunk and sat down. He took off his glasses with one hand and untucked his shirt with the other, squinting at me while he cleaned the lenses, rubbing the shirt corner between his finger and thumb. 'How about I give you something else? I know things. I could give you information.'

'You know things? Jesus Christ, Deeks, listen to yourself. You can't buy your way out of this. I want you looking over your shoulder the rest of your time, just like I have to. I like it you don't sleep at night.'

'How long you got left?' he asked, still squinting.

'Mind your own fuckin' business.'

'You think you'll stay out next time? Keep straight?'

I didn't answer.

'No, you'll be back,' he said sliding the glasses back onto his nose. 'It's in your blood. But I've seen the way you look at the old timers down in the centre,' he went on like he could see right through me. 'Sitting there in the high backed chairs, watching the telly like they're in the old folk's home. I swear I've seen some of them dribbling.'

I looked at him.

'That's you, that is. You're just like them. You think that maybe you'll make it, keep out of here, but you know you can't. People like you, Presley, they see something and they go for it. Can't help themselves.'

'What do you know about people like me?'

'I work for someone like you. He's just better at it, that's all.'

'What the fuck's that supposed to mean?'

'It means you're in here and he's not. He's counting his money, 'cause he knows a good deal when he sees one, and he knows how to keep out of places like this. He knows how to keep an edge.'

I lit a cigarette.

'You might've heard of him,' he leaned back in the chair. 'Guy called Montoya.'

'*Sawn-off* Montoya?' I'd heard of him all right. Everybody who wanted to be somebody had heard of Sawn-off Montoya. 'Kept that quiet didn't you? Something like that could work for you in here.'

'Not if people find out what I do for him.'

'Yeah? What's that then?'

'You want to hear something about him? The kind of thing he does? Could be worth knowing. Give you that edge.'

I laughed at that. 'Fuck off, Deeks.'

He held his hands up and protested, making out that I'd read him all wrong. 'No. No, really. I feel like I owe you.'

'Come on, Deeks, you're scared and you want to buy me off.'

'You don't understand. I find things out for Mr Montoya. We're very close. I collect information for him. But I *know* things. Things I'm not *supposed* to know.'

'Go on then,' I said. 'Like what?'

Deeks cleaned his glasses on the corner of his shirt again and leaned forward. 'Things that could be worth a lot of money,' he said. 'Interested?'

'How much money?' I pushed myself up into a sitting position.

'A lot. Maybe more than you can imagine.'

'I can imagine a lot, Deeks. How much?'

He reckoned about seven figures, minimum, and it took me a while to work out exactly how much that was, but when I did, I nodded and said 'Shit, go on.'

He paused for a moment, all part of the act, like he was thinking whether or not he should tell me and then he started. 'Okay, listen to this. Last year some guys from down south came here to lay low after a job they did, and they brought some kind of box with them. It looks like they didn't really know what they were doing, because when they realised what they'd nicked, they got a little bit uneasy. They squawked about a bit, argued amongst themselves, the whole Reservoir Dogs thing, and then finally came to a decision. They decided to get some advice from someone with experience, someone who *does* know what they're doing.'

'You're going to say Sawn-off Montoya, right?'

'Right.'

'But you're not supposed to know?'

Deeks shook his head and looked around. 'Well, anyway, Mr Montoya talks with these guys, gets to know them a bit, then says he'll see what he can do for them. He tells them he knows a few people, maybe he can sort something out. A few days later, he arranges a deal, telling them he's setting them up with a buyer.'

'But it's a different kind of set up.' I swung my legs over the edge of the bunk and looked down at him. 'More of a *fit* up.'

'You know him better than I do.'

'It's obvious, isn't it? I'd do the same thing myself.'

'Quite. So anyway, he arranges a meeting somewhere out of the way, and takes along these two guys he uses. The way I heard it, no money changed hands, a few people died, and Mr Montoya took ownership of the box.' Deeks stopped talking and looked at me like he was expecting me to cartwheel.

'And?'

'Well, don't you see? It's hot property. It's worth a lot of money. There's people out there who'd like to get their hands on it.' Deeks stood up. 'Police, dealers, other people like Mr Montoya.'

'Yeah. So why you telling *me*?'

He smiled at me like I was pulling his leg. 'Come on Presley, you know better than I do that it helps to have an edge. Information like that could be useful. It's up to you how you use it. Could come in handy next time you're in a tight spot with the law.'

I rubbed my eyes and shook my head. 'Like you wouldn't have used it already?'

'No way. I'm too close. If he got even a whiff that I knew about this, he'd kill me.'

'So you thought you'd drop me in it, then, did you? What am I gonna do, grass him up? Try to nick it from him? Or maybe you thought I'd go in there and try a bit of blackmail?'

'I hadn't thought of that.'

'Oh, fuck off, Deeks, that's probably the first thing you thought of, sneaky little shite like you. I can see where you're coming from. You think I'll leave you alone for a little bit of used information.'

Deeks sat down again and I lay back on the bunk, wondering what kind of idiot Deeks thought I was. What he'd told me about the box was interesting enough, it passed a bit of time, but it wasn't much use to me. On the other hand, Deeks himself might be of some use. 'So this guy Sawn-off,' I said. 'He probably keeps himself surrounded, does he? A guy like that always has people around him.'

'Mr Montoya?' Deeks took off his glasses rubbed his eyes. 'No. There's a couple of us he trusts, but mostly he likes to do things himself. No one to fuck it up that way.'

'So maybe he's looking for good people, then. People who *won't* fuck it up for him?' I leaned over to look at him.

'Maybe.'

'And I guess someone like that would need an introduction, right?'

Deeks smiled.

I lay back on my bunk and lit up. If I wanted to get out of this place, and not end up like those old guys with yellow patches on their uniforms, then I was going to need some money and some protection. I reckoned that working for Sawn-off Montoya would give me both. And if Deeks was going to be the man to put me there, then I figured that it was worth keeping him sweet. Maybe I could be nice to him for a while.

But I didn't get long to work on him, because a couple of days later, Cook went for Deeks with a homemade knife out in the yard. From what I heard, the little grease wasn't hurt too badly, but his application went through on the grounds of keeping good order. He was ghosted out as a Vulnerable Prisoner to the segregation block with the sex offenders and the grasses. Word was that he spent more time with the analysts than with the medical officers after the attack, but either way, I never saw Deeks again.

JACK

'I'm gonna have to borrow some of your clothes, Jack, okay?'

I was in the living room, about to make a call, but I could hear Sean rummaging somewhere in the flat and it was putting me off. 'Fuck me,' he was shouting. 'You've got some crap in here, Jack. Where d'you buy this stuff? Charity shop?'

It didn't look like he was going to give me any peace, so I hung up the phone and put it down on the coffee table, thinking I'd call her back later, when he was gone. Instead, I went through to the bedroom to find Sean sifting through my wardrobe, pushing hangers backwards and forwards. I stood beside him and gently shouldered him out of the way saying, 'When you've finished taking the piss out of my clothes...'

'She doesn't let you go out in this stuff does she?' Sean pulling out the sleeve of one of my shirts, holding it by his fingertips like it might be dangerous. 'This mysterious girlfriend of yours, I mean. She's not fussy?'

'Wear your own clothes,' I said pushing the shirt back into the wardrobe and straightening the hangers.

'Yeah, right, and smell like a tramp?'

'A tramp? Why?'

''Cause all my stuff stinks. What have you *done* to it?'

'I haven't touched it,' I said. 'Everything's exactly as it was.' The room was full of cardboard boxes, the ones he sent over before he went away. The ones I'd carted around with me from place to place until I found this flat. They were the kind you pick up at the supermarket, brand names printed across them – beans and bottles of wine – and they'd been closed up with brown packing tape. Most of them were still sealed but Sean had opened a couple since he'd been back.

'You didn't even open them to air, Jack. Didn't hang anything up. You want me to smell like a tramp?'

'Hey, I didn't know what was in those boxes. Christ, I didn't *want* to know what was in them.'

'What's that supposed to mean? What d'you think was in them?'

'Just be grateful I kept them at all.'

Still naked except for a pair of white shorts, Seán ran a hand across his chest and scratched his collarbone. 'I'm meeting Hornrim tonight. I'm going out, Jack. Fuck, I might even get lucky if I'm dressed sharp. No one's gonna go near me if I smell like a fuckin...'

'...tramp, yeah, I know, you said that.' I looked at him, standing there like that, his first night out of prison. He was pale, but he was in pretty good shape considering where he'd been. 'Look,' I said. 'I've got something for you. I wanted to get you something, you know, to celebrate your release. I was going to save it for Christmas but you might as well have it now.' I moved him away and reached into the bottom of the wardrobe, pushing aside a pair of steel capped work boots they'd given me to wear in the factory. I pulled out two parcels wrapped in silver paper and threw them over to Sean saying, 'Hope you like them.'

He caught the parcels and looked at me, his mouth hanging open like he wasn't sure what to say. Then he smiled and raised his eyebrows, sitting down on the bed to tear off the wrapping paper. He opened the first package and held it up in front of him, me thinking I'd never seen him so excited by something legal. The leather jacket had cost me just under a month's wages but I knew it would be worth it. It was the kind Sean liked, the kind he used to have, lapels and collars, like a regular sport jacket, with buttons down the front. When he stood up and put it on it fell below his waist. The black leather was soft.

'Man, this is style,' he said, looking a little odd wearing nothing but a leather jacket and shorts. 'You picked a good one.' It was as close to a 'thank you' as I could have hoped for.

The other parcel contained a pair of trousers, the kind with a straight leg and no creases down the front, and a t-shirt with a designer label. They hadn't come cheap. 'Fuck me,' he said dropping the paper on the floor. 'When did you learn to buy clothes like this?'

'I didn't choose them.'

'Well, I know what I'm wearing tonight,' said Sean.

'You'll freeze. It's snowing outside.'

'I'm not going to be outside; I'm going to be inside. Anyway, these are the best clothes in the house, I couldn't wear any of this other crap.' He swept a hand towards my wardrobe.

'I have to look good,' he said after he'd laid the clothes out on the bed, seeing how they went together. 'I need to borrow some shoes.'

I told him to take his pick. There wasn't much to choose from, but he could take what he wanted.

'How about the ones you're wearing?'

'The one's I'm wearing? Jesus, Sean.'

'Oh, come on Jack. It's my first night out, man. I need to look good.'

'All right. Take them. But they'd better come back looking like they do right now.' I shook my head but took the shoes off anyway, kicking them free just as the doorbell rang.

'That'll be Hornrim. Get it will you, while I put this kit on.' I didn't even reply to that, I just went to the door in my socks.

Hornrim didn't wait to be asked in. He stepped past me as if I wasn't there and walked straight into the flat, bringing a heavy smell with him. It was the smell that people carry when they live in damp, dirty houses. He stood in the hallway, hands in pockets, acting hard, saying nothing. I hadn't seen him for a long time and, although his appearance had changed, I could tell he was the same as ever - trying to look good but failing. He was wearing a dark pinstripe suit that was double breasted and didn't look good on him because he was too thin.

'You must be getting tough, Hornrim,' I said.

'Yeah? Why's that?'

'The guy you nicked that suit from must've been huge.'

He ignored that and pushed into the living room where he looked around for a moment, like he was deciding whether or not to give it his approval. Then he wandered over to the table and took a swig from my beer, making me wish I had cold sores or something.

Hornrim was called Hornrim because years back he had a habit of wearing thick horn rimmed specs, like the ones that Michael Caine used to wear. I heard that he faked his eye test so that he could blag some free glasses, then he'd popped out the lenses so that he could see. He wanted to look like he'd stepped out of the screen from one of those late sixties gangster films. He used to have the beige Mac, too, but he'd obviously changed his tastes since I'd last seen him because the glasses and the Mac were now gone. Now it was the badly fitting pinstriped suit, which looked just as crap on him. Sideways on he was like a pair of feet and a chin with a long space between them, and it was any wonder that his nickname wasn't 'Slim' or 'Macaroni'.

Like most of Sean's friends, Hornrim was lacking any decent personality traits. He was a cheap thug with nothing between his ears; the kind of person who followed Sean's lead and hung on his every word. I almost wished he'd died along with the rest of Sean's mates.

Eventually he turned around to look at me, wiping my beer from his lips with the back of his hand. 'So where is he then?' he said.

I was about to say something like 'What am I, his fucking keeper?' when Sean appeared from the bedroom.

'He-hey, you great long lanky streak of piss!' he said and they slapped each other's shoulders, shook hands and hugged each other like they were best friends. They called each other names for a while before things calmed down and Hornrim settled into an uneasy shifting from side to side. I suppose he didn't know what else to say so he waited for Sean to lead the conversation.

'So, how do I look?' said Sean lifting his hands in the air and turning around for his lackey to admire him. 'Am I the man or what?'

'You always were,' said Hornrim. 'Just like old times.'

The new gear looked good on Sean but the way they were acting, I had to shake my head at the pair of them.

'But I thought you wanted to go clubbing,' said Hornrim.

'I do.'

'Oh.' Hornrim looked like he was trying to find some words.

'Is there a problem?' Sean wasn't concerned.

'Well they're fuckin' picky these days. Especially on Saturday night. Most clubs, you can't get in without a tie. No t-shirts either.'

'Designer stuff, this,' said Sean pinching the front of his shirt and pulling it out for all to see. 'Expensive.'

'Don't cause any trouble,' I said to Sean. 'If you can't get in, you can't get in.' I've seen before what happens when Sean gets turned away from somewhere and it isn't nice.

'Don't be such a girl, Jack.' He looked across, his eyes fixing on mine, and he winked. 'Right then,' still looking at me. 'Let's go drink some beer. Sure you don't want to come, Jack? Last chance.'

I sighed and shook my head. 'Just be careful.'

'Yeah, later. Don't wait up, Mum.' Sean turned and walked towards the front door. As he passed the telephone table he picked up my car keys. 'You don't mind if I borrow your car.' It wasn't a question.

'Not if you're drinking.'

'Come on Jack.'

'Uh-uh. No way. D'you know how much that car cost me?'

'That heap of shit? It can't have been much,' he said. 'I'll get you a new one if anything happens.'

'I wasn't talking about money.'

'Whatever. Fine. If you don't want me to borrow your car, I'll borrow someone else's.' Sean nudged Hornrim and then turned to open the front door.

'All right,' I said. 'Take it. And take these so you don't wake me up.' I threw him a set of spare keys. He caught them in one hand and stuffed them into his pocket. Then he left without saying thank you.

MAGDALENA

I closed the door and turned the deadlock. Then I slid the chain across and allowed myself to breathe again. There was no sound in the hotel room, except the deadened white noise of traffic from outside and the metallic scraping of the door chain settling into place. I pinched it between finger and thumb and listened to the silence, staying completely still.

I waited for the stairwell door to bang open, or the lifts to stop on my floor. I listened for the sound of footsteps in the hallway or a light knock at the door but the silence continued.

As I began to feel safer, I put my eye to the door and peered through the spy-hole, taking in the goldfish view. I half expected to see that little face staring back at me, but from what I could see, everything looked clear and the corridor was as deserted as it should be. It had been a smart move using the stairs. I watched for a minute or two, my breath hot against the door, the smell of polish strong in my nose. Then I turned around and kicked off my shoes, beginning to relax as my feet felt the softness of the carpet.

I took a miniature bottle of Vodka out of the fridge, cracked the seal and poured it into one of the glasses. Then I dropped myself into the chair by the window, allowing myself to slouch, just a little, as I sipped my drink and ran trembling fingers through my hair.

Once my breathing was back to normal, I pulled a mobile phone out of my bag and held it out in front of me for a moment. There was only one number in the address book and I brought it up, thinking about making the connection. I took another sip of vodka and hit the dial button. It was a number I'd called many times before and the tone was reassuringly familiar as the numbers dialed through. Like always, it rang only once before it was answered. 'Hello?'

'Hi. It's me,' I said.

'Is everything all right? You sound different.'

'I think someone's following me.'

'When? This evening?'

'Just now in the hotel. '

'You sure?'

'Almost certain.'

'What happened?'

'I was in the bar, I needed a drink, and he was watching me from the lobby. He followed me in there but I think I lost him.'

'What did he look like?'

'Short, sweaty, nervous looking. A bit like a rat.'

'Leather cap and glasses?'

'That's him.'

'Sounds like Deeks.'

'What?'

'Jeremy Deeks. He works for your husband.'

'Doing what exactly?'

'He finds things.'

'Well he's found *me*. How long do you think it'll be before he finds *you*?'

'Your husband must know about the box already. We'll have to move fast...' the line went quiet.

'Are you still there?' I said. 'Hello?'

'Yes, sorry, I was just thinking. Did he see you go in? Does he know which room you're in?'

'No, I don't think so. I did everything you said.'

'You used the stairs?'

'Yes.'

'And you haven't signed for anything? Nothing with a room number on it?'

'No, but...'

'Look, stay where you are, I'll sort something out. Have you still got the things I gave you?'

I was silent for a moment. My throat had gone dry.

'Have you got them?'

'Yes,' I replied.

'Good. Keep them close, just like I showed you. If you do what I say, everything will be all right. I'll have you out of there by tomorrow night.'

'Tomorrow night? No, that's too late. I don't want to stay here that long, what if...?'

'If I could come right now, Magdalena, I would, you know that, but it's the best I can do for the moment.'

'So what am I supposed to do until then?'

'Nothing. Nothing at all. Watch TV. Read a book.'

'B...'

'Don't order any food. Don't leave the room. If you did what I said when you checked in, then they'll never know what room you're in, you'll be fine. They'll have to wait for you downstairs.'

'But...'

'Just stay where you are, it's the best thing for now. Trust me. It'll only be for one night and I'll get you out of there as soon as I can.' There was a noise in the background. 'Look, I've got to go. I'll speak to you later, okay?'

'Okay, just don't let me down.'

'I won't.'

'Promise?'

'Promise. Listen, I'll call back as soon as I can.' The line was killed from the other end. I put down the phone and closed my eyes. I never thought it would turn out like this.

JACK

I stood at the front door and watched Sean and Hornrim standing in the graffiti covered hallway, talking loudly while they waited for the lift. They looked happy enough to see each other and I suppose they had a lot to catch up on, but I still wasn't sure it was the right thing, them going out like that. On the other hand, I was glad to have the place to myself, even if it was Sean's first night out - it was going to take some getting used to having him around. I'd kind of hoped that he'd stay and talk about his plans, but I knew as soon as he got into the car that it wasn't going to happen. It was obvious he wasn't up for it, and there wasn't any point in trying to make him do something if he wasn't ready. Sean wasn't the kind of person to do anything unless he was ready, he'd been like that since I could remember. When we were kids we went through a lot of families because of Sean's attitude. That and the other stuff.

    I waited until the lift took them down and I was sure they were gone, then I shut the door and went back to the living room. I carried my bottle of beer to the kitchen, poured it down the sink, and took another one from the fridge, thinking how I didn't know what kind of diseases Hornrim might have. God knows he'd been beaten hard enough with the ugly stick, and that kind of thing might be catching.

BURN OUT

I took my fresh drink to the window in the living room and looked out. It was dark and the bright room was reflected in the window so I leaned closer to see the city. Shadowy high-rise buildings with dull windows banked roads that ran like rivers of traffic. Pedestrians everywhere, carrying bags of last minute Christmas shopping. Coloured lights climbing lampposts and running across lines over the streets. Snowmen twinkling in shop windows, presents glowing in trees, angels shining on wires. Horns blasting, engines roaring, alarms screeching, the place was alive and humming, but the noises which reached up to the apartment sounded dead in the snow. Snow had a habit of doing that; of making things seem quieter. Better, even.

It was still coming down pretty hard out there and the flakes were bigger now but that was okay by me, because it would probably be at least a couple of feet deep by morning. Then the city would be another place. Quieter and brighter. I liked the snow when it was fresh and clean, it hid the decay, but the grey sludge that came after it was different. That always made everything look a whole lot worse.

I pressed my face right up against the window, making light greasy patches where my forehead and nose touched the cold glass. My breath made a damp smell that brought back a few old memories of brothers peering out at the rain. I looked down at the steps at the front of the building and saw Sean run down them, leaving footprints in the settling snow. I thought that if he wasn't careful he'd slip and break his neck, Hornrim too, but then maybe that wouldn't be so bad.

They disappeared into the underpass, running like kids out of school, and emerged a few seconds later into the open car park on the other side of the busy road. They were laughing about something and looked like they were having fun; two boys out on the town. Once they found my car, they climbed in and settled themselves before Sean drove it out into the road. I watched as they joined the traffic and the taillights disappeared amongst all the others, then I looked at my watch. It was a little after eight.

I wanted to chill out for a while and put my new CD on the player, but I remembered I'd left it in the car, so I put something else on and turned the volume down before taking a sip of my beer. I struggled to think of a reason why I shouldn't call her, but couldn't come up with anything so I took the phone and made myself comfortable.

'Hello?' Her voice was sleepy.

'You okay?'

'Jack. I thought maybe you'd forgotten about me.' Even so, she perked up and sounded pleased to hear my voice. I imagined that she'd been sitting in the easy chair, phone in hand, thinking about calling. The television would be on, the sound turned down low and there'd be a glass of wine on the table next to her.

'Yeah, sorry I didn't call back, things have been a bit up in the air.' We talked for a while, but then talk wasn't enough, so I said I'd meet her. I could go round to hers.

'I thought you couldn't get here tonight,' she said. 'What about Sean?'

'There's been a change in plan. Things didn't turn out like I expected.' I told her that finding a taxi should be easy enough, so I grabbed my keys and threw on a coat as I was talking. She said she'd see me soon. I told her I'd be there in half an hour.

SEAN

I loved it on the quayside, it made me feel good. The smell of the river, the people, the sounds, the lights, the colours. It all just kind of merged into one.

It had changed since I'd last been down there, even more built up now, but it was still where the rich people came to burn their money and the regular people came to feel special. It wasn't like spending the night in the old down town bars, these were fresh and new; clean and fashionable. All lights and glass and steel. I guess they'd eventually go the way everything does, turn to shit, but for now the quay was the place to be seen if you were somebody - or even if you were nobody.

There were people all over the place, queuing outside bars, pouring out of taxis, standing in the middle of the road, laughing, running, shouting, scuffling, drinking. They were fucking everywhere, most of them pissed already, but I picked my way through the crowds, sometimes stopping to say something to Hornrim, but mostly I just ignored him and took in the sights. It was cold out there, colder than I liked, but these girls, they braved the weather in short skirts and open toed shoes, hoping that someone would notice how great they looked. Some legs were orange with fake tan, some might have been treated to a few minutes on the sun bed, but most were corned-beef red and white. Hair was bleached, dyed, permed, straightened.

Make-up was piled on thick and the air was heavy with cheap perfume and petrol fumes.

We didn't stay in any bar for more than one drink, I don't know why, it's just the way we did things. I drank Bud straight from the bottle and Hornrim had some sort of blue coloured drink saying, 'It's the latest thing, man,' and taking the straw out and leaving it on the bar. I told him it looked like a fuckin' girl's drink to me and he said 'No, honest Sean, everyone has 'em now,' like he was trying to justify drinking something that was electric blue.

'Blokes?' I said.

'Yeah, course blokes.'

'*Real* blokes? *North*ern blokes?'

'Yeah.'

'Then how come I don't see any of them?' I looked around.

'There's loads. Look there's someone over there.' Hornrim pointed.

'And why'd they put a fuckin' straw in it? They didn't put a straw in my beer.'

We managed to find a small round table next to the window in the corner of a heaving bar, so I sat facing out onto the river. I glanced at my watch and then back out over the water. I could see the floating nightclub on the other side. They'd tried to do it up with a few lights - coloured strings stretched from the mast to the bow - but from where I was it looked like nothing more than a rusty boat that was ready for a lick of paint. The gangplank was empty now but in a couple of hours it would be full of people waiting to go on board.

'So what's going on with Jack and Mandy Hepple, then?' I said without taking my eyes off the river.

'Dunno.'

'Don't give me that shit, Hornrim. You told me on the phone something was going on.'

'Yeah, but it's not like I hang around with them. They think they're too bloody good for us now.'

'They're probably right.' I looked at him.

He raised his eyebrows up and down. 'Yeah, well, word is he's giving it to her big style. Trying to keep it quiet, though.' He took some of his blue drink and smiled a toothy grin. His lips were wet and loose.

I asked him why they would try to keep it secret and turned my attention back to the coloured lights on the other side of the river. I used my nails to pick at the label on my beer bottle.

'I guess maybe they didn't want you to know,' he said.

'Didn't want me to know? Why should I care who my brother wants to screw?'

'No reason, I guess.'

'So what's the problem then? Why's he keeping secrets?'

'Hey, I dunno. Like I said; I don't even see him. Don't want to.'

'No, but you hear things, Hornrim. People talk.'

'Sometimes.'

'So...?'

'I dunno. Maybe it's serious.' He shrugged, the square shoulders of his suit lifting up around his ears.

'Well good for him, then.' I said nodding my head slowly. I was thinking about Mandy Hepple, trying to decide if I cared that my brother was seeing my old girlfriend, but I didn't find anything I didn't like. That was all over a long time ago. 'Why did we split up, do you remember?' I asked Hornrim and he looked surprised by the question, like he was thinking maybe I was getting soft.

'Sure, I remember. You said she was fuckin' around with one of the guys. Didn't know who at the time, but maybe it was your Jack. Maybe that's why it's such a big secret. Anyway, you got pissed off and broke her nose as I remember it.' Hornrim was smiling his loose-lipped grin again. 'Probably fuckin' deserved it though.'

'I broke her nose? I don't remember that.'

'We took a lot of junk back then, Sean, there's probably a whole shit load of stuff you don't remember.'

I drank some beer and wiped my lips, not wanting the wet look that Hornrim had going on. 'I remember we caused a bit of trouble,' I said putting the bottle down. 'And I remember a bit of rough stuff. A bit of dealing and a lot of fun. Hey, I even remember you had curly hair and thick glasses. And you had a funny smell about you, still do as a matter of fact, but I sure as fuck don't remember breaking Mandy's nose. No, I'd remember a thing like that.'

'Yeah, right. Yeah. You probably would. I must be thinking of someone else,' said Hornrim all sarcastic like he was about ten years old.

I *had* hit Mandy, I hadn't forgotten that, but I was sure I hadn't broken her nose like Hornrim said. No, I'd remember that. I must've just knocked her about a bit, teach her a lesson, something like that. But it was a long time ago, we were just kids then. I was going in a different direction now.

I downed the rest of my beer. 'Come on, let's go.'

*

We went to a few bars, places with names like 'Chase' and 'Martha's', the ones where other guys were drinking bottles of blue and orange stuff, so it probably made Hornrim feel at home. Me, I stuck to the Bud. Cold and straight from the bottle, exactly the way I'd thought about it when I was lying on my bunk trying not to hear Deeks tugging himself. By about half ten, we'd been to a few places and I was just starting to get into my swing. I was beginning to relax, feel like myself again. My head was light and everything was going to be okay. Prison was something that had happened to someone else. I was even having a laugh with Hornrim, telling a few jokes, talking about old times, remembering some of the things we'd done and thinking that maybe he wasn't so bad after all. Must've been something to do with all that beer.

'So what now?' he said when he came back from the bar with two full bottles. 'What you got lined up? Gonna try to go straight again?'

I didn't want to talk about it. I didn't want to think about anything my first night out, just wanted to get drunk and get laid, so I ignored him. But Hornrim kept going with it, saying, 'Nothing too shite, I hope. You're not gonna be stacking shelves or something? That's what you did that first time out, remember? Stacking shelves.'

I ignored him and looked over towards the door where a group of drunk girls had just come in. They were singing and waving their hands in the air. One of them was wearing a bridal veil.

'And then another time, you got that job testing fuses. Nearly drove you fucking mad and you only did it for like a day or something.'

The girl in the veil slipped on her high heels. Her legs went up in the air and she landed on her arse, her skirt hitching up around her waist.

'And what about when you were a waiter in that Italian place in town? Sacked you for pissing in the soup didn't they? You'd only been there a day or...'

'I'm going to work for Sawn-off Montoya.' That stopped him dead in his tracks. His mouth hung open, his eyes widened and in those few seconds before he spoke again, Hornrim had more respect for me than he'd ever had.

'Sawn-off Montoya? The guy who runs the clubs?'

I nodded.

'*The* Sawn-off Montoya?' Saying it like he didn't believe me.

I nodded again.

'Honest?'

Irritated now. 'Yes.'

Hornrim looked at me for a moment and then he said, 'So how did you swing that, then?'

'I got an introduction. Shared a cell with someone who's close to him. A guy called Deeks.'

Hornrim smiled. 'You're not gonna end up working behind the bar?'

'This guy owes me. He's going to set me up with something good. Sawn-off's looking for people he can trust.'

'You've met him?'

'Not yet.'

'So when's this going to happen?'

'Soon as I find Deeks.' I knew that if I couldn't find Deeks and lean on him a while, then I wasn't ever going to meet Sawn-off Montoya. And if that didn't happen, then maybe I *would* end up testing fuses again. Either that or I'd be back inside.

Hornrim went quiet for a while, nodding and sipping his drink before saying, 'I heard he owns that new club, 'Noir'. Heard he hangs out there.'

'Yeah? Maybe we should check it out then.' In the back of my mind I could see Deeks sitting at the bar, buying me a drink.

'See where you're gonna be working, you mean?'

'Something like that.'

Hornrim shook his head. 'It's one of those shirt and tie places. We'll never get in.'

'We could give it a try.'

'Why don't we just go to the boat. They'll let anyone in there.'

I looked at Hornrim. 'My mind's made up.'

*

We left the warm bar and picked our way through the streams of clubbers who were spilling out into the street. It was close to kicking out time, and the early birds were hoping to catch short queues. I turned up the collar on my leather jacket and dug my hands into the pockets, hunching my shoulders to stop the light snow from falling down my neck. I kept my head down but my eyes were scanning ahead and I walked at a good pace with Hornrim trotting along beside me, trying to be cool, but looking more like he was my pet.

We rounded the corner and saw Noir up ahead, standing at the dead end of the side street, nothing behind it but the mucky river. It was isolated from the main drag of bars and clubs, making it all the more exclusive, so the street was pretty quiet except for the sound of people queuing to get inside. The building itself was made out of red brick and sand coloured stone that looked fresh like it had just been cleaned up. On either side it was flanked by dark office buildings, gray and black. The front of the club had been removed and replaced with smoked glass that hid the levels of dance floors. Two flights of steps, one from the left and one from the right, rose to a point in the middle where they became one in front of the main door. Those steps were now crowded with people who were chatting and stamping their feet, waiting to be let in. Most of them wore coats and suits, there weren't any corned beef legs here.

I stopped a few yards away and looked up at the queue. When I was inside, I told myself I'd never stand in another queue again, all that waiting in line for showers and meals, standing for an hour to buy cigarettes. Seemed like I was going to have to rethink my promise though, so I lit a cigarette and watched for a while as the doormen checked membership cards and unclipped the red rope to usher people in. I could see they were wearing head mikes and earpieces, and it made me wonder what else had changed since I'd been away. I hadn't been inside that long, but blokes were already drinking blue stuff and now bouncers had technology.

One of the doormen was your typical meathead - no neck, wide shoulders, barrel chest, bald head. He was wearing a heavy coat and thick gloves. The other guy on the door was much smaller and younger, dressed lightly in a shiny black puffer jacket over the top of a white shirt and black tie. He was lean and carried himself like a hard-on but there was something in his face like he didn't really belong. I thought maybe he was green.

I took a deep breath and stretched my fingers out, making myself relax.

'What are we waiting for?' said Hornrim. 'It's fuckin' freezing.' He crossed his arms around his chest and started swaying from one foot to the other. 'Why don't we just go in? Hey, maybe if you tell them who you are, they'll let you go straight to the front of the queue.'

I looked at him for a moment, then shook my head and turned back to the club entrance.

'What?' he said. 'What's that mean?'

'Nothing.'

'No, I saw the way you looked at me. Like I said something wrong.' He shook his head a little, imitating how I'd looked at him.

'You know, you can be such a dick, sometimes, Hornrim.' I shook my head again.

'All right,' he said. 'Whatever.' Then he was quiet for about a second before he spoke again saying, 'So what are we doing, then?'

'Well, you're prancing about,' I said. 'I'm checking the lay of the land.'

'What for?'

I told him never you mind what for. 'Come on, let's go.' I flicked my cigarette into the empty street and made my way towards the club.

I climbed the set of steps to the right and joined the queue, thinking that once I was working for Montoya, *then* there'd be no more standing in queues for me. No, I'd just walk straight up to the front like I owned the place, and the bouncers would step back and let me in.

We waited for half an hour or so, and Hornrim kept trying to make conversation but I ignored him because my mind was on other things. I was wondering if Deeks was in the club right now. Maybe even sitting with Sawn-off himself. And when Deeks saw me, he'd invite me over and introduce us. We'd drink brandy or something and talk about what I was going to do for him. In fact, Sawn-off was just saying how much he needed people like me when we reached the front of the queue and bouncer number one, the big guy, let Hornrim through and then held out a gloved hand saying, 'I'm sorry sir, I can't let you in without a shirt and tie.' He clipped the rope back across the entrance.

'What?'

'Club rule,' he shrugged.

My eyes were about level with the top of the bouncer's chest and I could read his name badge clearly. 'Howard Taylor', it said. Fucking sissy name for a bouncer.

'Come on Howard,' I said. 'This T-shirt I'm wearing is Armani. And this jacket probably cost more than your suit.' I smiled, playing it cool.

'I still can't let you in without a shirt and tie. Club rule.'

'Well it's a pretty fuckin' stupid rule don't you think?' I smiled again.

He shrugged again.

'You seriously not going to let me in?'

Howard shook his head.

By now the queue behind me was starting to get restless, just like it did inside when you were in the shower or on the phone too long. Hornrim was uneasy too, so he came back over the rope saying, 'Come on, let's go.'

'How about you give me a tie from behind the desk, then?' I said. 'Places like this, you guys always have ties.'

A couple of people behind me tutted and groaned, so I turned around and gave them a look. People like that, nice people, they moan behind your back but when you face them, they don't know what to do. They just turn away and pretend they don't see you.

Howard looked up and raised his voice. 'I'm sorry, folks, we'll be with you in just a moment.'

'Come on, let's go,' Hornrim said quietly, touching my jacket. 'We'll go somewhere else. It doesn't matter.'

'I don't want to go somewhere else. I want to go here.' I pulled away from Hornrim and turned to the bouncer. 'I want to see *Sawn-off*.'

'I'm sorry, *sir*, I don't know anyone by that name.' It was the young one, this time, the smaller of the two bouncers. 'Joe' it said on his name badge.

Joe put his hand out to lead me away from the door so I pushed it off, but he just rolled his eyes and said, 'Time for you to leave,' and then he smiled, real cocky. After that, he reached out again and put his hand on my shoulder, applying pressure, trying to push me back.

'Get your fucking hands off me.' I moved to brush him off, but he caught my hand, pulling me, forcing me to take a step towards him. In a fraction of a second, he was behind me, holding my arm twisted up between my shoulder blades. Then he reached up with his other hand, grabbed the back of my neck and pushed my head forwards.

My face burned and I tried to stay calm, but I couldn't believe what was happening. I'd played it about as cool as I could. I'd been polite. I'd been nice. I'd *smiled* for fuck's sake. But now some kid was pushing me around in front of all these people. And Hornrim was standing right there beside me like he didn't know what to do.

I knew that rage wasn't going to help here but I could feel it coming so I close my eyes and breathed deeply, the cold air stinging my nose and throat. I relaxed my arm, allowing myself to be manhandled, but as soon as Joe's grip softened, I moved. I was going to push him away and leave with my head high, but when I broke the hold, pulling away and twisting around to face him, I was met with a solid punch straight to my chest. So quick and hard, the force knocked me back against the brick wall which lined the steps, my lungs gave in and the air rushed out of me. Just one hit and I was down and out but Joe didn't stop there. He took hold of my shoulder with his left hand and twisted me to one side, opening up my kidneys. He punched me at least twice, it could have been more, but I only felt the first one. Then he moved in to smash his elbow into my nose and I went over sideways, smacking my head against the steps, everything going fuzzy and slow like I was underwater. I remember thinking it couldn't have taken more than about five seconds to put me down, then I heard a voice say something like, 'That's enough, Joe,' and someone else might have said, 'Hit him again.'

After that someone dragged me to my feet and threw me face down into the snow.

Then it was just cold and dark.

JACK

I jumped out of the taxi and reached Mandy's front door almost exactly thirty-five minutes after I closed my own. It was an expensive ride, but it was worth every penny.

Mandy had been there a few years now, said she'd had enough of living in the city, and I can't say I blame her. I sometimes wondered if her moving might have had something to do with Sean and his crowd, but I never asked. Mandy and I talked about those days as little as we could – she'd pulled herself a long way out of that world and there was no going back for her now. She had a strong family who stood behind her, a good job and she worked hard. She'd managed to save a little money and now she even owned her own home. Done a lot of good for me too, and it was hard to imagine that she was the same person who'd been with Sean all those years ago.

It was a quiet village, a place people moved out to so they could raise kids, keep pets, look after their gardens and wash their car on a Sunday. It wasn't the best, but it was better than the run down high-rise where I lived. The houses were good, there was enough space between them so that people weren't living on top of each other and they were away from the city. Mandy had a porch, a small back garden with flowers and a fence, and there was a little green patch at the front which was now virgin white. She even had a small garage, where she kept her affordable car, and a path which ran from the road all the way to the yellow front door. All in all it was a happy place; the kind of place where people wave to each other as they leave for work, and look after each other's houses when they're away on holiday. My guess is that Sean would've hated it.

It was dark when I arrived and she'd left the porch light on for me so I pressed the doorbell and waited under the shelter out of the snow. I heard ringing somewhere inside and then faint footsteps on the carpet. The smell of Mandy and Mandy's home, like a mix of perfume and pastry, leaked out into the night when she opened the door. It was light and warm in the hallway, another world. I stepped onto the mat and turned around to bang the snow off my feet before closing the door, but as soon as I had my back to her, Mandy's arms were around my waist and her face was pressed between my shoulders. She made a happy sound, a kind of quiet moan, and squeezed me tight. I turned around and kissed the top of her head, breathing deep to smell the shampoo in her hair, then she looked up and kissed me hard on the mouth, warm lips against cold, then again more softly.

'Drink?' she asked, breaking away. She smiled and headed for the kitchen without needing to wait for an answer. I followed her, watching the way she moved, listening to the sound she made. She was wearing a baggy red sweatshirt and dark blue leggings. Thick blue socks on her feet and blonde hair pulled back into a ponytail.

'Thank God it's Saturday,' she said pouring a heavy amount of red wine into a glass and handing it to me. She put the bottle down and we touched glasses before drinking. 'So how's your day been?' her leaning against a cupboard now, reaching out with one hand and pulling me close. I put my arm around her waist and moved so that the tops of our thighs were against one another. My jeans were still cold from being outside, but her body was warm and it felt good.

'Oh you know,' I said.

'Not really, no,' she shook her head and a strand of hair pulled loose from the ponytail. I thought about reaching out and touching it, moving it away from her eyes, but I liked the way it looked so I left it, smiling and saying, 'No, I suppose not.'

'So?' she said. 'How was it? How'd it go?'

I pursed my lips and raised my eyebrows. 'Well, it was okay, I suppose. I mean, I picked my brother up from prison and listened to him slag off my life. Then Hornrim came round, and I listened to the pair of them insult each other. Then they went out, taking my car with them. Just another ordinary day.'

'My god. Hornrim? Is he still around?'

'Uh-huh.' I sipped my wine. 'And he's the last person I want Sean to be out with. Especially now, on his first night.'

'Don't worry about him, I'm sure he'll be fine.' The strand of hair moved, slipping across her face and arcing to point at the corner of her mouth.

'Sean or Hornrim?'

She laughed, 'both of them, I suppose,' and brushed the stray hair to the side of her face but it fell back so she tucked it behind her ear.

'Anyway, it's not really him I'm worried about,' I said. 'It's what he might do to someone else.'

'How d'you mean?'

'Well, you know what he's like. And it's been a while since he's been out.'

Mandy rolled her eyes upwards. 'You worry about him too much. Maybe you should just give up on him. Leave him to it.'

'Can't do that.'

'Course you can. He'll drag you down with him if you don't.'

'Maybe.'

'Definitely.' She paused for a moment, not long, and then said, 'so what about us?'

'Us?'

'Do we tell him?'

I nodded slowly. 'Yeah. I think so.' I told her I had a feeling he might have guessed already, that he'd been acting like he knew something and wasn't letting on, so she asked 'How come? How could he know already?'

'Well, he's been on the phone to Hornrim, hasn't he? You remember what that lot are like.'

Mandy sighed and said she thought she'd left all that behind, got away from those people, it was all such a long time ago. 'Sean and his bloody friends,' she called them.

We stayed in the kitchen and talked for a while, about all kinds of things – some important and some not - then we went through to the living room and talked there, but not as much. Things had moved on, taken a different turn, slowed down. The fire was on, the sofa was soft and there was quiet music playing. It was warm and comfortable.

We finished our wine upstairs.

BURN OUT

HORNRIM

I ran over to Sean and put my hands under his armpits, trying to lift his head out of the snow, but he was heavy and it was a struggle, but I had to do something. I had to get him on his feet and away from there, I mean, shit, I couldn't just leave him lying in the snow after what that kid had done to him, messing him up like that and pushing him down the stairs. At first I thought maybe I should call an ambulance, maybe it was serious, but then I reckoned Sean would probably kill me if I did that, me acting like he couldn't take what had just been dished out. 'Sean. Sean. Wake up will you.' I gave up trying to lift him and crouched down beside him, keeping my voice low, not wanting the bouncer to comeback and play hell with me the way he had with Sean. 'Come on, man, get up.' Now I was trying to turn him over, get him on his back, but all the time I kept my eyes on the bouncers by the club door, but they didn't look over, though, they acted like it hadn't even happened, like Sean wasn't lying face down in the snow, bleeding all over the place. 'For fuck's sake, Sean, get up.' I couldn't get him on his back, everything was getting cold, my fingers going numb, nothing was working properly, couldn't get a grip, so I shook him hard but he didn't move. Nothing. I put my hands on either side of his head and turned it sideways, lifting his face out of the snow and then I leaned down and stared right at him thinking, shit, he looked rough, there was fucking blood everywhere, all frozen and hard around his busted nose and mouth, and his eyes were swollen right up so that I wasn't even sure if they were open or closed. 'Sean? You alive?' I put my hand on his back, wanted to see if he was dead, felt it rise a couple of times, but it was weak and shallow. 'Fuck.' I gritted my teeth and sat down beside him, starting to think maybe I *should* call an ambulance. I looked back over at the club, wondering if they'd give me a phone to use or if they'd just let him die, and then I turned back to Sean just as he finally groaned and rolled over onto his back. For a while he stayed like that, lying in the snow, all spaced out and covered in blood. I sat beside him until my arse was so wet and numb that I had to stand up.

He was breathing hard now, his chest pumping up and down like he'd run a marathon and he stared up into the dark saying nothing, not seeming to notice the cold, I mean, he was lying in the snow for fuck's sake, like he was kind of dead, but not, if you know what I mean. Then, after a while longer, he touched his mouth and said something, I don't know what exactly, but it was something like 'fucking bastard', and I don't think he meant me, but he could've.

Then he pushed himself into a sitting position and looked up at me like he wanted to kill somebody. 'Thanks for stepping in, mate,' he said, his voice sounding different, muffled, like he had flu' or something and he hardly moved his lips.

'What could I have done? Get me head kicked in by Bruce Lee up there? Fuck that.'

Sean tried to stand up but it took him a long time just to get to his knees and he looked like he was in a lot of pain so I grabbed him with both hands. I pulled him to his feet and held him straight but he pushed me away from him, saying he could stand up on his own thank you very much.

After that, I knew he'd be all right. I mean, at least he was standing. And he could talk. Sean had been beaten up before, it was nothing new to him, it was part of the life. I remember one time he had to spend a few weeks in hospital, all rigged up to machines and instruments because he'd been beaten so badly - broken jaw, broken ribs, blood clots, you name it – but the guys who did it to him, though, they ended up spending a lot longer in there than Sean did because as soon as he was better he went looking for them. A few of us went along for support, but Sean did all the work.

He looked down at himself, dusting off the snow and said, 'Jesus, look at that. The stupid fucker's ripped my jacket. Look,' he held his arm up for me to see the rip under the armpit. The sudden movement made him lose his balance, his left foot twisting and giving in, but I caught him and held him up.

'Fucker ripped my jacket,' he said again. 'It was a fucking Christmas present from my *brother*.' He turned around and made out like he was going back to the club, trying to pull away from my grip, but he was weak and I kept a hold of him saying, 'Hey, you want the guy to kick you to *death*?' and that made him stop right where he was and turn to look at me like he was going to kill me for telling him not to go back. 'What?' I said letting go of him and holding up my hands. 'What did I say? Shit, man, go. Go back. I won't stop you.'

'Remember what you told me on the phone?' he said.

I put my hands down. 'You mean about Jack and Mandy?'

'No, the other thing'

'Oh, that.'

'You said you'd show it to me.'

'Yeah, but...'

'Well, now would be a good time.'

'Bu..'

'Get me back to the car. We're going to your place.'

RUBENO 'SAWN-OFF' MONTOYA

I fired off a few last emails and then took the computer off-line, unplugging the modem link from the wall socket and coiling it behind the machine. I couldn't see any sense in leaving a permanent connection, there were too many things on there that I didn't want anybody to see.

I liked the computer. At times it could be a little too technical for my liking, or it could run off with a mind of its own, but as long as you let it know who's boss, it had its uses. For starters, it was easy to keep track of business. I always knew where my money was and who owed me what. Just with a click of my finger, I could see what needed to be delivered, what needed to be collected, who needed to be paid or who was getting in my way. It saved on a lot of paper, too, which stopped all the clutter. Some of the games were good, especially the ones where you get to shoot people with big guns, and porn was always easy to find if you knew where to look. And then there was the word processor. For years, I'd been telling people they were on my shit list, but I'd said it to so many people that I kept forgetting who they were. The difference now that I had the computer was that I actually *had* a 'shit list', a real one, all listed out in order of preference and everything. That way I never forgot anybody and I could put you straight to number one using nothing more than my fingers. No one would go unnoticed. I'd even made the ones at the top stand out by colouring them red.

I pushed the swivel chair back from the computer station and wheeled it across the room. Once I was back behind my desk, I felt more like a tough guy called Sawn-off and less like a computer geek.

My office was more or less soundproof, but when the night was in full swing, I could always hear the dull pounding of the music that played in the club. Now the thumping was silent and my desk clock told me it was three am. There'd still be a few stragglers on some of the floors but they wouldn't evade security for long. Sledgehammer's boys would soon turf them out into the cold. The guests in the upstairs bar, on the other hand, could stay a while longer. A couple of slimy local politicians were having a few drinks more than they should, and I'd arranged for them to take one or two of my dancers home with them. One of the guests, some fat fuck freeloader called Wilby was well connected with the police so I'd organised some special treatment for him. You never know when you might need a guy like that, so I'd set him up with one of my girls, one who does the really dirty stuff but knows how to leave the curtains open just enough for prying eyes. That way, the guy I'd lined up to follow them home would be able to take a few good snaps. Wilby knew who I was and if he was stupid enough to accept favours of the flesh from me, then he should expect to be caught with his trousers down. I tried not to think about what that would look like, some fat sweaty bastard heaving over one of my girls, but I knew that he'd be a powerful ace to have up my sleeve. With dirty pictures of the politician and the lap dancer, Harry Milton wouldn't be such a pain in the arse. I could just see the headlines now-'*Wild Wilby in sordid sex soiree, exclusive pictures inside*'. The poor guy's wife would have a fucking hernia if she knew, and I was pretty sure that old Wilby would do just about anything to keep his dirty little secret quiet.

Now that everything was up to date, I was thinking about leaving for the night, but couldn't see any good reason to go home. It was warm in my office, I had a large glass of bourbon, and the rest of the bottle was still in the cabinet. It looked cold and miserable outside, all snow and slush, so I couldn't think why I should bother moving. Usually it would be the thought of Magda that would take me home because I was always feeling horny at that time of night, and she'd be ready and waiting; silk stockings and uplift bra. But she wouldn't be home when I went back that night. The house would be dark and empty and I'd have to sleep alone unless I took one of the girls with me. Magda used to like that.

I'd been trying to forget about her all night, but she'd gnawed at the back of my mind, and here I was thinking about her again so I closed my eyes, but all I saw was her leaning over into that car, and me wanting to know who was inside. Whose lips she was kissing, whose leg she was touching, maybe even whose hands she was putting the box into. My box. And every time I saw that played out in my head, I knew that if I could see that face, then I'd be able to finish it. Punishment would be given and the box would be returned.

I picked up a pile of papers that was lying in a tidy stack on the desk and flicked through them. Letters, bills, documents about the club, shipment details, all important stuff, but I couldn't fix on any of it so I loosened my tie enough to undo the top button of my shirt and pushed the chair away from the desk. I put my feet up and leaned back, taking a sip of bourbon. Right now, I could only think of a couple of reasons why she'd have stolen the box. Money's always a good one but Magda would never be able to sell it without the right connections. I couldn't think how she'd turn it into cash or favours unless she had someone lined up to do it for her, and that took me back to the figure in the car. If I could find out who *that* was, then I'd send Carpetto round to put another hole in their face – it would be worth the expense. The other reason, the police, didn't make a lot of sense either. We both knew that Harry Milton would do almost anything to snap his cuffs around my wrists, but if that's what Magda was planning, then she wouldn't have bothered stealing the box. She would've just left it where it was, passed on the information and Milton would've popped up with a warrant and my lawyer would be earning a fortune right now.

Even so, I was beginning to wish that I hadn't hit her.

JOE

All in all, it was a funny kind of night. After I gave that guy a hiding outside in the snow, I spent another hour on the door in the freezing cold with nothing much happening except for Hammer giving me dirty looks. He didn't say a word, wouldn't let me check any cards or talk to any of the customers, just had me standing there like a mug unclipping the rope every so often. I reckon he thought I went a bit too far with that guy but I only hit him a couple of times before he went down so it can't have been that bad. Maybe it had been a long time since Hammer had to turn someone away like that, so he might have been getting soft. Anyway, after that they sent me inside to watch the middle dance floor area for a while before going down to the lower bar and then back up again. I broke up one or two scuffles and chatted on with a few of the girls but other than that, the rest of the night was pretty calm.

Once the club was winding down and most of the customers had left, Hammer came over and tapped me on the shoulder. 'Follow me,' he said. 'Sledge wants a word downstairs.' He didn't say anything else, just gave me another one of his dirty looks and walked off. I watched his back as he picked his way through the last few stragglers, getting them to move on towards the door, then I shrugged and followed him.

Seeing the club after closing, with the lights up, was like waking up and seeing a one-night stand for the first time in daylight. Her make up was all streaked and you could see every pimple, every wart, every fault in what had looked so great the night before.

The fluorescent lighting was harsh and exposing, reaching into all the places that had been so secret in the dark, and the smell of stale tobacco and alcohol seemed stronger. There was no colour; there were no dancers; no drinkers, no staff, no music. The beige walls were splashed with ugly patterns from spilled drinks and scuffed in places where people had leaned against them or put their feet on them. The floor was streaked with dark stains and littered with crushed cigarette butts. Bottles were tucked into corners, dumped on any available surface or just rolling about on the floor along with cigarette packets and plastic shooter glasses. I clocked a bracelet and a watch amongst the debris under one table, a lost handbag on a stool at the bar, a coat draped over one of the cushioned seats. There was even a twisted pair of yellow knickers caught around one of the barstools.

At the far side of the titty bar, Sledge was sitting at a round table that he'd pulled away from one of the booths along the wall. He was drinking and chatting with a couple of the dancers, acknowledging his brother as he took off his jacket and sat down at the table.

'What's up?' I asked walking over, my footsteps feeling dead on the sticky carpet.

'Ah. Joe. Just the man I was looking for.' Sledge smiled at the girls and nodded, so they picked up their stuff and left us alone. When they were gone, Sledge pointed at an empty chair and said, 'Sit down.'

Hammer didn't bother to look at me, kept himself sideways on, facing out towards the small stage with the poles. Sledge took a sip of his beer and put it down on the table. Then he just stared at me for ages without saying anything. Didn't even move until I said, 'What?'

'D'you want to tell me about it?'

'About what?'

Sledge didn't answer, he just raised his eyebrows.

'Tell you about what?' I said again.

'About what happened on the door, Joe. Don't you remember me saying 'no rough stuff'?'

'Well...'

'Maybe it's me. You see, I'm sure I said 'no rough stuff.'

I sat back and crossed my arms saying, 'But the guy was getting abusive. He had to be taken down a peg or t...'

'No,' Sledge held up a hand and stopped me. 'We're not in the business of taking people down *any* number of pegs. We're in the business of making this a place people want to come to.' He spoke slowly like I was a moron or something.

'I...'

'You see, if people come here, then Mr. Montoya will make lots of money, and if Mr. Montoya makes lots of money, then he will need me to look after his clubs, and if I look after his clubs, *I* will make lots of money.'

'Yeah but...'

'Shut the fuck up,' Hammer finally shifted in his seat and looked me in the eye, so I held him to it, neither of us wanting to look away.

'Joe,' Sledge started again. 'Maybe you should look for a job at one of the other clubs. One of the rough ones uptown. I think that would suit you better.'

'Are you firing me?' I asked, still staring at Hammer.

'I'm telling you you're not for us. Go somewhere else,' he said.

'But I've only been here a few nights...' I started to argue but Hammer reached over and grabbed the collar of my shirt, pulling me across the table until his nose was about a millimetre from mine.

'Get - the fuck - out - of here,' he said, and I thought about breaking his nose like I'd done to that guy in the leather jacket earlier on but I knew it wouldn't make any difference. Besides, it looked like it'd been broken about a hundred times before already, so it probably wouldn't be anything new to him.

'Hammer. Leave it,' said Sledge putting one hand on his brother's shoulder. Hammer immediately let go and I dropped back down into my seat.

'You'd better go now,' Sledge still with one hand on his brother. 'I think it would be best.'

'Bu...'

'Just fuck off.'

I pushed back my chair, gave them the 'v' and headed straight for the stairs, thinking I should've broken Hammer's nose just for the hell of it. Sledge wasn't so bad, I reckon I could have been all right with him, but Hammer had been out for me as soon as I'd started. And I really wanted the job, too, I couldn't believe I fucked it up so quickly. As soon as I was out of sight, I kicked a couple of doors and punched the wall a few times to help me calm down a bit, and by the time I got to the main entrance, I knew I'd made a mistake by letting my temper go again. I shouldn't have done that guy on the door and I shouldn't have lost it with Sledge just now. I was starting to think maybe I should go back, hang my head and say I'm sorry, I won't do it again, I'll be a good boy. If I was lucky, I might be able to persuade Sledge to keep me on. I knew I had an attitude on me, but I'd tell him I'd control it. I could do it if I really wanted to, I could really make a go of it.

I thought I'd let them cool off for a bit first, so I hung about in the entrance on the main level, larking about with some of the staff and saying goodnight to the girls. Then I went back down to the lower bar but the brothers had gone and the place was empty except for one of the dancers. She was standing on the main stage, holding the pole, wearing a kind of glittery bikini thing that had nothing more than three small triangles of material at the front and a couple of bits of string round the back. She was singing to herself and swaying about so I thought she must be practicing a few routines or something. Didn't look the same, though, with the lights up like that.

'Hi,' I said.

'Hi back,' she looked me up and down, pouting her lips. I think she liked what she saw because she put her hands on her hips and stuck her boobs right out when she spoke to me.

I smiled again and looked at the floor, pretending to be shy because I knew the chicks loved that. 'You haven't seen the brothers have you?'

'You're the new guy aren't you?'

'That's me.'

'Joe, right? I'm Natalie. *Nat.*' She asked me if I was hanging around for a while, maybe we could have a drink when she was changed. I told her that sounded like a good idea, but that I needed to see the brothers first. I needed to see Sledge.

'I think he went up to see the boss.' She turned to one side and flicked her hair over her shoulder.

'Thanks. Maybe I'll go up and find him.'

'Sure you don't want a drink first?' she said, batting her eyelids, really laying it on thick now.

'You know what? I'd really like that but first I need...'

'Yeah, yeah, whatever. Don't be a stranger,' she said giving up on me. She turned on her heels and disappeared through the changing room door at the far side of the small stage.

So then I was alone and there wasn't any point in going up to find Sledge if he was in with Sawn-off, so I thought I'd wait where I was. When he came back down, I'd eat a bit of humble pie, say I was sorry, promise to do better and ask for my job back. Hopefully he'd come back on his own, but if he came down with Hammer then I'd have to deal with it.

I stood around for a few minutes but no one came, so I sat down at the table and looked at my watch. I leaned forward to drum my fingers on the wood. I leaned back and cracked my knuckles. I looked at my watch again. Then I was forward again, playing with the cigarette packet, standing it on its end and running my fingers down it. Turn it over and do the same. I looked at my watch a third time and wished Natalie would come back through, maybe wearing the same outfit she had on just a few minutes ago. She seemed pretty nice for a dancer and I could do with some company.

I sat back again and my elbow brushed the jacket hanging on the chair next to me. Something solid. I wondered if one of the brothers was packing and decided to have a quick look, kill some time.

I pulled the jacket away from the chair and peered down into the inside pocket. Jesus, I'd never seen so much cash in my life. It wasn't a wad or a load or even a pile, it was a fucking *shed load* of cash. Note after note after note, all in a tight bundle. There must have been fucking hundreds in those pockets and it was all begging to be mine.

BURN OUT

RUBENO 'SAWN-OFF' MONTOYA

I was leaning back, taking another sip from the heavy crystal when someone knocked on the door. I didn't answer straight away, it would've made me look like I had nothing to do, and even after three am, a man like me has to look busy.

Another knock, a little harder this time, so I took my feet off the desk, pulled the chair in and moved a pile of papers so that they were in front of me. I took the top off a pen and held it point down like I was working on something important.

Another knock and this time I said, 'Yeah. Come in.'

The door opened and Sledge lumbered in like one of those big ugly buffalo things they get in Africa, the ones that get eaten by giant crocodiles. He'd taken off his jacket, something he always did at the end of the night, and the sleeves of his shirt were rolled up past his thick hairy forearms. Like me he'd loosened his tie.

'How we doing?' I put the pen down and held my hands together on the desk in front of me.

'It's been a good night, Mr. Montoya.' Sledge moved his head from side to side like a boxer limbering up before he goes into the ring. Then he stretched his neck to the front and rubbed a hand across the ripples of skin on the back of his bald head. 'Busy. Not too much trouble.'

'How's the take? Anything in yet?' Sledge wasn't the manager but he always had some idea of how the night had gone.

'Entries on the door were up from last weekend.'

'Up by how much?'

'Don't know, but they reckon the bar take should be nearly half as much again.'

'Good.'

'Yeah, well, it'll cover that pay rise you were gonna give us.' He tried to make it sound like a joke, but with Sledge there's always a reason behind the comment, so I told him not to push his luck. There were one or two things in the pipe line but he'd have to be patient for now. 'Besides,' I said. 'Let's see how you get on with the return of my box, shall we?'

'You're the boss,' he said.

'Yes. I am.' I thought for a moment and sipped my drink. 'Okay. So, we clear downstairs?'

'More or less. Just a few of your personal guests still hanging about in the private area. Maybe I should ask them to leave? It's getting late.'

I nodded, yeah he should go ahead and move them out, I didn't want to give Harry Milton any reason to drop down on me. 'Make sure we get those Wilby pictures, though.'

'All taken care of. Got some pretty good ones already.'

The conversation was over as far as I was concerned so I picked up the pen and pretended to write something on the top of a note block. I drew a cube, not a very good one. Sledge didn't leave, though, he stayed where he was, taking up too much space in my office. 'What?' I looked up from my cube. 'Something else?'

'Yeah,' he touched his hand to his forehead. 'D'you know anyone who drives a light blue Ford?'

'No. Should I?'

'Jamie's been on the radio saying there's one parked outside with the motor runnin'. Been there a while, apparently.'

I downed my bourbon and looked up at Sledge again. 'Show me,' I said and pushed the chair away from the desk.

We went to the window and I opened the blinds enough to peer out. 'There,' Sledge pointed.

I nodded. The window from my office on the top floor looked out directly over the front steps and along the quiet street. The end of the road was intersected by one of the busier roads on the quayside, and one or two cabs and a few straggling pedestrians passed by on their way home. Other than that, the night was still and the road in front of the club was dark except for the no good orange spots from the street lamps. I'd asked the city council for better lighting but none had ever been put in. I don't think they knew what to do - me asking them for lights -probably nearly shit themselves. Or pissed themselves laughing, but either way, I didn't get the lights.

There was a car parked up between two of the spots of orange glow, and at first I thought maybe it was empty, but when I leaned right up to the glass, I could see that the motor was running, the gray fumes from the exhaust clear enough once I'd spotted them. The last of the staff were making their way down the street towards the car park, but none of them turned to look at the Ford as they passed. No headlights were on, not even sidelights, so I was thinking that whoever it was didn't want to be seen. Maybe someone like a policeman who was trying to keep an eye on me. It made me wonder what Magda might have told them but I knew that didn't make sense. The box would be more incriminating if I still had it in my safe when Milton turned up holding his warrant. Unless she'd given them something else, of course, and Christ knows there was plenty. Either way, I knew I'd feel safer once I had my hands on those Wilby pictures.

'How d'you know it's blue?' I said. 'Looks gray to me.' I didn't think that Harry Milton drove a blue Ford, but it could've been a pool car or something.

'One of the boys on the door saw it pull up a while ago, said it was blue. Would've seen it when it passed under the light. You want me to get someone to check it out?'

'Yeah. In a minute.' I watched the car. I couldn't see any movement and it was impossible to tell how many people were inside. Then I saw a cigarette end glow in the dark, someone taking a good long drag, and I knew it couldn't be Milton because he didn't smoke. Sanctimonious cop probably didn't even have to shit like the rest of us. No, it wasn't him. I breathed out hard. 'Probably just a ride waiting for one of the staff. Jesus, Sledge, you nearly gave me a fuckin' heart attack.'

Sledge looked at me sideways, pulling his head away from the glass. 'What's the matter, Guv? Something you want me to handle for you?'

'No, you're okay for now,' I said. 'Let's wait and see what he's up to.'

Still, I didn't want to take any chances, so I grabbed a pen and paper from the desk saying, 'Can you see the reg?'

Sledge was still at the window so he nosed forward and squinted. He said nope, it was too dark to see anything, then he told me to hang on a minute, he'd find out. He took a radio from his belt and held it to his mouth. 'One to Jamie,' he said. 'You still down by the door, big guy?'

'That's a yes,' came the reply and there was a slight crackle, but other than that it was crystal.

'Can you see the plate on that car?'

'Yes to that.'

'Without being seen?'

'That's a yes.'

'Read it out for me.'

He read it out and I jotted it down. I'd get Deeks to check it out, find out who was hanging around. If it *was* just a ride, then they'd be okay. If it was someone else, then I'd have to deal with it.

I folded the paper and slipped it into my pocket just as Hammer came in, knocking on the already open door and saying, 'Oh, there you are,' and then seeing us both looking all serious, his brother still peering out into the street, he said, 'Hey whatcha lookin' at?' and came over to the window.

'That car out front. Trying to figure out who it is,' said Sledge. From behind, both their faces pressed to the glass, they looked like a pair of bowling balls.

Hammer asked if I wanted him to go down and take a closer look, drag someone out if necessary, but Sledge answered for me, saying, 'Already offered. Mr. Montoya says he wants to wait. Got the number, though.'

'Well, you just let us know if you want us to do anything, Mr. Montoya,' said Hammer.

'I will.'

'Fine.' He left the window and made for the door telling his brother , 'Don't be too long, mate, beer's getting cold.'

'I'll come now,' both of them moving away from the window now, and then Sledge turning to me saying, 'Just call down if you want us to...' he stopped and whipped around to look at his brother. 'Hey, where's my jacket?'

'Downstairs.' Hammer looked puzzled for a second and then realisation spread across his face. 'On the chair.'

Both brothers moved quicker than I'd ever seen. They didn't bother to close the door behind them and I was left alone in my office listening to the sound of giants trampling down the stairs as fast as their legs would carry them.

I smiled and turned back to the window to take another look at that car, just in time to see the new kid, Joe, appear from the alley beside the club. I wondered if the car was there to give him a lift, but he was acting twitchy, turning this way and that, holding his jacket tight – not walking over to it like someone *expecting* a car waiting for them. When he noticed it, hiding in the shadow, he hesitated and then looked about. He crossed about a couple of yards of snow-covered street before the car door opened but the light inside didn't come on and it was too dark for me to see much of the person who climbed out. Joe obviously knew who it was, though, because he stopped dead in his tracks. Then the figure in the leather jacket stepped forward into the dull light and although I couldn't see his face, I knew what he was going to do as soon as he took his hand out of his pocket and extended his arm at Joe.

Jesus, I couldn't believe that shit was happening on my own doorstep.

SLEDGE

All the time I was talking to Mr. Montoya, up there in his office, I was thinking about my money, down there in my jacket. It should've been all right, I mean, my brother was looking after it. My brother the security guy. Except now he was here, right in front of me, standing in the office, bold as brass, looking out the window.

Bollocks.

We raced down the stairs and headed for the bar where I'd left my jacket, where I'd specifically told Hammer to keep an eye on it. '*Keep an eye on it,*' I'd said. '*Don't forget about it,*' I'd said. '*No problem,*' he'd said. So what did he do? He forgot about it. Great advert for Sledgehammer Security - can't even look after our own fucking money.

We came down the stairs and burst into the bar like a pair of idiots but the place was empty except for the two bottles and the packet of cigarettes we'd left waiting for us. And my jacket, which was still draped over the back of one of the chairs we'd pulled out. I slowed to a walk, crossed the bar and picked it up. It felt light. I slid my hand into the inside pocket and shook my head at Hammer. 'Gone,' I said throwing the jacket back onto the chair. 'All of it.'

Hammer kicked the chair nearest him ' Shit,' and then sat down on it saying, 'Sorry mate. I just didn't...' he swore a few times, getting it out of his system, while I went through everybody in my head, thinking who might have done it. There were so many, though, bar staff, security, maybe even a clubber who'd managed to avoid the final clear through.

It was Hammer who said, 'Joe. I bet it was that kid, Joe.'

'Joe?' I thought about it and then shook my head 'No, can't be. We sent him packing ages ago. He'll be long gone. Anyway, how would he know about the money?'

'I dunno. Maybe he got lucky. Maybe he came back to see what he could take with him.'

'No. I mean he was hot-headed, yeah, but...'

The door, which was hidden in the wall to the right of the stage, opened and one of the girls walked through from the changing room. We both looked up, watching her move past the poles towards us. She was wearing a long coat and trainers, carrying a sports bag, her hair scraped back and pony tailed. She looked tired and pale.

'Hey, Nat, anyone else been down here?' I didn't think any of the girls would have rifled my jacket. They spent the night with their tits in people's faces while sweaty hands squeezed money into their g-strings - they didn't need to nick money from the likes of me, they had enough cash of their own.

She looked over at me but kept on walking, the trainers squeaking on the waxed wooden floor. 'Nope,' she said. 'Just some of the other girls, but I'm the last.'

'Okay, thanks. See you tomorrow.'

'Yeah. G'night.' She stepped down from the stage and made her way to the bottom of the stairs where she stopped and turned around. 'Oh, I tell you who I *did* see earlier on. That new one. Young dishy one.'

I could feel Hammer's eyes on me now but I ignored him and said, 'Joe?'

'Yeah. Joe. Nice buns.'

I asked how long ago that was.

'Ten minutes?' she said it like she wasn't sure. 'Maybe less.'

'What was he doing?'

'Not much. Said he was looking for you.'

'What you tell him?'

'Bloody hell, what *is* this? Twenty questions?'

'It's important, Nat,' said Hammer, his voice edgy, impatient.

She sighed and put her hands on her hips. 'I told him you went up to see Mr. Montoya.'

'That little bastard,' said Hammer turning to me. 'I'll bloody kill him.'

And then we moved. Together, at the same moment, both of us thinking the same thing. If we were quick enough we might catch him. We pushed past Nat and rushed up the stairs hoping to find Joe somewhere by the main entrance, or maybe halfway down the street. Whichever it was, we'd chase him down and beat the money out of him if we had to. Thing is, though, we had no way of knowing what was waiting for us out there.

DAN SMITH

JOE

When I saw all that money, I nearly shit myself because I knew straight away that I was going to steal it. Well, maybe not straight away, because I did think, just for a split second, that I should leave it where it was. Get up, walk away from the table, go find Sledge, talk to him just like I'd decided, and ask for a second chance. But sometimes you can't fight your genes, you just act on the fly and do what comes natural, so I pulled the money out of the pocket and tried to slip it into my own.

There was too much, the guy must've had big pockets, so I divided it up, all the time scanning the room and listening for footsteps. I shoved some of it into my inside pocket and managed to get some of what was left into the top pocket of my shirt. The rest I folded and stuffed into my trousers, making me feel like a walking money belt. After that all I needed to do was get out of the club, which was easy enough, I just slipped out the fire exit. You weren't supposed to use it, but I'd seen one of the girls go out that way the night before so I knew it wasn't going to set off any alarms.

Outside, the cold was harsh, so I pulled my jacket tight and thought about all that money burning a hole in my pocket. I might not have had my job but I sure had a lot of cash and I was already deciding how I was going to spend it. I was thinking that one of those smart new MP3 players would be cool, but as

I got to the end of the alley, and was checking everything was clear before making my way out into the street, I began to realise what a stupid thing I was doing. It seemed to me that Sledge was a pretty cool guy, tough but cool, and I wanted him to give me a job, not kill me. I mean, sure, Hammer was a pain in the arse and I'd like to have a crack at him but those guys *did* have a hard reputation. Maybe they'd even killed people, I don't know, but I'd heard rumours and I probably didn't want them coming after me. Of course, they'd never be able to prove I'd taken their money unless they actually caught me, but they didn't seem like the kind of people who'd worry too much about proof. Besides, I needed the job.

I slowed down as I thought about it. I couldn't take the money, it was crazy. I'd done it again, acting without thinking. I wondered if I'd have time to put it back. Maybe if I could get back into the club the way I'd come out and if the boys hadn't turned up yet, I could just put it back. If they *were* there, then that could be more difficult but maybe I could make something up. Or even just own up. Yeah, that was it, I'd own up if I had to, they were bound to go easy on me if I went back with the money, saying I'm sorry I've been an idiot.

I stopped in the middle of the road, about to turn around, and something caught my eye. The blue car. I was no more than a few yards away from where it was parked between two streetlamps. There were no lights on inside but the engine was humming and the exhaust was chucking out fumes. It was strange, there not being any lights, so I moved closer, trying to get a better look, the thought of money slipping right out of my mind.

When the door opened and the guy stepped out, I knew who it was straight away. I couldn't believe he'd come back. I'd given him such a beating and here he was, back for more, probably wanting his revenge. He'd have to know he didn't have a hope, so I was betting on him having a crowbar or maybe a knife, but that didn't worry me, so I stayed right where I was. But when he took his hand out of his pocket, raised his right arm and took a couple of quick paces towards me, I knew I didn't have a chance. There was nothing I could do other than hope that he wasn't serious. Or that he couldn't shoot straight.

But he was. And he could.

I heard the first shot and felt the bullet make contact. The first thing it touched was the cloth of my jacket, then the stolen money which filled my inside pocket. The bullet whacked a hole straight through both of those, slowing a little and shifting its path as it went. After that, there was only my flesh and bone in its way, so the lead punched through the right side of my chest, picking up a spin and tumbling between two ribs. It cracked both of those and went on to puncture my right lung, drilling through the meat and stopping only when it reached my ribs round the other side and lodged between them.

I felt like I'd been hit by a train and my legs gave up, crumpling beneath me and dropping me to the ground in a heap. I tried to move once I was down, maybe get away if I could, but nothing seemed to work all that well, and things were starting to go numb. That might have been the cold, I don't know, but it was probably the bullet.

I'd heard somewhere that if you don't die straight away from a gunshot then you stand a good chance of surviving provided you don't bleed out, but things weren't looking good for me because Leather Jacket was coming right up to me now, still holding the gun out in front of him. I was trying to ask him to stop, but no words were coming out of my mouth, and that's when I knew it was over. As soon as I was having trouble breathing, I knew it was the end. After that, all I could do was drown in my own blood.

SEAN

When Hornrim helped me out of the snow, my mind was so full of rage I couldn't think. Christ, it felt like everything inside burned white-hot and was ready to explode. I could have shouted till my eardrums burst. I could have torn my hair out in chunks. I could have stamped my feet, kicked and punched and ripped someone to fuckin' pieces. I *had* to deal with this, I *had* to make things right. I wasn't going to let *any*body blackjack me like that and get away with it.

Hornrim was no use when it came to a stand up fight - he'd already shown that much - and he was only slightly better when it came to helping me into the car. He half dragged me back to our parking place and manhandled me into the passenger seat. He strapped me in, slammed the door on my elbow and then ran around the other side to take the wheel. Shit, he was never going to be a paramedic. 'Back to yours,' I told him. My mouth felt thick and full, my jaw ached and it hurt to talk.

'Maybe we should go to the hospital?'

'Just fuckin' drive, will you. We're going to yours. There's something I want.'

'Are you...?'

'Drive.'

Hornrim rammed the car into gear and did like he was told.

There's no point trying to think straight when you're raging inside so I worked hard to stay on the level. I concentrated on the radio, hearing the pounding music without knowing what it was, I closed my eyes and pushed the seat back as far as it would go, I chained enough cigarettes to make my lungs scream for air, I drummed my hands on my knees, I tapped my feet, I squeezed my fists, I ground my teeth. And finally the red mist started to clear. By the time I reached Hornrim's flat, I was coming back down. Cool. Everything was under control again. Oh yeah, and I'd decided what to do. Joe would be making his exit from the world that night, I was sure of it. I even knew how I was going to show him the door.

The first thing I did at Hornrim's was find the bathroom. It was dirty and the toilet hadn't been flushed, but it was enough for what I needed. Right now, I couldn't smell anything anyway, my nose was so packed full of dried blood. I filled the basin with cold water and held my face in it until it started to feel numb again. Then I wiped the mirror clean and looked myself in the eye.

It wasn't good, but it would've been worse if I hadn't fallen face first into the snow. Both cheekbones were blue and pink with angry bruises, my chin hurt like hell, and it looked like someone had tried to take off my nose with a baseball bat. I ran my swollen tongue around my mouth and lifted a fat lip to look at my teeth in the streaked mirror. None were broken at least, but a couple seemed loose. I pulled up my shirt and checked my ribs and chest. They were blooming with roses of purple where the blood had welled under the skin but I was sure that the bones were intact. I'd broken ribs before and they didn't feel like that now. I was satisfied that nothing was seriously damaged, so I tidied myself up, blew the blood from my nose and dusted myself down.

I wandered through to check myself out in the full-length mirror which was hidden behind piles of dirty magazines and even dirtier clothes in Hornrim's small, sweaty bedroom. I thought I looked pretty good. Hard and mean, the bruises adding to the image.

I sat down on the end of Hornrim's bed, opposite the mirror, and watched myself smoking a cigarette while he made something that smelled a bit like coffee. I could hear him moving around in the kitchen, making more noise than he needed to, pacing the floor, maybe wondering what I was going to do while all the time knowing what I wanted from him.

When I was done, I added to Hornrim's mess by grinding my cigarette butt into the worn carpet and then went out into the living room. It was cold and he'd turned on the gas fire which glowed red and hissed but didn't do much else. It definitely didn't kick any heat into the filthy room, that's for sure. I pulled my jacket tight and puffed a mist of breath into the air just as Hornrim came out of the adjoining kitchen. He handed me a chipped mug full of something muddy that steamed warmth into my face and smelled about as good as I could expect. It might have been coffee or it might have been gravy, I didn't know which, but I took a sip anyway and winced at the pain in my mouth. 'Fuckin' hell, Hornrim, you trying to save money?'

'What?'

'On your gas. Turn it up a bit, it's fuckin' baltic in here.'

'Give it a minute,' he said. 'It'll be warm as toast. Takes a while, that's all.'

'Yeah, right,' I looked around. It was nothing like Jack's little pad. Jack's place was a penthouse next to this. Here the furniture was worn and mismatched, like it had come from a tip. There were a couple of high backed chairs - the kind they used to have in the local - with stretchy floral covers that had faded to a kind of dirty pink with flecks of orange. Dark stains on the backs, where Christ knows how many people had rested their greasy heads, suspicious marks on the cushions. The couch had probably been blue at sometime, or maybe green, but had turned brown somewhere along the line. The T.V. that backed onto the curtained window was one of those ancient cupboard jobs with oversized clunky buttons and fake wooden paneling. One of the doors was hanging at an angle, ready to come off, and slouching on top of the whole thing was a strange lump of melted black plastic that coiled around itself like a snake and glistened like fresh guts. Over-stuffed ashtrays puked butts into all corners of the room and I think there was a coffee table in front of the couch, but it was hard to tell because it was littered with plates of half-eaten pies and fish and chips. There were a couple of mugs on there too, and I noticed that one of them had green fur spilling out of the top.

The cold, damp air was rank with the stink of rotten food sneaking in from the kitchen, and from where I was standing I could see that the plastic pedal-bin was overflowing with meal-for-one cartons and something that could have been cat litter.

I looked into the mug I was holding and decided it was better off with friends, so I dumped it on the table. Hornrim hadn't changed at all; he still lived like a pig. I told him it was no wonder he couldn't get laid but he just laughed like he was proud of it. I shook my head and moved a damp newspaper from the couch, thinking about sitting down amongst the crushed cigarette packets and socks.

'So where is it?' I said, still standing.

Hornrim dropped onto the couch and swept his arm across the coffee table to clear a space. 'Right here,' he placed the bundle in the clearing. 'Siddown.'

I said I wasn't going to sit in his shit-heap so he shrugged 'suit yourself' and started to open out the folds on the bundle. Slowly like there was something delicate inside. 'Where d'you get it?' I asked and picked it up before he'd finished unwrapping it.

'I know a guy.' His eyes followed my hands.

'You know a guy? Jesus, since when did you know people?' I took the grease-cloth off the weapon and wiped it down before holding it out with both hands and looking down the barrel. It felt familiar and comfortable, like it could have been made for me. 'Can it be traced?'

'Doubt it.' Looking up.

'Why?'

'My guy doesn't sell traceable weapons.'

'*Your guy?*' I had to laugh. 'Jesus Hornrim, you're priceless.'

'What? It's true.'

I shook my head again, but it made everything hurt, like my brain had swollen inside my skull or something.

'It's a Cougar,' he said. 'Beretta.'

'I can see that,' I lied. I'd used guns before but all I knew about them was that you point them at people and they either do what you say or they piss themselves and get shot. I liked it, though. The Cougar. It was black and glistening, like the guts on top of Hornrim's television, and it smelled of oil. It was short, with maybe three or four inches on the barrel but it looked like it meant business and its shape was smooth and snag free so it would easily slip in and out of my pocket without catching. I gave it a try, perfect, then I handed it back to Hornrim so that he could give me a run through, show me how everything worked, but I didn't like to see him hold it - he seemed to dirty it, somehow.

I took it from him, the handle warming up now, and pulled the slide a couple of times to feel the action. Then I unwrapped the magazine from another greased cloth and slid it into the gun. It felt a little heavier now, but not too much. 'What about bullets?' I asked.

'There's some in it already,' he said without taking his eyes off it.

I looked at him.

'What, you need more? What you gonna..?'

'I don't know how many I'm going to need, Hornrim. The way I feel right now I could use about a fuckin' million.'

His eyes widened then he lowered them a little and nodded. 'Hang on.' He went into the kitchen and I heard him rummaging through cupboards before he came back in again to hand me a clear plastic bag - a baggie, the type that seals across the top. It was filled with shiny brass shells.

'They're forty-fives,' he said, sounding like he was some kind of expert. 'There's about fifteen or so in there. It's all I've got.'

I stuffed the bag into my trouser pocket. 'Ta.'

'Yeah.' His eyes shifted away and his voice was tight. 'You sure you...?'

'I'll see you later,' I said. 'Don't wait up.' As I moved, the Cougar settled down into my pocket and I liked the way it pulled my jacket to one side. 'I'll call you tomorrow.' I didn't wait for him to come to the door; it hadn't been a social visit.

*

I drove Jack's car straight into town and headed for the quayside. The gritters had been out and all that was left of the day's snow was the gray sludgy stuff that ridges up along the white lines and sprays out when you steer through it. Reflections from the yellow streetlights burned across the wet tarmac, broken up by the white glare from the few cars that were still on the roads. Here and there, groups of people hung around outside bars and clubs, saying their goodbyes and then weaving off to hail a cab or maybe take the long walk home. Couples got it together in doorways, drunks pissed into the openings of dark alleys and scruffy students looked for safety in the lights and warmth of late night kebab joints. I took everything in but ignored it. I even passed taxi ranks without turning my head to look at the short-skirted tarts who rubbed their naked knees and stamped their high-heeled feet.

I thought about Joe and coasted down the bank towards the club. Once there, I pulled onto the curb where the shadow fell between two well spaced streetlamps. I killed the lights but left the motor running so that the heater kept on blowing warm air at my face. I reached up and switched off the inside light, I didn't want it coming on when I opened the door.

Time crawled and it began to snow again.

For what seemed like hours I watched the front of 'Noir', but the digital clock on the dash told me I'd only been there half an hour. I smoked a Regal and switched on the radio. Some teenage no-hoper singing crap, so I turned him off again and listened to the night until it deafened me. Then I tried the CD but it was Simon and Garfunkel, so I turned that off too. I wasn't in the mood for those guys. Shit, I wasn't *ever* in the mood for those guys. I thought about looking for another CD but it was too dark. I felt around inside the glove box for something to eat, but all I found was gloves. I took the cougar out of my pocket and checked out the way it felt in my hand.

I smoked another Regal.

Eventually the staff started leaving the club, coming out the main entrance and making their way down the street, none of them turning to look at the car. At first they came out in a group, maybe ten people, something I hadn't thought about. In my mind I saw him coming out alone, just me and him in the street, but now I was thinking he might be with others and it wasn't going to be so easy.

I leaned closer to the window, checking the faces in the group, but the kid wasn't with them so I ignored them as their sounds faded behind me. After that, the place was quiet again. A couple of girls came out together, one or two people alone, then nothing.

I was beginning to think that I'd missed him, that maybe I'd have to come back tomorrow, when a door opened in the alley and a knife of light cut across the darkness. I sat up straight and watched as Joe came out looking uneasy, his head left and right, checking this way and that, like an animal keeping an eye out for trouble. He was holding his jacket tight around him.

Not long after I spotted him, he noticed the car and stopped in his tracks. He stooped a little and cocked his head, trying to see into the darkness behind the window, edging closer.

When he was just a few yards away, I opened the door and stepped out onto the deserted road. I dug my hands into my jacket pockets, tightened my fingers around the warm handle of the Cougar and looked at Joe.

I waited until he recognised me, then I slipped the gun from my pocket, took a few quick steps towards him, raised my hand and shot him in the chest. Easy as that.

The bullet dropped him straight to the ground, and for a moment he lay there, still, lifeless, just a dark shape in a sea of white. Then he began to twitch, his legs flicking about, and he gulped at the air making a strange sucking noise.

Not caring that someone might've heard the gunshot, I went to him and crouched down beside his writhing body. I watched the blood bubbling from his mouth and nose, thinking that maybe he was trying to say something but all I could hear was that sucking noise.

'About now, you're probably wishing you'd been a bit nicer to me up there by the door,' I smiled, but he didn't say anything, he just gurgled and jigged about some more.

Then I stood up and raised the Cougar in both shaking hands. I shot Joe in the face and something warm and wet sprayed my cheek. I felt good, though, not bad at all.

Then the sound of heavy footsteps caught my attention and I turned to watch two men in dark suits appear from the entrance to the club, one of them the big guy from the door earlier on. They began to run out, but when they saw me move to face them, they hesitated for just a second, a million things probably flashing through their little brains. I shot at Howard a couple of times as quick as you like, and blood clouded out around him as he fell back behind the wall which lined the steps. I'd like to have gone over to see him die, but the other one was starting to shout something that sounded like '*Hammer*', and he looked like he was torn between saving his mate and saving himself, so I turned the Cougar on him and put him down on his arse screaming like a girl and grabbing his stomach. He slipped about halfway down the steps before he managed to stop himself by wedging his feet against the club wall and I reckon it was pretty funny seeing such a big guy writhing about like that.

I dropped the magazine into the palm of my left hand and counted how many bullets were left. Three was more than enough, so I strolled over to the bouncer who was complaining about his stomach and shot him in the face, like I did with Joe, thinking it could be my trademark or something. I missed, though, he was moving about so much, or maybe it was because I was shaking, and that pissed me off so I tried again. I steadied myself, holding the Cougar in both hands, but the second shot missed too, so I knelt down on one step, pushed the barrel of the gun against his forehead and finished him off.

All empty, I retraced my steps back to the car and lit a cigarette before climbing in. My ears were ringing like fuck and my nose was filled with the sharpness of gunpowder, but I felt good. I closed the door and took the Ford out onto the deserted quayside. I wondered if someone from the club would call the police. Maybe even Sawn-off himself, but I didn't think so. A man like him wouldn't want the law sniffing around.

SUNDAY 19TH DECEMBER

BURN OUT

JACK

Morning arrived late, just how I like it, easing us into the day without the need for an alarm clock. I pushed myself up in the bed and opened my eyes to the brightness around the curtains, lying there for a while, clearing my head, enjoying the lateness of the day. It made a change from going to work in the cold and the dark. Sundays were lazy days, nothing to do, nowhere to go, it was part of our routine now. Spend Saturday night together, have something to eat, maybe go out, sleep well, get up late and chill out. We'd been doing it for a while now, it was what we did. I would've skipped it for Sean, though. I'd been prepared to miss out that weekend, spend some time with my brother now that he was out, but part of me was glad he'd gone with Hornrim last night. Everything seemed more normal that way.

While Mandy dozed, I went down to the kitchen and made us something to eat. Toast and tea. Everything went on a tray, along with marg, honey, jam, chocolate spread for Mandy, and I carried it up to the bedroom. I put it in the middle of the bed, kissed her on the forehead and sat back to watch her wake up.

Being with Mandy had changed me and I sometimes wondered what I'd done to deserve it. I had a crappy job in a cold factory, working for peanuts and not a word of thanks, but I had Mandy. I guess there's always a balance, good with the bad. You work hard, get a whole load of shit dumped on you, so life gives you a sweetener to help you along the way. I suppose it's one way of looking at things.

After breakfast in bed, we brushed toast crumbs from the sheets and showered together, taking our time under the warm water. Then I went out to buy Sunday papers from the local shop while Mandy made fresh tea. It was quite a walk in the cold, a good fifteen minutes there and back, but the snow was holding off and the sun was showing just a bit.

By the time I came back, my fingertips were tingling and my nose was running, but it was worth the trip just to be welcomed back into the warmth.

We spent the next few hours chilling out in the living room, drinking tea, reading the papers, watching T.V, until I eventually looked at my watch and said, 'I suppose I'd better head off.' I was lying on the sofa, flicking through a magazine. 'It's nearly lunchtime so I guess Sean'll probably be up and about. I want to spend a *bit* of time with him.'

'I'm sure there'll be plenty of time to see him,' said Mandy. 'Knowing Sean, he'll be crashing at yours for a while yet.'

'Hmm.'

'Why don't you stay for lunch?' she said looking up from the paper which was spread out in front of her. 'Go home afterwards.' She was lying on the floor with her legs out to one side and her chin in her hand. Her elbow was propped on the soft carpet. She was wearing an old rugby shirt with faded lettering on the back, and the way she was lying made her jeans pull tight around her thighs. Her hair was loose and fell forward so that it just touched the newspaper. Her feet were bare.

I thought for a moment. 'No. I'd love to, but I'd better not. I need to spend some time with Sean. He needs me to sort him out.'

'Sean doesn't need *any*one to do *any*thing for him. There's no way you're going to keep him straight.'

'He's not *that* bad,' I said.

Mandy widened her eyes at me.

'Well, all right, he *is* that bad. But he's still my brother.'

'You don't owe him anything Jack.'

'Yeah, maybe,' I said sitting up on the couch. I leaned over and brushed her hair behind one ear saying, 'But I have to try.'

She looked good sitting there on the floor, just natural like that, and I couldn't help myself wanting to be with her so it didn't take much to persuade me to stay a while longer. We had a late lunch and then I went home to see Sean, full of food and Sunday evening blues.

*

The cab dropped me off a few yards from the front door of Lowdean Court - my own personal shit hole - and sped away as soon as I'd handed over the money. The guy didn't even offer to give me the change.

Lowdean Court was built over one of the main roads in town, and looked like a monster rising into the skyline. It was one of those places they built in the sixties, back when they thought the twenty-first century was going to be all high-rise buildings and flying cars. Maybe the place had been okay in its day, but now it was over a main route through town and all those cars and busses crawling under Lowdean had left their mark. Twenty-three storeys of steel framed windows, which didn't open and were never washed, were now streaked from years of traffic and bad weather, and the gray bricks were starting to look black. It wasn't much better inside, some of the flats themselves were falling to bits, no one living in them, but it was cheap and it was a start for someone like me. The warden told me that they were thinking of buying us all out, turning the place into luxury flats, but I reckon they probably wanted to pull it all down.

I used the underpass and then climbed the steps and swiped my card to open the main door into the building, all the time looking around to make sure I wasn't being followed. You don't want to let anybody get too close behind you in a place like that, you never know what they might be after. Sometimes people tried to con their way in, maybe they just wanted a little shelter, others, they saw the place as ripe for house-breaking. You had to be careful, though; few weeks ago, someone from floor five tried to stop someone following them in and was left with a dirty needle stuck in their back.

Inside, the dark gray marble effect floor was chipped and scuffed and smeared. The warden cleaned it, I guess, but it never seemed to make any difference. The once cream walls were now a mess of endless layers of graffiti and marker pen swear words that the guy from the council washed off every six months or so. The stairwell smelled of whatever was the latest thing to be dropped, dumped, spilled, pissed or puked onto it and was dimly lit with emergency lights only. The two lifts were small and creaky and smelled pretty much the same as the stairs. You wouldn't want to get stuck in one, that's for sure. I took a deep breath and braved one up to my place, but by the time I reached my floor, I'd pulled the collar of my jacket across my mouth and was breathing through that.

I came out of the lift gasping for breath and still looking around to make sure no one was about when I let myself into the flat. Once inside, I was pleased to close the front door and shut all the crap behind me.

'Sean, you up yet?' I called out. 'You have a good time?'

The flat was silent. Nothing.

A quick scan of the few rooms I had and it was obvious that Sean had been in at some point. His bed had been slept in - and left unmade - and most of his boxes had now been opened. In the kitchen, the fridge door was open and there was an empty mug on the side, along with some tin foil containers. The living room smelled of takeaway Chinese food.

I thought maybe he'd gone out for cigarettes or something so I pottered around the flat and tidied away any rubbish before making myself a coffee and sitting down to read the book which Mandy had given me. But after twenty minutes or so, Sean still wasn't back and I was beginning to think maybe he'd gone out with Hornrim again.

Another twenty minutes and I was half reading, half deciding whether to call Mandy and go back round to hers when the doorbell rang. It was strange, hearing that sound when I wasn't expecting anyone. The only people I really knew, people who would come to the flat anyway, were Mandy and Sean. But

Mandy was at home and Sean had keys, so I was just starting to convince myself that I'd imagined it, when the bell rang again. This time, I put my book face down on the sofa and went to the door. I pulled the vertical blind which covered the slit window to one side and looked out into the corridor.

The man was standing a couple of feet away with his hands in his pockets, he looked smart, presentable. He took a gloved hand out of one pocket, held up a printed card and then slipped it away again, out of sight, quick as you can.

'Police,' he said. 'Detective Harry Milton. I'm lookin' for someone goes by the name of Jack Presley.' His voice was muffled through the door but I could hear him well enough.

I asked him why he was looking for Mr. Presley and he came back saying, 'It's better we talk inside, there's been some trouble.'

That made me think of Sean, wondering what he'd done now so I quickly straightened the blind, slid the chain onto the door and opened it as far as the brass links would allow. '*I'm* Jack Presley.'

'That name for real?' he said. 'Presley, I mean?'

'Can I help you?'

'You the owner of a light blue Ford?'

'Yes.' I thought of Sean and visions of accidents ran through my head. Something had happened to him.

'I think I'd better come in then,' said the detective.

'Okay,' I replied, my mouth dry. I closed the door, slid the chain off and then opened it fully.

I *knew* that I should've asked for identification, I'd seen it on TV and read about it often enough. Always ask for ID. The guy could've been anybody, and what's worse is that when I thought about it later on, he didn't even *look* like a police detective. Looked more like an Italian gangster. Too late now, though.

As soon as the door was open far enough, he smacked me hard in the face with something cold and solid. It hurt like hell and I fell back and hit the floor, everything becoming pain and darkness. I blinked my eyes hard, trying to make them see but nothing came. I felt him push past me and close the door. Then he was sliding the chain across saying, 'Now it's just you and me.'

I don't know what he did next, I don't remember so well. I think he might have kicked my head. Anyway, there was a lot more pain.

DAN SMITH

MAGDALENA

I woke at around nine that Sunday morning and lay in bed for a while dozing and watching satellite television because there was nothing else to do. Tony had told me to stay put, so there was nowhere for me to rush off to, but I didn't expect to have to wait so long. I checked that my mobile phone was charged and left it on the bedside so that Tony could contact me at any time.

Hotel rooms are boring. For starters, they're too small. Then there's the layout. Double or twin beds, whichever it has, they generally have a cover that is either gold or beige. Those are the standard hotel colours - gold and beige. Or maybe sometimes you get brown, but mine was beige. Beside each bed there is always a cabinet with some sort of lamp on it and there's always a bible in one of the drawers. There is a dresser of some description with a mirror over it and a television to one side. The drinks fridge is in the cabinet underneath and to the side of the mirror. It is, more often than not, unstocked unless requested and the contents are always, *always* over priced. Miniature bottles of vodka, gin, white wine, foil packets of nuts. Sometimes there is a small round table and two chairs. The art on the wall is always dire.

There can be slight variations, perhaps a different colour here or a new angle there, but on the whole, hotel rooms are all the same and I could think of a hundred places I'd rather be. I just wasn't used to slumming it like that.

Of course, I'd wanted to rent the suite, go for the best like I *was* used to, but Tony told me it was a bad idea. I was supposed to be hard to find and people who stay in hotel suites are never hard to find - they stick out.

By ten, my stomach was starting to complain but I resisted the urge to order any food because Tony had said not to. If that rat from last night was still hanging around, it's the kind of sign he'd look for. He'd be interested to know who was ordering from their room because it would tell him who didn't want to be seen. At least, that's what Tony said, but I wasn't completely convinced. I'd be willing to bet that quite a number of people would order breakfast in bed on a Sunday morning. I was sure I wouldn't be the only one.

I'd already eaten the peanuts and the pretzels from the mini bar and I'd drunk everything alcoholic it contained before I went to sleep last night, so now there was nothing left. The cupboard was bare, and that was not good. A lady's stomach should never have to grumble and it was affecting my mood. I even went as far as to look through the order menu but I supposed there wasn't any point in taking the risk. Tony *had* said not to. So I hid the menu away - it was just making me feel even hungrier. For now I'd have to go without, smoke instead, and Tony could stand me a good lunch later on.

By eleven I was sick of television. There were more channels than I cared to count, but none of them was worth watching. Cartoons, pop music, cheap shopping channels, God programmes, woodwork and fishing seemed to be all there was. I left it on, just for the company, and soaked in a hot soapy bath but the tub was far smaller than I would have liked, and the hotel staff must have forgotten to put out the bathrobe and slippers.

Feeling clean, but still hungry, I dried and brushed my hair. I put on a dark burgundy trouser suit with a white blouse and a patterned silk scarf, and I applied make-up, careful to cover the bruises which Rubeno had left on my cheek. Then I packed all of my belongings into the small suitcase that I had taken with me when I left the house. I slipped one or two things into my handbag and snapped the catch shut.

I left the suitcase near the door, ready to take it or leave it, depending upon what Tony told me to do, and I placed my handbag and mobile on the table, within easy reach. Then I sat on one of the uncomfortable chairs, switched the television off, and waited for Tony to call.

It was two hours before my mobile vibrated on the table and started to ring, and in all that time I did nothing other than stare at the wall and smoke.

I picked it up and put it to my ear. 'Hello?'

'Magda, it's me.'

'Finally.'

'Is everything okay?'

'Well, it's not exactly swinging.'

'You're alive and you're safe, that's the main thing.'

'Mm, but I might as *well* be dead. I'm not designed for sitting around in hotel rooms, you know darling. Not like this one, anyway.'

'Don't say that. Anyway, it won't be for much longer. I have a job to finish and then...'

'My suitcase is packed, I'm dressed and I'm ready to go. I've done everything that there is to do in this room and I've eaten everything there is to eat. Tony, I'm hungry and I'm bored. Don't make me stay here any longer than I have to.'

'I'm getting you out tonight.'

'To*night?*'

'It's the best I can do.'

'Okay,' I sighed. 'Tonight it is.'

'I'll meet you at the station. Eight o' clock by the coffee place. Costa's, isn't it? Take a cab.'

'What if I'm followed?'

'You will be, but don't worry about it. I'll deal with it when you get to the station.'

'When I get there?'

'Trust me. Everything will be fine.'

'Why don't you just meet me *here*? I'm not sure I can cope with all of this cloak and dagger. It's just not me.'

'We can't afford for me to be seen at the hotel. If your husband finds out it's me, then it's all over. You do *know* that, don't you?'

'Yes, I do.'

'Okay. And did you put the box where I told you?'

'Yes,' I said. 'Should I leave it there?'

'For now. Look, I have to go. I'll see you tonight okay?'

'Okay.'

'And don't worry. Everything will be fine.'

And then I was alone again.

JACK

It was cold and someone was slapping my face.

'Wake up. Wake up.' The voice was unfamiliar, grating. 'Time to wake up you little fuck.'

The slapping stopped. Something creaked. I could hear the beat of music somewhere in the distance. Or it might have been the blood in my ears.

'Hey, fuckin' wake up!' Shouting this time, but still unfamiliar, still grating.

Another two slaps, one across each cheek.

I tried to lift my hand to my face, I needed to stop the slapping, but my arms were paralysed, nothing seemed to work. I moved my head from side to side, but that was all I could do.

'Ah, there you are,' said the voice. 'I was worried I might've killed you.'

I was worried I might have been dead.

'I don't want you to die just yet,' said the voice.

I didn't want to die at all.

'I've been waiting for you to wake up.'

I tried to think where I was, to remember what had happened, but it took me a few moments just to know my name. I squeezed my eyes and wondered how long I'd been out for. It could have been a while, my whole body hurt and

I had what I assumed to be blood on my face. It had dried and tightened, pulling across one cheek. I tried to move again but couldn't, so I guessed I'd been out long enough at least for someone to tie me up. I forced my eyes to open and tried to focus on something but I didn't like what I saw.

My ankles were bound to the legs of the chair with tea towels.

My wrists were tied behind my back and whatever it was that had been used to fix them was cutting into my skin. I could feel warm liquid, sticky in the palms of my hands and I imagined it to be red.

I took a deep breath that caught in my chest and then I raised my head. Sitting two feet in front of me, on a similar wooden chair, was the man who had called himself Harry Milton. The man who said he was a policeman. His suit was smart and when I looked down I could see a pair of highly polished shoes reflecting the ceiling light. They looked expensive. He had taken off his camel coat and it was now draped on the arm of the sofa. Next to it, on a well-fluffed cushion, was a sawn-off shotgun.

I was pretty sure that the man in my living room was not a policeman.

'So, pencil-dick, you know who I am?' He leaned forward and held my chin up with one hand. He'd covered it with a handkerchief to prevent the blood from touching his own skin.

I just stared, nothing working.

'Do - you - know - who - I - am?'

My mind was dull, slow. I couldn't think.

He dropped my face, walked around behind me, out of sight, and I heard a metallic rattle just seconds before feeling a tremendously sharp stinging sensation in the back of my head. I screamed and my vision disappeared. Everything went black. Nothing except for a ringing that wanted to burst me from the inside out.

Another slap.

Then the ringing died and the music came to back to me again. It was definitely music, the beat had changed.

'When I ask you a question, it's best you answer.' The voice swam out to me in the darkness and I heard him walking backwards and forwards behind me, the footsteps soft on the new carpet. 'What's that smell?' he said. 'Vanilla?' The footsteps stopped. 'Bit strong for my liking.' I vaguely wondered if the blood would come off. 'Nice view, though. Mind you, what I could never understand is why they let people like *you* in these places. They could do them up nice and charge good money for them.'

My vision started to return with a painful brightness. Everything was surrounded by a blurred light and then reality came back to me. The man was still behind me.

'One good thing though,' he paused. 'Listen to that music,' he paused again so that I could hear the bass pounding somewhere in another flat. 'Sounds like someone's having a party. No one's going to pay any attention to your noise. You know, screaming and stuff.'

As if to make his point, he walked around into view and I heard the metallic rattle again. He flicked a telescopic steel baton from the palm of his raised right hand and brought it down on my knee. The swishing sound it made was quite dramatic and the pain was breathtaking.

'So, pencil-dick,' he said after I stopped screaming. 'I'll ask you again, do you know who I am?'

'No.' I could hardly speak, my breath coming in short sharp gasps as the pain rippled out from my knee. 'I don't know who you are.'

'Really?' He looked down at me and tapped the tip of the steel whip gently in the palm of his hand. 'Take a good look.' He took my chin in his hand again and lifted my face. 'How about now?'

'Yes...no...I...I don't know.' I could taste blood. 'You said you were a policeman. Milton, I think.'

'Did I?' He took his hand away. 'Yeah, I suppose I did.'

'You're not?'

'Do I look like a fuckin' policeman?' He pushed the telescopic whip back into its handle and slipped it into his trouser pocket. It ruined the line of his suit but it didn't matter, I wasn't going to tell anyone.

'No.'

'Good, 'cause I hate the fuckin' police. They're a pain in the arse. I've had that prick Milton all over my club this morning.' He sat down. 'Some do-gooder reported a 'disturbance' last night, but then you'd know all about that wouldn't you, Jack?'

'What? No.'

'Liar!' He slapped my face, but it didn't hurt as much as the steel whip.

'I had to clear your mess up. I can't have that shit on my doorstep, bringing the police crawling round, sniffing into every little corner. Do you have any fuckin' idea how much trouble you've caused me?' He stood up and walked around behind me again so I closed my eyes, squeezing tears down my cheek, waiting for the sound, waiting for the pain.

'So, kid, you got a hammer?' It sounded like he was asking for a light and it took me by surprise.

'I...'

'Do - you - have - a - *hammer*?'

'No.'

He put his hands on the back of the chair and leaned in to whisper in my ear. 'You should know that I'm going to look for one anyway.' The smell of his aftershave was strong. 'If I find one and you didn't tell me, I'll be very pissed off.'

I couldn't see his face, but I could hear well enough. '*Pissed off*' meant pain. 'In the kitchen,' I managed. 'Cupboard under the sink.'

'Good boy,' he said sitting back down in front of me. 'Already found it, though. Just testing.' In his right hand he was holding a hammer, my hammer, the one with the black rubber grip, and in his left hand he held a four-inch nail. He reached forward and touched the tip of the nail to my knee, pushing down hard enough for the point to pierce my jeans and touch my skin. Then he raised his right hand.

'Please! NO!'

'Then stop fuckin' lying to me!'

'I'm not, I'm *not*. I don't know who you are I fuckin' swear it I don't know who you are I don't know anything about the police I don't know anything about any trouble I swear please don't...'

'Oh, for fuck's sake...' He stood violently, pushing his chair back so that it fell over onto the floor. '*I don't want to do this, kid!*' He held out the hammer, waving it in my face. 'And I'm pretty sure *you* don't want to do this. What the fuck is wrong with you? Just tell me what you were doing and let's get this over with.'

'But I...'

'Shut up! *Shut the fuck up.*' He held his hand up and walked away from me, going over to the dining table at the far end of the room. He rested his hands on it and leaned forwards, head down, letting out his breath. He ran one hand over his hair and shook his head. He straightened his tie, smoothed down his suit. When he came back, he righted his chair and sat down, leaving the hammer and nail on the table.

He put his hand inside his jacket and removed a cigar. With the other hand he snapped open a gold lighter and touched it to the tip, sitting back and puffing until it was alight. It smelled sweet. 'D'you smoke?' he asked.

'Sometimes.'

'Do you fuckin' smoke, Jack? Yes or No?'

'Yes.'

'Cigars?'

'No.'

'Cigarettes then?'

I nodded.

'Want one?'

'Please.'

He took a pack of Dunhill cigarettes from his pocket, stuck one in my mouth and lit it. Then he leaned back again, puffing his cigar and watching me like a snake while I drew on the cigarette. I looked at his shoes until he spoke again.

'Look, Jack, I'm getting too old for this. I've done it far too long for me to have fun anymore. I'm tired and I want to go home. Do you understand?'

'I think so.'

'Okay, so there's two ways this can go. In both of them, I live. You only live in one of them. Do you understand?'

'Yes.'

'And you *do* want to live, don't you?'

'Yes.'

'Okay then. Good. Already that's much better. We understand each other. So why don't you start by telling me exactly who you are?'

'I'm...I'm no one.'

'C'mon Jack, we're just starting to make progress here. You have a girlfriend, right?' He raised his eyebrows.

'Yeah, but...'

'And you want to see her again?'

'Yes. But I...you know who I am. I'm Jack Presley,'

He took a long drag on his cigar and puffed out blue smoke in a sigh. 'Okay, Jack Presley. I'm gonna make this easy for you. Last night, you came to my club, you tried to get in the door, you threw my name about, you got turned away. Little while later you came back for some payback. Does that help?'

I looked down and shook my head saying, 'No,' but I was thinking about Sean.

'How does that *not* help? You fucked up three of my bouncers for Christ's sake.'

'What? I...no...I...what?'

'Three bouncers,' he repeated, puffing on the cigar. 'And one of my girls saw the whole thing - something else I had to take care of.'

'Wh..?'

'One of them recognised you, Jack. Needed treatment, so it took him a while to remember, but he got there in the end. Said it was the same guy who came asking for me earlier on.' He bit the cigar between his teeth and stretched out his hands. 'Well here I am, Jack.'

'What...?'

'Got to hand it to you, though kid, you don't look like you got it in you. I can normally tell.'

'I...'

'But that doesn't change the fact that you were at my club last night, asking for me.' He leaned forward and looked at me, eyes narrowed. He reached out and took the cigarette from my mouth, giving me a chance to breathe properly, and then he put it back in again. 'Caused me all kinds of trouble. Had those guys lined up for something special. You really...' he paused like he was thinking, like maybe he'd just thought of something hugely important. 'Or did you?' he said under his breath. And his whole face relaxed downwards before lighting up into a smile that glinted diamond. 'Oh dear, oh dear, oh dear, you poor miserable fuck. You poor - miserable - little - fuck, Jack.' He sat back in the chair and crossed his arms. 'You poor, poor bastard. It really isn't your day at all, is it?'

I stayed quiet.

'I had a feeling about you, you know,' he said nodding his head. 'The minute I laid eyes on you, I didn't think you were a hard-on. Didn't think you could do it. Not the type. I get it now, though. It all makes sense now.'

My head was starting to clear, beginning to relax. My mind was working again and my body was trying to cope with what was happening to me. It was all starting to make some sense.

'How about this for size?' he said. '*Someone* came to my club last night. Someone who wasn't very bright, see, because they came in your car. Your blue car. The one with the registration written on this piece of paper,' he pulled a scrap of paper from his pocket and held it in front of my face. 'So what I want to know, Jack, is if *you* didn't come, then who did?'

I didn't know what to say. Sean was my *brother* for Christ's sake.

'Who was it borrowed your car, Jack?' He reached over and touched the shotgun with his fingertips. 'Who was it?'

I shook my head and looked down. 'No-one. Me.'

He picked up the shotgun and popped it open to check the load. He took his time, sliding out the cartridges, holding them up for me to see, dropping them back in again. Then he snapped it shut and pointed it at my mouth saying, 'Who?'

'Please.'

He stood up.

'I suppose you've never seen what this does to a man's head.' He flipped off the safety and turned his body away from me, holding his left hand in front of his face, palm out, like it would stop him getting sprayed.

'Please.'

'Well, it's been nice talking to you kid. I hope whoever you're protecting is worth it.'

'Please.' I closed my eyes and waited forever. 'Don't.'

'Come on, Jack,' said the voice. 'Give me one good reason not to do this,' and the way he said it, the tone of his voice, I really believed that he wanted a reason, that he *really* didn't want to kill me. He was giving me a chance. Just one good reason not to die.

But I couldn't think of *any*thing.

SEAN

'Honey, I'm home!' I closed the front door behind me.

'In here!' It was Jack's voice, but he sounded different. Weak.

I kept my jacket on and didn't bother taking off my boots even though they were still wet from the snow and slush outside. I dropped Jack's keys on the telephone table and left damp tracks down the short hallway into the living room, shouting, 'Hey, how's it going bro...' but I stopped as soon as I saw him.

Jack was tied to a chair in the middle of the room, his face and hair thick with dried blood. Opposite him was another chair, empty, and my first thought was that it was for me. I didn't speak, I just held a finger to my mouth and shook my head. 'Shh.'

'He's gone,' said Jack.

I ignored him, looking left and right, but there was nobody else in the room. Nothing was out of place except for the hammer on the table, and the rusty-brown spots on the carpet, spraying outwards around my brother. One or two of the larger ones were smeared, like maybe someone might have walked in them.

'Untie me, Sean.'

I checked the kitchen without saying anything, moving slowly, not making a sound.

'Sean; he's gone.'

I checked the bedroom. Inside the wardrobe, under the bed, behind the door.

'Sean.'

I checked the bathroom and the spare room.

'Sean.'

After the checks were done, I went back into the living room and sat down on the edge of the chair opposite Jack, leaning forward and saying, 'What's going on?'

'Cut me loose, Sean.' Jack looked rough; all scabs and cuts and shit. Like looking in the mirror last night; before I went back to the club to see Joe.

'This some kind of kinky game?' I said. 'Should I be looking around for oranges and paper bags?'

'Cut me loose,' he said it again, his voice calm but his eyes giving him away. Made me wonder if I wanted to cut him loose, I'd never seen that look on Jack's face before. It reminded me of myself.

'*Sean.*' Insistent now, teeth gritted, lips tight.

'Okay.' I stood up. 'It's done.' I took a knife from a drawer in the kitchen and went back to the chair. I sat down holding the blade. 'You *sure* there isn't something you want to tell me, Jack?'

He breathed deep and closed his eyes. 'Cut me loose, Sean. Just cut me the fuck loose.' Looking right at me now. 'I've been tied to this *fuck*ing chair for about as long as I can *fuck*ing remember and I don't want to sit here *any*more. Just *cut me the fuck loose.*' He struggled and rattled on the spot, some of the dried blood around his mouth cracking into tiny creases and flaking off. The legs of the chair lifted off the floor and I had to reach out to stop him from toppling over sideways.

'Okay, okay, I'm sorry.' I went round behind him, feeling bad when I saw how raw his wrists were. I cut the plastic ties that were biting into his skin and straight away, Jack bent down to claw at the towels around his ankles. It was no use, though, his hands were dumb, fumbling uselessly, so I knelt beside him and used the knife. I sawed at the material until the blade cut into the leg of the chair, then I moved back to give him space. Jack stayed where he was, bent forward, breathing heavily, his chest resting on his thighs and his arms hanging down. After a few minutes, he pushed himself up, trying to stand, but his knees buckled and he tipped, making me think Christ, he must have been sitting like that for hours, his legs frozen into place. I caught him and held him until he could stand on his own. Then, without saying anything, he left the room. I thought about following him, but didn't. I reckoned it was safer that way because how he looked right now, he might've killed me; taken that knife out of my hand and stuck it right in my eye. Instead I went to the kitchen and helped myself to a beer from the fridge. I put the knife back in the drawer and went to the window to watch the world while Jack sorted himself out.

He moved between the bedroom and the bathroom for a while, maybe an hour, and when he came back he was looking better. He'd changed his clothes, his face was clean, his hair was wet and although the cut across the bridge of his nose was still angry, at least it had stopped bleeding. My brother looked calm now, maybe a little too calm considering the circumstances, and I wasn't sure which I like best. I watched him go to the kitchen and put ice in a fresh tea towel which he held against his swollen eye. He took a handful of painkillers and chased them with water straight from the tap.

'Look, I'm sorry man, I...' I started, but he held up a hand, sat down on the sofa, and took a cigarette from the packet of Dunhills on the table. I'd never seen him smoke that brand before, I reckoned they looked a bit flash, but they might be worth a try so I helped myself and Jack lit us both with the Zippo. I thought maybe I shouldn't have given it to him.

'You want to tell me what happened?' I said blowing smoke at the ceiling.

He looked over at me without moving his head, his eyes right over to the side, as far as they would go. 'I might ask you the same thing.' His voice was steady, no tone in it, making me wonder what was going on.

'How's that?'

'Your face.'

'Oh, yeah,' I touched my nose. 'That. It's nothing really. Had a fight last night. Nothing I couldn't handle.'

'That would've been at the new club, then? Noir. That's where you went isn't it?' His head turning in my direction, his eyes right on me now, one of them so full of blood I could hardly see any white.

'Yeah. Yeah, sure, we went there. Well, we didn't get in but...yeah...why, what's the big deal?' I took a drag and went back to the window, not looking at him.

'I heard there was a bit of trouble.'

'Yeah? Well, I wouldn't know about that.'

'I heard some bouncers got hurt.'

I turned around, leaning against the window, feeling it cold on my shoulder. 'Yeah, well, like I said, we didn't get in. Some stupid rule about ties. Anyway, after that we found a couple a bars open near the station, had a few more drinks, ended up in The Lizard Lounge and Hornrim picked a fight with some guy, so I helped him out. That's it.' I'd practiced it, even been round to see Hornrim that morning, tell him what we'd done last night if anybody asked.

'Don't lie to me, Sean. You've been out one day, *one day,* and look what you've done. You've just got out for doing this exact same thing.'

'Same thing?'

'I know you were there, Sean, you were seen. What the fuck were you thinking?'

I sat down on the edge of one of the slatted chairs and took a long drag on the Dunhill before saying, 'Seen?' and wondering what would be worse; having the police after me or having Sawn-off Montoya on my case.

'You were in *my* car, Sean. They got the number and it led them right here to *my* flat.' He shook his head. 'But guess what? They thought it was me. So some guy pushes his way into my flat saying he's a policeman...'

'And you let him in?'

'Yeah, I let him in and...'

'You didn't ask for ID?'

'No, I didn't ask for ID. He had the registration and description of my car. I thought something had happened to you. I thought he was for real.'

'So who was he?' I asked the question but already knew the answer.

'Some guy called Montoya.'

'What'd he want? What d'you tell him?'

'He wanted to know who I was, Sean. He wanted to know why I was asking for him and why I drove to his club to beat up his bouncers.'

'Beat up his...?' I stood up and turned around. 'Beat up his bouncers?' Maybe Sawn-off didn't tell Jack exactly what happened, or maybe he didn't understand. Either way, I had to know what they talked about, so I went to the kitchen to buy a little thinking time and took a couple of bottles out of the fridge. I popped the tops on the edge of the sink and went back in to the living room. I put one of the beers in front of Jack but he just looked at it and shook his head.

He waited until I was sitting down again before he spoke. 'He was going to hammer a nail through my knee,' he said.

'What? For beating up his bouncers? He must've liked them a lot.'

'No, I don't think he cares too much about *them*. It was what they were going to do for him.' Jack closed his eyes again and breathed deeply. I reckon he was trying hard, he always does. When he opened them again, he held out his wrists and stared at them. They looked sore as hell. He turned them over and checked both sides, his eyes distant, like maybe he was remembering what Sawn-off had done.

Then he looked up and said, 'Are you going to tell me about it?' so I acted all sorry and told him the truth, more or less. I didn't lie; just left a few things out. I told him that I was looking to find work with Montoya, that I'd heard of him but didn't know much about him, and that Deeks was going to set me up. I told him what happened on the door of the club and that I went back to kick seven shades out of them. And the whole time he sat there shaking his head, judging me, thinking what an idiot I am, until I asked how come Sawn-off didn't pull that trigger. It was like he hit rock bottom then, worn down as far as he could go, and he just sighed and said, 'I have to get something for him, Sean. Then he'll leave me alone.' He lowered his hands and looked at me. 'Leave *us* alone.'

'Us? He knows about me?'

'He knows *I* didn't do anything, Sean. Said he could tell straight away. Apparently I'm not the sort. But he thinks I know who *did* go to his club.'

'You didn't tell him, though?' Maybe my brother was tougher than he looked. Maybe he was more like me than I thought. Maybe he was more like me than *he* thought. He'd been in a tight spot with a guy who'd killed more people than fucking anthrax, and here he was to tell me all about it. I had to admire him for that.

'He says I owe him, Sean - and that means you owe *me*.'

'Okay, what is it? What does he want from you?'

'A box.'

'What box?' I asked, keeping cool.

Jack shook his head. 'All I *know* is where it is and who's got it. All I need to *do* is get it back.'

I could hardly believe my luck. The box Deeks told me about inside. I started thinking that maybe it was *meant* to be mine. It was being paraded under my nose by Sawn-off Montoya himself. It had to be fate. It had to be. If I could get my hands on it, then Deeks and Sawn-off and everybody else could go shove their jobs and their deals and everything else. 'So where is it?' Still sounding calm.

'His wife's got it.'

I thought that over for a while, smoking the cigarette and trying to make sense of what Jack said but eventually I had to ask him. 'I don't get it. If his wife's got it why doesn't he just take it?' I leaned back in the chair for the first time since I sat down, and the Cougar, which I'd tucked into the back of my trousers, dug in, as if to remind me it was still there.

'He's not with his wife any more. They're separated,' said Jack.

'So?' I folded my arms and shrugged. The gun was uncomfortable against my spine, it wanted to be in my hand.

'What do you mean, '*so*'?' he said.

'So what difference does that make? I mean, if he knows where she is, and he knows she's got it, why doesn't he just take it?' I was wondering if Jack was thinking straight, if he knew what he was talking about. He *had* been in a bit of a state when I found him.

'He thinks if he goes after her, she'll disappear. Thinks ...'

'I still don't get it.'

'Well, if you let me finish,' his voice raising and then coming back to normal like he's catching himself, controlling himself. Jack touched a hand to the cut across the bridge of his nose and a pinprick of blood oozing from one indented edge. 'He's had someone following her, but he got spotted, so now she's scared and'll probably run. He wants someone who she won't recognise.'

'And that's us?' It made some sense, but I couldn't believe that Sawn-off would leave the box in Jack's hands unless he was desperate. Even so, I nodded and said, 'Okay, so where is she?'

'Staying in some posh hotel downtown. But we need to be quick before she disappears again.'

'Okay, so what do we do? Go in there and get rough or...?'

'No, Sean. I mean, I'm not sure I even *want* your help.' He started to shift about, like he was going to tell me something I wouldn't like. He looked away. 'You're starting to scare me, Sean. Maybe I don't know you so well anymore.'

'What you talking about, Jack? Course you know me. Nobody knows me better.'

'Well, maybe *that's* what's worrying me. Maybe I know I shouldn't trust you with something like this.'

'Course you can trust me,' I said looking hurt. 'Come on Jack, we'll do this together. It'll be fine.'

Jack was quiet, taking a drink of his beer and then saying, 'Look, Sean, I don't know how I got away from that guy, but I don't think he'll let me go next time.'

'What next time?'

'Listen to me, Sean, I want you to understand that this guy is a complete fucking psycho, and I want you to keep that right at the front of your mind, because he was going to kill me. He beat me with a steel whip and then he was going to kill me. And if I don't get him what he wants, he'll come back. But not straight away, because first he's going to find everyone I know and hurt *them*, and I'm pretty sure he can do that, Sean, I believe him. He traced my registration to this flat easy enough. And once he's hurt everyone I know, *then* he'll hurt me. Now, I don't reckon it would take him too long to work his way through my friends 'cause I don't know a whole lot of people, but the people I do know? Well, I'd like to keep them alive thanks very much. And remember, you'll be on that list too.'

But Jack wasn't thinking about Sawn-off coming back and killing me. Oh no, he was thinking about his girl. Mandy Hepple. And right then, I think Jack's mind was giving him a pretty good idea of what Mandy would look like with a sawn-off shotgun pointed at her face. Maybe it was even showing him what she'd look like with half her head gone and her brains falling out around her shoulders. I held up my hands. 'Don't worry about it. I want this to go as smooth as you do.' I was telling the truth. 'You can trust me.'

I was eager to go to the hotel, but knew I'd have to play it calm for Jack's sake, I didn't want him to worry, so I sat down on the edge of the chair, trying to avoid resting back against the Beretta, and acted relaxed. Anyway, I needed some time to figure out a way of persuading Jack to keep the box once we had it. He already said that he didn't know many people, so Sawn-off wouldn't be kept too busy killing them when we decided to keep it. That meant we'd have to act quick. Mandy Hepple would be a problem, though; I'd have to deal with that one sooner or later. I thought maybe we could bring her in on it too - after all, seven figures is a lot of money in anybody's book. Or maybe she'd be better off out of the picture altogether, I hadn't decided. 'Right then, we need a plan,' I said.

Jack stood up and went to the bookshelf. He picked up a small, passport sized photograph and gave it to me saying, 'That's her. That's his wife. Magdalena she's called.'

I looked at the photo. 'Nice,' I said and passed it back.

'There's something else you need to know, Sean.'

'Yeah?'

'Yeah. Whatever we do, we can't hurt her.'

JACK

Darkness came down early that Sunday afternoon and the roads were as quiet as I'd ever seen them. The only thing that broke the silence was the odd car splashing past in the opposite direction and the occasional dirty yellow truck spraying grit and salt. Sean rolled my blue Ford across town and I sat beside him, rubbing my hands together against the cold, waiting for the heater to warm the inside of the car. I was trying to bring everything together, but it was all slipping away.

Just as we'd been about to leave the flat, Hornrim had turned up, smiling his gawky smile and shuffling his lanky legs, saying, 'Fuckin' hell, guys, matching black eyes. Nice. Maybe you could start a tag team or something.' He was still wearing the same suit that he'd had on last night.

'Yeah, yeah, very funny,' Sean looked over at me. 'What d'you say we give Hornrim a shine? I mean, we wouldn't want him to feel left out, now would we?'

Hornrim backed away, losing the grin and holding his hands up, saying, 'Aw come on, guys, I was only joking.'

'You have first shot, Jack,' said Sean.

I thought about it - laying one on Hornrim might have made me feel better - but that seemed to be my brother's answer to everything. Instead, I watched as Sean pretended to go for him and the two of them ended up tousling in a sort of self-conscious way, like blokes being blokes but trying not to act too close, if you know what I mean. I couldn't believe Sean was so high after everything that had happened. Me, I just felt sore and numb.

Anyway, we tried to get rid of Hornrim. He asked if he could hang about with us for a while but we both said no. We didn't want him around, and we didn't want him to know what we were doing. But then he said something to Sean, something about last night - '*Still got the cougar?*' I think it was - and gave him a kind of knowing look, raising his eyebrows. After that, I couldn't tear them apart and before I could stop him, Sean was inviting Hornrim to come along for the ride, telling me, 'It'll be all right, Jack, he'll just sit out of the way.'

'No way, Sean, I don't want anything to screw this up. Especially not him.'

'He won't.'

'How can you be so sure? I mean, just look at him for Christ's sake.'

Hornrim was standing by the front door, picking his nose and checking the contents. He held up his finger for me to see, and pulled a face.

'He won't,' Sean said it again. 'I'll kill him if he does.'

'I'll be cool, man, I promise,' Hornrim flicking his fingers at me, both hands. 'Come on Jack, I haven't got anything else to do. Be a mate. Go on. It's just me.'

'And he might come in handy,' said Sean. 'Many hands and all that.'

I lowered my voice and pulled my brother closer. 'Look, Sean, I'm worried *you're* gonna fuck this up, I don't want to have to worry about him too.' I stared at Hornrim and pointed a thumb, not caring that he could see me.

'Don't be such a girl, Jack. All he's gonna do is sit in the car.' Then Sean looked at his watch and tapped the face.

I couldn't think of any good reason to take Hornrim along, and I tried to stand my ground but before I knew it, he was lolling in the backseat of my car, smoking my cigarettes and crawling under my skin. 'Don't drop ash on the seat,' I told him.

'Whatever you say.' There was an edge to his voice, like he was taking the piss, so Sean laughed and Hornrim saw that as an opening.

'So what we doin'?' he said. 'Where we goin'?' He was excited, like a kid on a mystery tour. I half expected him to ask if we were nearly there yet, but Sean cut him down by telling him, 'Shut the fuck up and sit tight.'

Hornrim didn't reply, he just did as he was told. He hooked an arm around each front headrest and poked his face between the driver and passenger seats like a turtle out of its shell, making me wish that Sean would step hard on the brakes.

By now the heater was on full, pumping hot air into the car, but I still couldn't get warm. I checked all the dials and moved all the vents so they pointed at me, then I looked over at my brother. 'Let's do this right, Sean.'

'Yeah, yeah. You keep saying that.' He took his eyes off the road and looked back at me. 'What d'you think I'm going to do, anyway?'

I just sighed and rubbed my hands together, turning to watch the lights from the window.

'It'll be fine, Jack. Don't worry about it.'

'Uh-huh.'

'Oh, come on you guys, what we doing?' said Hornrim, his head twisting from side to side as he looked from me to Sean and back again. 'Where we going? Come *on*.'

We both ignored him, so he flopped back in the seat and sulked. I imagined him glaring at the back of my head and tapping cigarette ash onto the seat.

The light traffic on the roads meant that it didn't take long to cross town, but once we reached the rich part of town, there were a few more cars about. It was a part of town that I didn't see much; the place where people with money came to live, work and spend up. Expensive, designer apartments with fashionable names and waterfront views. Windows that were clear and lights inside that looked warm and bright. The cars that lined the streets weren't rusted and old, like mine, and people weren't afraid to go out after dark. It was the right side of town, the place where people 'did lunch' and went to the gym after work. Shit, even the snow looked cleaner down here.

Sean pulled up on the side of the road opposite the main doors of the hotel and killed the lights.

We sat for a while and listened to the engine ticking.

Cars splashed past.

Hornrim fidgeted.

I smoked a cigarette.

'Okay, so you know what to do?' I broke the silence, my voice sounding flat.

'Sure.'

'Tell me again.'

'Jesus, Jack.'

'Tell me again, Sean.'

'Okay, okay, chill. I'm gonna wait here for you to come out with the woman. You get her away from the hotel - no cabs - I pull up, we get her in the car, find somewhere quiet and then we get it. She walks, we disappear, end of story. Simple.'

'That's right,' I said. 'Simple.'

'Just one thing, though,' said Sean.

'What?'

'How you gonna get her away from the hotel with you? What if she goes for a cab out front? How you gonna stop her?'

I unclipped my seat belt and looked at my brother. 'You just leave that to me.'

'Uh-huh. Okay.' He studied my face. 'You sure you don't want *me* to go? I *can* do this.'

'No. It should be me. It's better that way.'

We looked at each other for a moment.

'Well, I might as well do it, then,' I took a deep breath and popped the door handle.

'Yep,' said Sean.

I opened the door and stepped out, pulling my jacket tight. As I waited for a car to pass, Sean leaned over and wound down the window. 'Hey, Jack.'

'What?' I turned around.

'Good luck.'

'Thanks.'

'And...'

'Yeah?'

'And don't fuck it up.'

JACK

My face was fixed as I crossed the road, all the muscles feeling paralysed, rubbed with ice, so that my cheeks thudded with every footstep. I blinked heavily, my eyeballs as dry as my mouth and I could hear the blood rushing in my ears. I was cold all over, my stomach hurt and I needed to pee. The cut underneath my left eye had closed overnight and I'd cleaned myself up as best as I could, but I still looked rough around the edges. My nose was a little bigger and a lot more crooked than usual, and I limped on my right leg, a reminder of what had happened last night when the steel whip left my knee bruised and tender. The weapon had split straight through, parting the skin, drawing blood, but it looked worse than it really was. Anyway, I tried not to think about it because every time I did, I saw a hammer and nail hovering over my knee.

My boots crunched hard snow when I stepped up onto the pavement, my breath plumed up and out around me. Cars passed behind, tyres scrunching snow and splattering sludge, but I ignored the sounds, my eyes staring straight ahead, and tried to concentrate on the job at hand. I had to find Magda. It was the only way to keep everybody safe.

The hotel driveway ran parallel to the main road - the one Sean was parked on right now - giving an area for cabs and limos to pull up and drop their fares into the lap of luxury. The stonework was lined with a train of tiny white lights, criss-crossing here and there, and twinkling cheerfully, reminding me that Christmas was just around the corner.

I made my way directly under the awning where two black cabs from one of the expensive companies were standing idle, and I ignored the bored stares of the drivers. One or two guests bustled out of the main doors as I approached, but none of them headed for the cabs. Instead they turned down the street and made their way into the night, chatting and laughing. They were probably headed towards the cafes and restaurants, where the lights were flickering and the rich folks were gathering like moths, but I watched them without really watching them, because somehow I didn't feel like me anymore; like I was walking in someone else's shoes.

*

When I stepped into the warmth of the hotel, the voice took me by surprise.

'Evening, Sir.'

It dragged me away from my thoughts and I turned to look at the doorman. He was an older guy, friendly face, wearing a long green overcoat and a black top hat. 'Oh. Yeah. Good evening,' I said and turned my head to the left in the hope that he wouldn't notice the cut under my eye. I wanted to look as if I knew where I was going, so I quickly scanned the area, deciding where to go first. Ahead of me was a small area of shops selling newspapers, magazines, watches and clothes – the usual kind of gift stuff, probably expensive from the look of them. Around the lobby, comfortable chairs were arranged, providing places for guests to relax, drink coffee, watch the world pass them by and do whatever it is that people do in hotel lobbies. Topiary cut trees in purple pots stood in discreet corners furnishing the area with tasteful decoration. The shaped animals, mostly reindeer, twinkled with white lights that matched the piped Christmas music.

I made my way across the marbled floor and aimed for the cocktail lounge that took up the left hand side of the huge lobby. I had no idea how I was going to make contact with Magda, I didn't know which room she was in, or whether she was even still staying in the hotel, but I guessed that if she was still there, she'd have to come down to the lobby sooner or later. So it looked like I'd have to watch and wait, and the cocktail lounge seemed to be the best place to do it. It was fronted with floor to ceiling glass, stood directly opposite the reception area, and looked secluded and private enough for me to disappear into. Once inside, I'd have a good view of the lift doors by reception and I'd be able to see the stair exits, too. I'd wait for Magdalena in there.

Close to the lounge entrance, a black notice board was propped up by one of the newsstands. The removable plastic gold lettering told me that there was a singer on that night and when I pushed open the glass door and stepped in, I was met by the sound of Ella Jones. I'd never heard of her.

The singer was at the back of the lounge, standing on a small stage, and looking the part in the silver sequined dress which fell to the floor and ruffled around her feet. She was perfect cocktail hour material, like something out of a hundred cheesy movies. Her hair was piled high on her head and her nails were painted dark purple. There was a slight sway in her heavy hips. In front of her was a microphone stand which she held in one hand while the other waved around in the air, up and down, the way that singers do when they're acting like no one else is watching. Her eyes were closed and she looked like she was in a different place from everybody else. She sang 'Mad about the boy' which I recognised from an advert on the television, way back, but I couldn't remember what it was for. Behind her, wearing tuxedos, a small group of musicians pushed out the tunes for her.

The bar was filling up, but I found a place near the window without too much trouble. I ordered a coke from the waiter who came to the table and then I sat quietly, picking at the funny coloured peanut things and smoking cigarettes. I turned away from Ella Jones, so that I could watch the lobby.

Under the table, I slid the photograph of Magdalena Montoya out of my pocket and held it in one hand, checking it every minute or so, trying to memorise her face. Occasionally a woman would come out of the lifts or the doors leading up to the stairwell and I'd look at the picture again, just to make sure it wasn't her, but I knew it wasn't. I'd recognise her straight away, I was pretty sure of that. I'd know Magdalena Montoya when she showed her face, I had to. Mandy's life depended on it. My only problem was what I was going to do when I saw her. Sean and I had talked about it, trying to decide the best thing and, of course, he'd wanted to do it hard and fast, scare her, his way. I told him I wanted to come clean, be up front, but Sean said I was mad, he knew these people better than I did. Said he'd been dealing with their kind all his life, saying it like I was going to congratulate him. It was a risk, but in the end we decided to do it his way. I'd follow her out of the hotel, get her to move away from the main entrance. Whatever happened, I had to get her onto the pavement, beside the road. All I had to do then was keep her there long enough for Sean to pull up. We'd both get her into the car and persuade her to give us the box. Once we had it, she'd walk.

*

Ella Jones was singing 'Piece of my Heart' when Magdalena finally appeared from the lift, but the music didn't swell, there were no loud trumpets, no thunderbolts, no electrical storms, no nothing. Just Magdalena. She simply stepped out, carrying her suitcase, and walked across the hotel lobby. I didn't need to check the photograph.

Her suit was pressed and her boots were polished. The scarf and jewellery matching her outfit. Not one hair on her head was out of place and her make-up was fresh. She held her chin high and her shoulders well back. She looked strong, the way she walked like that, striking out like she wasn't going to take shit from anybody, and I could see why so many of the men in the lobby turned to watch her. She had a pretty face, but that's not all. The way her jacket bulged at her chest and the long legs that strode across the lobby, that's what everyone was looking at, but I was watching her eyes and they said something else. Her eyes were everywhere, looking into every corner, every shadow, checking every face, every movement. She was looking for spooks who hide in dark places. She was expecting somebody.

In her right hand she was carrying a medium sized soft suitcase that was swollen around the sides like it had eaten too much. The brown leather straps were buckled tightly and it must have been heavy because it pulled her to one side, affecting the way she walked, and she had to balance herself with the other arm, holding it out just a touch. Over her right shoulder was a small handbag that probably wouldn't hold much more than a purse and some make-up. Maybe a packet of cigarettes and a few other bits and pieces but not much else.

I tried not to look right at her, watching only from the corner of my eyes so that I didn't meet her sweeping gaze. As she crossed the lobby, her head turned towards the lounge and she looked close to where I was sitting behind the glass, but her eyes swept over my head and searched the dark corners of the bar. I hoped she didn't have a meeting arranged; it would make things more difficult.

I watched her move past until I was looking at her back, seeing her hips swing as she headed towards the doors. She was leaving. I crushed my cigarette into the ashtray and started to lift myself out of the seat, knowing I had to follow her out of the hotel, as close as I could. If I was going to catch her, I'd have to be careful not to let her leave too far ahead of me. But instead of heading directly for the sliding doors, she crossed to reception, and stopped at the high stone counter to speak to one of the women standing behind it. The assistant smiled, nodded. Magda put the suitcase on the floor and slid it right up against the reception counter. She stepped forward and pressed her shins against it so hard that the muscles in her calves must have tightened like knots.

I sat back in my seat and listened to Ella Jones sing 'My baby just cares for me' while I watched the silent conversation between Magda and the woman on reception, feeling like my insides were about to turn to treacle and leak out. Papers were passed, Magda leaned onto the pale marbled counter and signed something. Something was filed away in a drawer. Papers were passed back. Something was slipped into her pocket - credit card, I guessed, or maybe a receipt, but either way, I was sure she was checking out.

When she finally looked like she was ready to leave, I left some money on the table and stood up, picking my way around and through the other tables in the lounge. The place was now bubbling with drinkers, most of them ignoring the singer, trying to talk over the music, so I apologised to those who

I knocked and asked several to move their chairs so that I could pass. All the time I kept the reception area in view to my right. When I reached the dark polished bar, racked with glasses and multi-coloured bottles, I worked my way out into the main lobby and allowed the lounge door to swing closed on the sound of Ella Jones. I stayed around the newsstand, pretending to study the headlines, and waited for Magda to finish her business.

At last she nodded to the assistant, smiled, lifted her luggage into her right hand and made her way to the main door, fending off the bellhops who offered to carry the suitcase. I watched as one tried to take it from her, but she refused, shaking her head once and pulling the luggage away from him. When she was close to the exit, I followed, timing my approach so that I reached the sliding doors at exactly the same time as she did.

*

Standing beside Magdalena, waving her through the door like that, pretending to be polite, I realised she wasn't as tall as she'd looked. Her shape and the way she carried herself made her look tall, but she was a good few inches shorter than me, even in those heels. She nodded once, looking up at me with a vague smile, but not seeing me, not making eye contact, and then stepped through the door in front of me. I followed close behind her, not feeling the cold.

I'd spent a lot of time in the car and in the cocktail lounge thinking about what was going to happen next. I was going to have to talk to her, say something if I was going to keep her away from the cabs, get her out onto the pavement and make her stop. I didn't know *what* I was going to say, but it didn't have to be much, just enough to get her attention, Sean said. Then we'd do it, snatch her, push her into the car, frighten her and force the box from her. Sean said it would be easy. Watching her in the lobby, though, I thought about just grabbing the suitcase and making a run for it. Maybe it would save us some trouble, me and her; I wasn't so sure that I could do it the way we'd agreed. Hitting her, attacking her, mugging her, frightening her. I tried to work myself up to it, be angry with her so that it would make it easier for me, but actually being there, actually putting a person to the name and the picture – and actually *seeing* her right beside me, well, that just blew it wide open because up close, she looked afraid. Alone. And when she looked up at me like that, with the vague smile, those eyes, that's when I made up my mind what I had to do.

'Mrs. Montoya?' I said as she walked towards the first taxi. She stopped in her tracks but kept her back to me, waiting for something to happen. Maybe a knife in the back or a bang on the head, just like we'd planned. 'You *are* Mrs. Montoya aren't you?' I kept my voice polite and easy, but I could feel a tightness in my throat.

She turned around and looked at me for less than a second before her eyes shifted away and her head turned, searching for a way to run.

I held my hands out, to show her that they were empty and said, 'I need to talk to you. It's about your husband.'

We looked at each other for a beat before she said, 'My husband?' and her left hand went to her face, where a bruise was just visible, a dark patch under the make-up. As soon as she realised I'd noticed, she dropped her hand and shook her head at me. 'There's nothing I need to say about my husband.' She spoke with the slightest hint of an accent, maybe French or Spanish, I couldn't say for sure. 'Tell him to...'

'Maybe not. But there's something *I* need to say. Can we talk?' From the corner of my eye, I could see my blue Ford parked on the other side of the road, just one amongst a line of others which had parked along the curb.

'No. Tell him to stop following me. I don't know what he wants. Leave me alone,' she turned away, a little clumsy with the heavy suitcase, and the doorman glanced over when he heard the sharpness in her raised voice.

'He knows about the box,' I said and looked towards my car, shaking my head, not yet. Once again, Magdalena stopped in her tracks. 'He wants it back.'

The doorman shifted his weight and held up a hand as if he were about to come over, but Magdalena failed to notice him and turned around to face me, her eyebrows low, saying, 'Who are you?'

'Nobody. Look, we need to talk. There's something I need to tell you.'

'No. I'm meeting someone. I don't have time. I'm *expected*.'

'Then we'll take a cab.' I lowered my voice, took her elbow and guided her away from the doorman. 'We'll talk in there.'

Magda pulled her arm from my grip and looked down at my hand as if to ask how it had dared to touch her. 'You think I'm just going to get into a cab with you?' She glared, indignant and unhelpful, so I took a step away from her, telling her that bad things were going to happen if we didn't talk. All the time I kept my voice calm.

'Bad things?' she said. 'To me? Is that a threat?' Her face was hard, her whole manner changing from that first encounter.

'No. Not to you. To me.'

'To you? Then why should *I* care? I don't even know you.'

'No but...'

'You're nobody. You said so yourself.'

'Not just me,' I said. 'Other people too. My girlfriend. My brother.'

She shrugged one shoulder, the one not carrying the weight of the suitcase, and her head tipped to the side. 'So what does it have to do with me? Why should I talk to you?'

I thought about telling her that there were two men in the car parked over the street. I thought about telling her that all I had to do was signal to them and they'd come screeching over, force her into the car and then who knows what would happen. I thought about telling her what kind of people she was dealing with, but what I said was, 'Because I think you're as scared as I am.'

As she considered this, one hand moved to her cheek, hesitated, and then swept through her hair. We looked at each other for a long while, both of us wondering what to do next, but it was Magda who spoke first. 'Okay,' she said, letting out her breath. 'How about we compromise? I won't get into a cab with you, but you can walk with me for a while. We'll head towards the station and I'll hail a cab further down.' She put one hand on her hip and waited for my reply, more confident now that she seemed to have dismissed me as a threat.

I nodded in agreement, knowing Sean would be watching, and thinking it was better if we were on the move.

As we started walking, I looked down at the suitcase. 'Help you with that?' I asked her, but she told me she could manage on her own thank you very much. I liked the way her mouth moved as she talked and I noticed the way her nose pulled down slightly when she spoke the letter 'm'. Her eyebrows were neatly plucked and the skin around her eyes was tight. The bruise on her cheek was even more noticeable up close. 'He hit you?'

'What's it to you?' She tensed up again so I shrugged like it was no big deal. She didn't want to talk about it, that was fine by me.

'Not any more,' she said relaxing a little, but I wondered if she was putting on an act. Trying to look tough, like she could cope with anything.

'How come?' I said.

'Because I'll never see him again.'

'I meant how come he hit you.'

'It's the kind of thing he does.' Then she nodded her chin towards the cut under my eye. 'Is that where you got *your* war wounds?' It was a nice way of putting it. War wounds. Like a mother talking about her kid's playground injuries, a few cuts and scrapes from falling over.

'Yeah, but that's only what you can see. You don't *want* to know what else he did.' Saying that made me think of my knee.

'So what exactly is it you want from me?'

'I want you to give me the box,' I said, thinking there was no point in hanging around. Tell it like it is.

'What box?'

'Oh, come on, I know you have it. Your husband told me. You give it back, he leaves us both alone. He doesn't want to hurt you, he just wants it back.'

She looked down, shook her head and then raised her eyes again. 'Okay. Let's say for the moment, that I *do* have it.'

'Okay let's.'

'Which I don't.'

'Of course.'

'I wouldn't give it to you,' she said.

'You have to.'

She just shook her head again and turned her face away from me, her pace faltering. I thought she was going to turn around and go back to the hotel but instead, she caught herself, picked up her pace with fresh energy.

'Please,' I said. 'Don't just walk away.'

'Then you'd better give me something else.' Her tone was sharp, impatient.

'Like what?'

'Do you have any idea what that box is worth?'

'I don't even know what it is.'

'Don't you want to?'

'No. All I know is how much it's worth to *me*. That's enough. That's all I need.'

'You ask for the box without knowing what it is? You've come with nothing to offer me?'

'Look,' I grabbed her elbow again but she pulled away once more. 'This isn't a bargain. I'm not here to make a deal. I'm here for the box and you should be glad it's me and not someone else. When your husband realised you'd taken it, he hired some people to take it back.'

'Sounds like him.'

'And they were bad people from what I heard.'

'So where are they, then?'

'Something happened to them. Lucky for you I'm here instead. Things could have been much worse.'

'*He* sent you or you came on your own? You made something happen to these bad people?'

'That's what your husband thinks. Says I owe him. And the only way I could stop him from hurting me was to promise I'd get this box back for him.'

'So you're doing this to save your own skin, you mean?'

'No, I'm doing it to save my *girlfriend's* skin.'

'He said he'd hurt her?' Magda's step slowed a little. 'And you believe him?'

'Yes, I do. Especially after what he did to me.' I paused and swallowed before asking, *'Would* he?'

'Yes,' she said. 'He would.'

I tried hard not to think about Mandy, didn't want to see her face in my mind right now, and we walked in silence for a while until Magda said, 'So who did he send after me?'

'I don't know. Does it matter?'

'Hmm. Well, I suppose you must be some kind of tough guy if *you're* here instead. Are *you* going to hurt me, tough guy?' She sounded playful now, she was growing more confident with every step. She was in control.

'Am I going to have to?' I took the opportunity to make a cheap threat that didn't work. I'm not the threatening type and she must've spotted it a mile away. She just smiled and laughed through her nose, a quick rush of air that puffed out into the cold.

We'd walked quite a distance now and came to a junction where it was intersected by another road. There was a crossing with lights so we stopped as the traffic trickled past. Along with one or two other people we waited in silence for the green light to let us go. Magda reached into the bag that hung over her shoulder and took out a silver cigarette case. She put one in her mouth and then offered them to me. I accepted and lit them both with the Zippo Sean had given me. The light changed to green, we crossed the road and continued to walk. 'I have something we both want,' she said, punctuating the remark by exhaling cigarette smoke. 'We also both have a thorn in our side,' she took another drag straight away. 'Maybe I could give you the box. And maybe you could do something in return.'

I asked her like what? I couldn't think of anything I could do for her, and she came back saying, 'Oh, I don't know. Maybe you could organise world peace, make me rich and happy, feed the poor. Or maybe you could make my husband go away.' She looked right into my eyes. 'Permanently.' Then she paused, more for effect than anything else, and said. 'That way you'd get the box and I'd get my money.' She slowed, moved to one side of the pavement and put her suitcase down against the wall. She stood with her back to the brick but her calves were pressed against the case. I stopped in front of her and we faced each other.

We weren't far from the first of the restaurants - an Italian from the look of it – and beside us a dark alley ran back between the buildings. The smell of warm food and decaying rubbish tainted the cold air. 'You mean you want me to...? Jesus, what do you think I am?'

'I thought you were a tough guy,' she said, giving me a look like she was daring me.

'Yeah, but I'm not a *hit man*.'

She took a drag and smiled, but it wasn't a proper smile, it was just a movement of her mouth coupled with a distant stare, like she was thinking of something else. 'Shame,' she said. 'I like a hit man.' Then she blinked and tossed her cigarette down into the snow saying, 'look, darling, I don't want you to kill my husband, it was a joke...'

'I don't have time for...'

'...but I don't think I can give you the box. I'm sorry about your girlfriend, I really am, but there's nothing I can do. And it won't make any difference; once he gets the box he'll probably kill you, anyway.'

I looked away from her, staring down the street and clenching my jaw.

'What's your name, sweetheart?'

'Jack,' I said still staring. 'Jack Presley.'

'For real?' she asked, her head tipping slightly to the side. 'Like the King?'

'Yeah, for real,' I said.

'You change that yourself?'

'No.'

'Okay then, Jack Presley, I can see you're in a lot of pain over this. What's your girlfriend's name?'

'Mandy.'

'She the real thing?'

'Yeah,' I said without looking at her. 'She's the real thing.'

Magda sighed. 'Well let me think,' she said. 'Maybe there's a way around this. Maybe we can work something out.'

BURN OUT

SEAN

'C'mon, man, what's the crack? What we doing?' Hornrim was still leaning forward between the seats like a nosy kid. He wanted to climb over into the passenger side but I told him to stay put in the back, I didn't want him right in my face.

'Business,' I said.

'What kind of business?'

'Not yours.'

'Aw, man!' Hornrim sighed and sat back in the seat. He folded his arms and sulked, probably wishing he hadn't come. I ignored him and kept on watching the hotel door. Every so often a limo or a taxi pulled up, sometimes two, and dumped passengers under the grey awning in front of the hotel. Important as they were, the passengers stood by, not lifting a finger, while green-coated doormen unloaded their bags. They watched as the bellhops, just kids most of them, struggled with their bulging suitcases. Then everything calmed down until the next load arrived.

From time to time, couples or groups left the hotel and headed towards the West End where all the shops and restaurants stood waiting for them to spend their oily cash. You just knew that those places would be full of waiters, bowing and scraping for the smallest tip. 'Yes, sir, right away sir' and all that shite. Some people would call that honest work, fucking mugs.

In the distance I could see all the signs of Christmas and goodwill. Coloured lights chasing each other around shop windows, decorated trees flashing on the pavements, lampposts shot with tiny white lights. The scene wouldn't have looked out of place on the front of some crappy Christmas card and If I'd listened hard enough I'd have probably heard fuckin' sleigh bells. But I paid no attention to those things. There'd be plenty of time for that once I had the cash that the box would bring. Then I'd be spending time in the expensive part of town and people would notice me. They'd want to be with me.

For now I was fixed on the hotel door. I was waiting for Jack to come back out with the woman and I didn't want to miss him. I slumped down in the seat and switched the CD on, but turned it down as soon as the music came on. Simon and Garfunkel were still in there, ready to ambush me with curly hair and jangling guitars. I ejected it and threw it onto the dashboard. Not my style - especially not for a job like this. I reached into the door pocket and pulled out Jack's CD case. It was a bright green rubbery job that I guessed Mandy must have bought for him, I couldn't see Jack buying something like that. I tossed it onto the back seat.

'Ow!'

'What?' I asked without turning around.

'Hit my fuckin' head.'

'Stop moaning and pick some tunes.'

'Like what?'

'I dunno. Something good,'

I heard Hornrim pop open the case and flip through the leaves which held the CDs. After a while he leaned forward and held one in front of my nose. 'There you go, mate.'

I looked down. 'Celine Dion? I said *something good*, dickhead! I can see I'm gonna have to have words with Jack about his music collection.'

Hornrim laughed and the CD disappeared.

'How 'bout this?' he said leaning forward again.

I glanced at the disc. 'Better.' I took it and slid it into the slot so that the old CD player could suck it in. The raw sound of 'Know Your Rights' filled the car and I pressed the repeat button so that the CD would loop. I liked 'The Clash', they were right for a job like this.

'This is where it's at!' said Hornrim. I didn't turn around but I shifted my eyes to watch him in the rear view mirror. He was nodding his head up and down and pretending to play the drums.

'Fuckin' Celine Dion,' I said under my breath.

'Hey, I thought you might like that crap.' Raising his voice a little now, so I could hear it over the music,

'Yeah, that's right Hornrim. That's me all over,'

'Well, I thought you might have softened up a bit - you know, all that time inside.'

I said uh-huh, it's pretty obvious you never did bang-up and he came back with, 'I thought being inside was a holiday camp for guys like you.'

'It's a fuckin' pleasure cruise compared to sharing a car with you.'

'Yeah, yeah,'

'You know I envy you, Hornrim, you're a lucky guy,' I said, not looking back.

'You mean with me being so good lookin' and everything?'

'No, because you've got me for company when all I've got is you.'

We kicked lines off each other for a while until Hornrim couldn't handle it any more, couldn't stand the pace, and sulked again. After that we just listened to 'The Clash'. It seemed like I'd been spending a lot of time sitting and waiting and listening.

After an hour or so, Jack came out of the hotel.

I sat up, lowered the volume and watched him make contact with the woman. They stopped just beside the first waiting cab. I rubbed condensation from the side window so that I could see better. They talked for a while but it didn't seem to be going too well. It looked like she was going to give him the bum's rush, walk away from him.

'C'mon Jack, don't be such a pussy,' I said under my breath. 'Get her away from the hotel. Doesn't have to be far.' I turned the key in the ignition, sparking up the car, just as Jack looked over in my direction and shook his head enough for me to notice.

'Who's that?' asked Hornrim, leaning forward between the seats so that his face was beside mine. He was too close and his breath was bad.

'Never you fuckin' mind.'

'But...'

'C'mon Jack, what're you doing?' again under my breath.

'Who's he talk...?'

'Fuckin' hell Hornrim, you ever considered brushing your teeth?' I shifted my face away from his but kept my eyes on Jack and the woman.

'What?'

'I said 'you ever think about brushing your teeth'?'

'I heard what you said, but what d'you mean?'

'Your breath, man, it smells like shit.'

'Oh, cheers; like you're Mr. fuckin' Hygiene.'

'What's that supposed to mean?' I asked, shifting my eyes to watch him for a second, and then I was looking at the hotel again. I was surprised that Hornrim had even heard of 'hygiene', I'd seen his flat, remember.

'Nothing,' he said.

'No, come on. What d'you mean?' Eyes still on Jack, but concentration fading.

'Well, you didn't wash the sink in my bathroom. There was blood in it.' He was sulking again.

'Jesus, Hornrim, you're some boy, you are. Not 'Mr. Fuckin' Hygiene'? A little bit of blood in your sink? You've got some nerve, I'll give you that.'

'How's that?'

'How's that? Man, you should take a good look at yourself.'

He said 'What?' like this was all some kind of news to him.

I went on. 'Look around, big guy. Start with the toilet and move outwards. Finish in the kitchen. *Then* tell me I'm not 'Mr. fuckin' Hygiene'. Compared to you, Hornrim, I'm Mr. Fuckin' *Domestos*.'

'Wha...'

'Shh!'

'Bu...'

'Shut the fuck up, Hornrim, you're getting in the way.'

Hornrim had broken my concentration too much. I'd been distracted from what was important. I put my hand full on his face and pushed him away.

I focused again.

'Shit! They're moving,' I said aloud. 'This is us.' I indicated to pull out, and as I edged into the light Sunday evening traffic, I saw Jack and the woman start walking. It looked like she had the upper hand, like Jack wasn't coping too well without his little brother to keep an eye on him. I kept my cool and waited until they were a good way down the street before I pulled right onto the road and joined the other cars, driving slowly so that I could keep an eye on them and not pass.

I would've killed to know what they were saying. They were gassing like old women, but she still looked like she was the boss. She was no pushover - I could tell by the twist in her hips and the sway in her walk. I could tell by the way she flicked her hair and by the way she looked at Jack like she was a fucking tiger hiding under all that make-up and fancy clothes. She was going to lead him down the path, I just knew it.

I tried to keep the car behind them, keep them in my sight. 'What the fuck're they doing? I thought he was gonna get her to stop. Get her away from the hotel and stop. That's all he had to do.'

'What *is* this? What's going on?' asked Hornrim.

'Never you mind. I wasn't talking to you.'

'Who *were* you talking to, then?'

'The only person in here who counts for shit, that's who.'

Jack and the woman stopped at the lights on the intersection, but the traffic was building behind me, forcing me to drive past them. I pulled in and double-parked a little further up, watching them in my mirror as they lit up, sharing the flame on *my* lighter. It wasn't long before the lights changed, but Jack didn't notice me when they walked past.

I checked her out, eyes up and down her as she walked. She was pretty good for her age. Tall, strong, good legs - I preferred them a bit skinnier but had to admit that she had something about her. She looked confident and charming and her face was warm - friendly, even - but I knew that this was no time to be sentimental. She'd twist a guy round her finger and drop him like a broken doll, anyone could see that except Jack.

They stopped by the entrance to an alleyway just a few yards in front of the car, deep in conversation, her leaning back against the suitcase. She was using her charm all over him, the two of them starting to look a married couple and me not liking it one bit. She was even smiling and that was all wrong. She should have been in the car, quaking in her size fives, begging Jack to take the box - '*please* take it' - pleading with him to leave her alive, not to put a bullet in her face, not to tear her to fucking pieces finding the box. There was no way he was going to get it by greasing up to her like that and I could see that I'd have to step in. I wasn't as easily fooled by a big smile and a great pair of tits.

'Who's the chick?' said Hornrim. 'Nice arse.'

'No one,' I said and opened the door. Cold air rushed in. 'Just stay in the car.'

I walked flat-footed to avoid slipping on the icy crust over the snow and closed the distance between the car and Jack in just a few paces. As I went, I pulled the forty-five from its nestling place in the small of my back, gripping it firmly in my right hand and stepping up close beside the woman. I pressed the short barrel into her ribs just enough to make it hurt. 'No more fuckin' about. Get in the car. Jack, get the suitcase.'

I put my left arm around the woman's waist, keeping the gun in place, and walked her over to the back of the car. 'Open it,' I said, and when she did, Hornrim looked at her with wide eyes.

'Move along,' I told him. 'Make some room.'

He shuffled along the seat.

To her, 'Get in.' I said it mean, so she'd know I'd kill her in a blink. If the woman had been around enough tough-guys to know that Jack wasn't one, then she was sure as hell going to know that I was.

She was good, though. She kept her poise when she climbed into the back of the car beside Hornrim, and she watched with cool eyes as Jack dithered on the pavement. At least she knew enough to keep her mouth shut and her head down, which was better than Jack was doing. He was starting to look like a headless chicken, flapping about round the back of the car. I even thought for a moment that he was going to open the door and let her out.

'What the fuck you doing?' I said. 'Put the suitcase in the car and get in. You drive.' I threw the keys to Jack but he fumbled them and they went down into the snow by the curb. For a second he just stood and looked at me and I prayed for his sake they weren't lost. 'Keys, Jack. Just get the fuckin' keys.'

He went down on his knees, out of sight, and popped back up again a few seconds later with cold hands and a set of car keys.

'Well done,' I said. 'Now get her stuff in the car and let's get the fuck outa here.'

Jack stumbled to the car and pushed the suitcase onto the floor by the woman's knees. He looked at her. 'I'm sorry, I...' he started.

'Save it, sweetheart,' she said. 'We'll work this out.' She was cool, I'll give her that.

'Jack, get in the car and stop pissing about.' I slid into the back seat, forcing the woman and Hornrim closer together, then I leaned over to open the driver's door. Jack walked around the car and climbed in.

'What are you *doing*?' he asked when he was behind the wheel.

'What we agreed. C'mon, let's drive.'

He reached down for the lever to pull the seat forward. 'This isn't what we said. This isn't right.'

'Yeah, yeah, whatever, Jack. Drive.'

'So why don't we...'

'Let's go.'

'Sean...'

'Just drive Jack. Let's get out of here.'

Jack did the right thing. He put the keys in the ignition. 'Where to?' he said turning around to look at me. 'Where are we going?' And that's when he first noticed what I had in my hand.

'Jesus Christ! Where did you get that?' he stared at the Cougar which was tucked neatly under the woman's armpit.

'Never mind that, just fuckin' drive will you?' My patience was slipping - it had been a long weekend and I had a feeling it wasn't even close to being over.

Jack turned back to the wheel and bowed his head. He clenched his jaw and rubbed his face with both hands. He pressed his fingers into his eyes and then turned the key to fire up the engine. 'Okay. Where?' he said as he guided the car out into the traffic and over the ridge of sludge.

'Anywhere,' I said and turned my attention to the woman. 'Where is it?'

She ignored the question so I pushed the barrel of the Cougar tighter against her ribs. She sucked in a sharp breath, like a back-street mechanic about to give me some bad news. 'Where's what?' she said.

'Don't fuck me about.'

'I don't have it,' she said.

'Yeah?'

'And I wouldn't give it to you if I did.'

'Well, let's see shall we?' I said. 'Jack, head down to MacFarlane's.'

He eyed me in the mirror, saying, 'Sean, this isn't right. Don't make this any worse than it already is.'

'Don't be such a girl, Jack. There's only one way we're going to get what we want from her.' I nudged her with the gun again.

'We were about to work something out,' Jack said.

'Did she say she'd give you the box?' I asked.

'Well, no, but...'

'Exactly. Just head for MacFarlane's.'

MacFarlane's was an old warehouse sitting on the top of a low hill in a part of the quayside that still hadn't been redeveloped. Years back, it was a storage facility for shipbuilding equipment, but it had been empty for years. Mostly it was hidden from view on the town side of the river, but anyone motoring over the bridge could see it if they looked down. It wasn't a pretty sight, like a war-zone with its rusted corrugated iron roof all peppered with holes and dents. The forecourt was littered with rotting wooden palettes that had probably once been stacked in piles. Twisted metal, decaying containers, old girders, mattresses, shopping trolleys, blankets, bicycles. Almost everything you could think of - and lots you couldn't - had been dumped over the bridge by kids just for the hell of watching it crash down. It was a dangerous place full of potholes and pitfalls, and it was the sort of dive that you knew would smell of old piss and human turds.

But the heavy fall of snow made it look a whole lot better. Rusted barrels full of dirty rainwater looked somehow clean with thick ice covering the surface, and the forecourt junk was now hidden by the fresh fall and topped with a crust of diamonds. Even the building was completely different now that the overhanging roof was lined with icicles and the graffiti on the outside walls was covered with snow. It looked kind of nice.

Jack guided the car up the bank towards the front of the warehouse, avoiding the potholes where he could, but the going was tough. The back wheels skidding and gliding most of the way and we traveled sideways as much as forwards. Jack tried to push the car a little harder, but there are some things you just can't fight. The snow on the ice-hardened muddy path was virgin and it was clear that no one had been up there for a while. Even the druggies and the vagrants didn't bother with the place anymore. It seemed that only the rats still used MacFarlane's. Rats and me, that is.

Jack pulled up at the front of the warehouse, between two piles of soggy palettes, and cut the engine. There was no light around the building so he left the beams on, cutting into the darkness.

'What now?' he asked lowering his head into his hands and rubbing his forehead. 'What do we do now?'

I pushed the gun into the woman's ribs. 'Now we get the box.'

'She already said she doesn't have it, Sean.'

'Oh really?' Looking at her.

'Yeah.'

'And you believe her?'

'Why not?'

'You see, that's your problem, Jack; you're a sucker for a pretty face and a good pair of tits. What do you think Hornrim?'

'Erm, yeah. Yeah, whatever you say, Sean. Yeah, she's got good tits.' Hornrim sounded scared, but there was something else mixed in there, excitement maybe, and his eyes were crawling all over the woman. I noticed he'd dropped his hand so that it rested on her thigh.

'No, dickhead, I mean do you think she's got it or not?'

'Got what? I don't even know what you're talking about.' Still looking at her, having to lean away a little so that he could fit her all into his picture.

I opened the car door and backed out, keeping the gun pointed at the woman. My shoes sank and the snow was cold on my ankles, but I ignored it. No time for cold. 'Out,' I said to her.

She did as she was told, I guess that's the power of the gun.

'Hornrim, bring the suitcase out here.'

Hornrim pulled out the suitcase and walked around to the bonnet of the car where I was standing with Jack and the woman.

'Open it.'

Squinting against the car lights, Hornrim placed the suitcase on the bonnet and tried to open the catch, but it wouldn't budge. 'It's locked,' he said looking at me. 'It's got a combination or something.' He held one hand up to his face so that he could see me without the glare of the headlights in his eyes.

I nudged the woman with the barrel of the gun and she recited the combination. Hornrim thumbed it in and flicked open the catch. He lifted the top of the suitcase asking, 'What am I looking for?' Everything in the suitcase just looked dark. It was almost impossible to make anything out.

'Take everything out,' I said. 'I'll know it when I see it.'

Hornrim took the stuff out of her suitcase, piece by piece. A fur coat that could have been real, a black dress, shoes, underwear and a few other bits of clothing. Hornrim checked them all, squeezing them in his hands, taking too long over the underwear, and dumped them in the snow by his feet. Then he took out a large jewellery bag which he placed on the bonnet.

'Open it.' I stayed calm. There was no point in over reacting but I couldn't help feeling that I was close.

Hornrim snapped the catch and opened it. He lowered it towards the light. He stared in there for a while, gave the bag a shake and turned his head this way and that. 'Just a few rings and bracelets,' he said looking up. 'All this for a few rings and bracelets?'

'Take them out,' I told him. 'I want to see everything.'

'Everything?'

'Everything.'

'Okay, here goes.' Hornrim took out each piece of jewellery, one by one and held it up to the light. I knew nothing about stones and gold but l knew that none of them was what I was looking for. I wasn't there to waste my time with keepsakes and bits of jewellery. Every time Hornrim held something up I shook my head and it disappeared into his pocket. When the bag was empty, he turned it upside down to show me and then dropped it in the snow along with the rest of her shit.

'So where the fuck is it?' I said. 'Where's the box?' I sniffed and wiped a hand across my nose. The cold was starting to make it run. My cheeks and the tops of my ears were burning.

'What box?' She was too calm for my liking.

'Don't give me 'what box'. You know damn well what box.'

'I already told you. I don't have it. Not here anyway.'

'I've had enough of this. Maybe I'll just kill you for the fuck of it.' I took a step away from her and pointed the gun at her face. 'How about that, eh? Just to see you bleed.'

'Sean, put the gun away. Magda says she doesn't have the box here; just let it go,' Jack said.

'Oh, it's 'Magda' is it? Getting a bit friendly are we?'

'Oh, for fuck's sake, Sean.'

'I won't let this go, Jack.'

'This isn't the way. She hasn't got it. Anyway, come on it's freezing out here. Look, it's starting to snow again.'

I'd hardly even noticed that the snow was coming down. At first it was just a powder, whipped up by the wind, but soon the flakes were heavy and light at the same time. Our hair turned white and it was probably too cold to be outside, but all I could think of were the seven figures that the box would bring. Fuck Sawn-off, fuck Deeks, fuck the job; the money was in my sights, right on the cross. 'So if she hasn't got it here, then where is it?'

Jack's breath almost glowed in the beam from the headlights. 'It doesn't matter, Sean. It doesn't matter anymore.'

'Of course it fuckin' matters. I'm not giving up without it.'

'No one said anything about giving up. We'll find another way, that's all.'

'What other way? There *is* no other way. *This* is the way it's got to be. You don't know what this is about. You think...?'

I was interrupted by the sound of music. The theme to the Godfather was dampened by the weather, but it was unmistakable.

Jack looked around and so did Hornrim, but I never took my eyes off the woman. I went to her and slipped my hand into the folds of her jacket. It didn't take long to find the mobile phone. God I hate those things. They always ring at the wrong moment - in the cinema during a movie; at the restaurant when you're hungry; when you're about to cap some bitch for being too cool and not telling you what you want to hear.

I pressed the pick up button and heard a voice say, 'Magda, where are you? I'm waiting.'

'Wrong number,' I said and hung up the phone. I switched it off and stuffed it back into the woman's pocket. 'Your friend's waiting for you. So why don't you just give us what we want and then you can go.' I tried to sound calm, but I think she knew what was coming because she took a step away from me and backed into Hornrim who had moved away from the car. His steamy breath snaked from his mouth and licked around the woman's head.

'Hey, maybe it's in her little bag,' he said. It was the first good idea I'd heard all day and I couldn't believe it had been his. He stayed behind her, holding tight around her waist, the fingers sliding up and down, one hand coming round to pull her jacket to one side. His chin was on her shoulder, his face angled in towards her neck.

'Maybe it is,' I said. 'Why don't you show us what you've got in your little bag?'

She shrugged the bag from her shoulder, catching Hornrim's chin at the same time, banging his teeth together and making him take a step away from her. He pulled his hand out from under her jacket as if something in there had just snapped shut on his fingertips. Then she held the bag up in her left hand, looking straight at me like I was something that would slide out of her poodle's arse. I played it cool, though, motioning with the gun, telling her everything she needed to know.

She opened the zip with her right hand.

'Come on, come on. Open the fucking bag.'

Slipped her hand inside.

This was it. It had to be. The moment I'd been waiting for. I was thinking the box must be a lot smaller than I expected, but then the smallest things are the most valuable, that's what they say, and any moment now I was going to be a rich man. Fuck Mandy, and fuck Sawn-off; the box was mine. I'd earned it. It was *mine*. And when I had it in my hands I was going to slot that bitch straight through the eye just for giving me the fucking run around.

It didn't happen like that, though. I'd lost my focus and that's why she surprised me. I never expected her to have a gun of her own. When she pulled her hand out of the bag, she was holding a tiny silver pistol. It glinted in the light of the headlamps and then she kicked it into action.

Two shots.

The first was mine; the second was hers.

Hers missed. Mine didn't.

DEEKS

I wasn't surprised when my phone rang and Sawn-off's number came up on the small screen. Last night, when I told him that his wife had given me the slip, he just waved me away saying that those two idiots would take over. I'd found her, that was all he needed, now it was up to someone else. I tried to tell him that I thought there was more to it, that someone might be helping her out, but it was like he didn't want to know. You've done your bit, here's your money, now fuck off. But I knew that Sledge and Hammer would screw it up. They didn't have the subtlety. They didn't have the flair.

So, I let my phone ring a few times, watching it move about as it vibrated on the table, before I picked it up and heard his voice say 'Deeks?'

'Yeah.'

'Where are you?'

'In the pub.'

'The pub? What the fuck are you doing in the pub? It's the middle of the afternoon.'

'I'm having a drink,' I said. I mean, what the fuck did he *think* I was doing in the pub? 'I don't have anything on this afternoon.'

'Well you do now, so put your drink down. I need you to do something for me.'

I sat back and smiled but tried to sound concerned. 'Oh. Okay. What is it?' I sipped my drink.

'Don't give me that tone, Deeks, just get your fucking skates on. Do this right and there's something in it for you.'

I sat upright again. 'Like what?' The pulling sensation starting in my cheek again.

'Money, Deeks, what d'you think?' The line was quiet for a moment, then he said. 'Something's happened to Sledgehammer. They won't to be able to do that job for me.'

'Something's happened to them?' I pushed my drink away, leaving a trail of beer across the table. 'You mean something permanent?'

'Maybe.'

'So what was it? Was it her?'

'Doesn't matter,' he said. 'You don't need to know.'

'Hey, if you want me to do something here, then I need to know what I'm getting into. I don't want to go down there and...'

'Deeks. Shut up. It wasn't her. It wasn't anything to do with her. Just listen...And don't fuckin' 'hey' me. Who d'you think you're talking to?' I waited while he pulled himself together and said, 'All right, look, I've got someone else to step in for them.'

'You got someone new? You couldn't have given this to me?'

'This isn't the time, Deeks. Anyway, it's hands on stuff, it's not your thing. And they're not exactly willing.'

'Not willing? So what makes you think...'

'Deeks, what the fuck is wrong with you? Keep your mouth shut and listen. It's all under control. You don't even need to think about it. All you need to do is keep an eye on him.'

I stuck my middle finger up at the phone, said, 'Okay, who is it?' and then listened as he gave me a car registration and a name. Jack Presley, he said. Like the King, he said.

I looked up at nothing in particular. '*Jack* Presley? You sure that's *Jack Presley?*'

'Yeah, why?' he said. 'You know him?'

'No. I mean, I don't think so.' I held one hand to the right side of my face, trying to rub the twitch away. '*Jack* Presley, right?'

'Yes.'

'What's he look like?' The rubbing didn't work.

Sawn-off gave me a description, bruises and all, but it didn't sound like the Presley I knew, so I relaxed a little and asked, 'There's just this one guy, right?'

'Don't know. Should be.' It wasn't like him to be unsure.

I shook my head and rolled my eyes. 'Okay, why am I watching him? Is there something I'm looking for?'

Sawn-off told me that this guy Presley was going to go to the Monterez and that he was going to make contact with her. 'He's going to get something from her, and I want you to watch him and keep me up to date. That's all.'

'What's she going to give him?' I asked

He hesitated and said, 'A package.'

'Yeah? What kind of package?'

'A never you fuckin' mind what kind of package.'

I pushed him a little further. 'So how will I know if he's got it?'

'Don't be a smart arse, Deeks, you'll know.' He told me that she might not want to give it up straight away, that he wanted to know if anything happened to her, but I wasn't listening too closely. I wasn't thinking about Sawn-off's wife, I was thinking about that package. I was thinking that I might know which particular package he was talking about. And then I'm wondering what it would be like to have that kind of money. Seven figures. I could have anything I wanted, do anything I wanted. I imagined an island in the sun; I imagined suntan oil and bronzed girls with thongs and bare chests. Then I imagined Sawn-off popping out of a piña colada and cutting my throat, so I tucked the thought away for a while, keep it on the back burner. You never know when an opportunity might arise.

I found the blue Ford in the car park by Lowdean flats and waited for the guy Sawn-off had put me on to. I'd been sitting for a while and was starting to think that maybe he'd given me the wrong details when finally things began to happen. Sawn-off had said that there should only be one guy, but now there were three dark figures coming through the snow and climbing into the car. I was too far away and the light was too poor for me to get a good look at them but it didn't really matter. All I was supposed to do was follow the guy, make sure he did what he'd been told.

They went straight through town without stopping and parked up over the road from the Monterez where I'd found her the day before. It still pissed me off that the bitch had outsmarted me - well, maybe not out*smarted*, but she'd definitely given me the run around - and I couldn't help wondering if she would still be in the hotel. She'd been pretty clued up from what I could tell, and I was sure that somebody had put her on to me otherwise she wouldn't have noticed me. With no one watching the place after Sawn-off pulled me out yesterday, there was no way of knowing that she hadn't run already. It made me glad that all I had to do was watch.

Opposite the hotel, just a few cars back from my quarry, I stayed in the car and slipped down in my seat. It wasn't too long before one of them climbed out of the Ford, and from the description Sawn-off had given me, he was the one I was supposed to keep an eye on. I was relieved to see that he wasn't the Presley I knew. This one was tall too, about six feet, but he wasn't as broad and he had the kind of hair that isn't dark and isn't light - somewhere in between - but I suppose it was light enough to call blonde. He might've had a look of Sean Presley about him, but it was hard to be sure because he had a black eye and a nasty cut across his nose.

Blondie was slow crossing the road, and when he reached the other side he stopped and looked up like he was asking for help, but he mustn't have got any answer because after a couple of seconds he went into the Monterez and the doors slipped shut behind him.

I turned on the radio and adjusted my position so that I could look from the Ford to the hotel without having to move my head. Sawn-off wanted me to keep an eye on him, then that was what I'd do. Just keep an eye on him, make sure he got the box.

When Blondie finally came out of the hotel with the woman, I sat up. I watched them talk for a while under the canopy over the main entrance and then they started to walk. The other two, the ones still in the car, waited and then followed. I did the same. Once the blue Ford was on the road, I moved out into the traffic a few cars behind. It was difficult to move slowly without attracting too much attention but they weren't looking for a tail. They were too busy watching the lovebirds.

About half way down the road, the Ford drove on ahead of the two who were walking, pulled over on the side of the road and parked up with the motor running. I did the same and waited to see what was going to happen. In my rear view mirror, I saw the lights change. Blondie and the woman stopped at the crossing.

I felt calm and the twitch, which had been jumping in my face last night, was nothing more than a slow waltz right now. I hummed along to the Christmas carols that were on the station I was tuned to. I could see snow, decorations and I could hear carols. It was all very Christmassy. Nice.

The lights at the crossing changed and Sawn-off's wife walked over, still talking to Blondie. They passed close by me and I watched the way her arse rolled about in her trousers. It looked damn good, moving this way and that, firm but soft. If I'd opened the window I could have reached out and touched it.

The two of them carried on past the blue Ford and then stopped. The woman put down the suitcase and leaned up against the wall giving me a good view before Blondie moved in the way. They were deep in conversation, everything looked relaxed, and I was just beginning to wonder where all of this was going when Sean Presley stepped out of the car.

I recognised him immediately and my twitch went into overdrive. He looked like he'd been in a fight and his eyes were badly bruised, but I would've known him anywhere. Tall, lean, straight-backed and confident.

Seeing him brought a lot of memories pouring back, and I remembered what I'd told him all that time ago when life seemed to stand still. About Sawn-off, about the box. That was the problem with prison, nothing seemed real, and you got so you'd say things you knew you shouldn't. It was like there was no other world, nothing else mattered. And now it had come back to bite me.

Presley was across the pavement in a flash. He grabbed the woman by the elbow, pushing his right hand into her ribs, and took to her the car. He shoved her in the back seat and started shouting at Blondie who took care of the suitcase. It was a busy part of town and the raised voices attracted some attention, a few people glancing over in their direction, but no one seemed too interested. It was where nice people came to eat and drink, and nice people always look away.

Once they were sorted and finally pulled away, I crunched my own car into gear and followed.

*

It was more difficult once we were away from the traffic but I managed to keep with them all the way to the MacFarlane's turning. Then I hung back and watched them make their way right up to the old warehouse. Their taillights crawled up the hill, chasing the main beams, the brake lights popping on and off, flashing bright red in the night. It looked like the going was icy, so I decided not to follow them all the way up, waiting until they passed over the lip of the hill and disappeared from view. Now all I could see was a faint glow in front of the dark shape of MacFarlane's.

I drove closer to the bottom of the hill and parked away from the main route to the warehouse before taking a couple of things from the aluminium case I kept in the boot. I left the car unlocked and pulled my jacket tight, fastening it up to make sure that no light clothing was visible. I switched off my mobile phone, clipped it back to my belt and then continued on foot, wishing that I was wearing boots instead of shoes. I used any cover I could, keeping behind the rubbish, even though I didn't expect the kidnappers to be watching. They'd taken the woman right there on the street, so they obviously didn't know what they were doing, and that meant it was unlikely that they would be watching their backs.

When I reached the lip of the hill, I crouched behind a stack of wet wooden pallets and tried to ignore the pissy smell that stung my nostrils. The light from the Ford was bright and I had a reasonable view of what was going on, but I wanted to see closer. I reached into my inside pocket and lifted the small scope to my eye. I flicked on the light amplifier with numb fingers and watched what was going on in front of the warehouse. The night vision cast everything in an eerie green-gray, and the headlights pointing away from my position caused a bit of interference, but I could see clearly enough. I increased the magnification and watched as the third guy, the skinny one, rifled through the woman's belongings. I could see that Presley was carrying a gun, nothing too big, probably a nine, but the other two looked clean. I zoomed in on each of their faces, one at a time. Blondie looked green and shiny, and there was a lot of wobble at such a high magnification, so it was difficult to read him but I thought there was a reluctance there. The other guy didn't even seem to know what was going on; he was confused and responded only to Sean Presley who looked like he was enjoying himself, waving the gun around, telling people what to do.

Presley seemed to be getting agitated so I popped the magnification back out again, just in time to see him push the woman into the skinny one's arms. He pointed the gun at her chest and I could hear him shouting something, short commands, the sound of his voice carrying in the quiet. The woman removed the handbag from over her shoulder, put her hand into it, and I wasn't entirely surprised when she pulled the gun out, but Presley was. He froze just long enough to give her time to squeeze off a shot. Her arm jerked, a flash, a small wisp of smoke, then the sound of the crack reached me. Unlucky for her, though, her aim wasn't so good and the bullet cut wide of its mark, giving Presley the wake up call he needed. He fired back.

I felt like I'd swallowed a ton of concrete when Magda's hands went to her stomach. She dropped onto that lovely arse of hers just as the sound of the second gunshot reached me. Sitting there, she looked at Presley with a blank expression on her face, and all I could think was that the box was gone and that Sawn-off was going to fucking kill me. She wavered for a moment, like a drunk trying to keep upright, and then lost her balance as her life drained away. She fell back into the snow and more or less disappeared from view.

The skinny kid who'd been standing behind her was also on his knees in the snow. I could hear him screaming and I guessed that the bullet must have passed straight through her and into him. Looked like I wasn't the only unlucky one tonight. His hands were clasped around his left thigh and he rhythmically bent forward and straightened from the waist like he was trying to pump the pain out of his body.

It was time for me to get ready to leave. If those idiots had any sense, they'd be in their car, putting as much distance between them and MacFarlane's as possible, and I intended to be right behind them. I skidded and fumbled my way back down the hill as quickly as I could, and climbed back into my car to wait for the blue Ford to pass me. I slowed my breathing and tried to straighten out my mind.

Two things, Sawn-off had said, just two things. Make sure Blondie brings back the box, and make sure his wife's okay. He wasn't going to be very happy.

RUBENO 'SAWN-OFF' MONTOYA

The television was on and I was looking at it, but I wasn't watching it. I was lying back on the leather sofa, remote control in one hand, staring blankly at the plasma screen, thinking about Magda and how I was getting too old for this.

My mobile phone lay on the carpet beside the sofa and the condensation marks from my warm fingers were fading from it now, the sound of Deeks's voice still in my head. It couldn't have been much worse. He was still on them, had followed them down from MacFarlane's, so if they'd recovered the box, then at least I'd get that back, but Magda was never going to come back. Not in this lifetime. Not the way Deeks told it. I should never have taken pity on that kid, Jack Presley, should never have given him a chance. I should've used the nails, and found someone else for the job.

Deeks was right when he said this wasn't a simple follow job anymore. It wasn't a straightforward case of leaning on someone, either. Now it was more complicated, and it was time to call in some expensive professional help. It was time for revenge and retribution, hellfire and brimstone. It was time for Carpetto.

I'd used the number a few times before, and it was burned into my memory - in case of emergency, break glass - so I pushed myself up on the sofa and swung my legs around so that I was sitting properly. I couldn't concentrate if I was lying down, and I needed to be sharp when I spoke to Carpetto.

*

After the call, I made a few arrangements and then waited. I moved from the living room, across the open hallway and into the study. In the study I walked once around my desk and then back out into the hallway. Next I went into the games room, clacking the balls around the snooker table and knocking down about an inch of neat vodka, Swedish I think. When I went back into the kitchen for the second time, I took off my shoes because they made too much noise on the gray-green marble flooring which ran through from the hallway. Normally I liked the sound, it made me sound like someone, but it was too loud tonight. Tonight I was listening for the sound of wheels on gravel.

I kept on pacing, the tiles hard and cold on my feet.

I calmed my stomach with another couple inches of vodka, thinking the last time I felt like this was when that deal had gone down with Vaughn a couple of years back. That was the last time I'd used Carpetto.

Vaughn was a small time tobacco smuggler who'd been trying to break into the big time by getting himself connected. I suppose you could say he was looking for a partner in crime but he wasn't in the right league, shooting way over his head. Vaughn liked to dress big and talk big. He surrounded himself with cheap tough guys and even cheaper firepower, trying to make himself look important, but anyone with half a brain could see that he was a small fish.

We did a few deals, nothing major, just a bit of stuff, but before too long Vaughn was telling people that we were like *that*. Brothers. Me and him, him and me, and while that kind of talk might not sound like much, it can put a lot of noses out of joint. Especially when there are other people involved; people who've paid their dues and are longer in the tooth than Danny Vaughn.

So, I had a meet with him - try to sort things out. I had to make him understand that you either work your way up to the top by earning a reputation or you blast your way in, and wipe out your competition. Vaughn didn't have the know-how to do the blasting and he'd have to settle for making a rep for himself so I was going to make him see that.

The meet went as planned and I was impressed at the way he handled the whole thing. He was calm, collected, cool even, and agreed to back off a little. Said he'd lie low, give his respect where respect was due. I even agreed to do a little more business with him when the time was right.

So the deal was done and hands were shaken, all smiles, but two days later my wife disappeared.

For the first time, I'd underestimated one of my business rivals - something I seemed to have done with little Jack Presley. Anyway, after Vaughn took Magda, I called Carpetto straight up. Expensive, but good, Carpetto always got the job done. It was three weeks before I saw my wife again, but Carpetto kept me up to date, and when she came back, Danny Vaughn was out of the picture and Carpetto was handsomely rewarded for a job well done.

They found him all burned up - Vaughn, that is - and I liked that, it had a kind of justice. The tobacco man got smoked.

JACK

I knelt down beside Magda and pulled open her jacket. 'Jesus.' I looked away, caught my breath and then turned back to her. It was everywhere. Her clothes were warm and wet, like she'd been bathed in the stuff. 'Jesus Christ, Sean.' It was all over my fingers, too. I held them up to him. 'What have you done?' I wiped my hands in the snow. 'What the fuck have you done?'

Sean tucked the gun into the back of his waistband and stared at me. 'We'd better go.' He turned away and started for the car.

'Yeah. Yeah, you're right.' I stood up. 'We've got to go. It's finished. We'll go to the police. Tell them what happened. Get it all straightened out. They'll...Jesus Christ Sean, what were you thinking?'

Sean stopped. 'No police, Jack. No way.' He turned to face me. 'No police.' He made a cutting motion with one hand, the heel of his palm coming down hard as he spoke the words. 'What we need to do is get the fuck away from here, right now. As far as we can go. Just fuckin' drive and never look back. You go to the police and we'll go down for*ever*. No way. No police.'

I took a step away from him. 'But she's dead, Sean. You fucking shot her. She's dead,' and pointed at Magdalena, slumped back in the snow, her head twisted sideways on, her legs buckled underneath her. 'And what about him?'

Hornrim was quiet now except for a low, continuous moaning. 'He needs a doctor or...or...I don't know, a fuckin' hospital or something.'

'Yeah, well, I didn't like her much. Him neither. Anyway, you saw what she was going to do.' He shrugged and looked down, before motioning with his head, his voice lower and more sympathetic as he said, 'Come on Jack. Get in the car.'

I didn't know what to say. Standing there in MacFarlane's yard, a place that looked like it was built from junk that had fallen from the sky in a storm, blood on my hands, ringing in my ears, Hornrim's moaning spinning about in my head. I didn't know what to say. Christ, my brother talking like that, I didn't even know what to think.

Sean moved closer, coming into my space. 'We have to go, Jack. We have to go *now*.' Saying it with insistence; urgent but calm like he'd done it a hundred times before and would do it a hundred times again. 'We have to get as far away from here as we can.'

But I knew he was wrong. He was wrong about running. Not because of Hornrim, though. Not because Magda was dead and Hornrim was bleeding, but because of Mandy. I shook my head at my brother, trying to clear away the unwanted images of what could happen. 'We can't run from Montoya,' I said.

Sean's voice hardened, his eyes tightened. 'Of course we can, Jack. We get in the car and we drive. That's all there is to it. We just fucking drive.' And then he's turning back to the car and I can see that the jacket I gave him is hiked up and one corner of leather is tucked into the back of his belt, and the handle of his gun is winking at me.

'He'll come after us,' I said, my eyes on the gun, wanting to look away from the blackness of it. I wondered where it had come from, how long he had owned it, why he was carrying it. What else he might've done with it.

Sean reached behind him to pull the jacket out of his belt. 'He'll never find us, Jack.' The soft leather dropped back down over his waist and the gun was gone.

I shook my head. 'No. I have a girlfriend. He knows her; knows her name, where she lives.'

Still with his back to me, 'Mandy Hepple, right?' Sean stopped and looked down at the snow like he was waiting for me to be surprised that he knew about her. Or maybe he wanted me to say something, anything, but I didn't speak - the only sound came from Hornrim, that terrible moaning - so he sighed hard and said something under his breath; something that sounded like 'Fuck her.'

I straightened myself up. 'What? What did you say?'

He shrugged, turning around but not meeting my eye. 'I said we'll *take* her. She means that much, Jack, we'll take her with us.'

'She'd never go.' I said, and Sean dropped his shoulders like he'd just taken on a load. Like the criminal when Colombo stops at the door, cigar in hand, and says, 'There's just one more thing'.

'Then leave her,' he said, his eye contact direct now. 'We'll have to leave her,' he said it without blinking, giving the words as fact, keeping his lips taught, his mouth thin.

'No.'

'One way or another, we have to get the fuck out of here, Jack. You don't want to run, then maybe you should tell me what you *do* want to do, because...'

'The police,' I told him. 'We go to the police. There's no other way out of this. We go to the police, tell them what happened...'

'I'm not going back inside, Jack.'

'...and they'll protect Mandy. They'll keep her safe.'

He laughed at that - 'You fuckin' think so?' - and my plan started to melt into the snow.

I tried to keep hold of it saying, 'Well, yeah...Why not?' and told him it made sense. Montoya said that the police wanted something on him, that they wanted to put him away, that they'd do almost anything. He even said that one guy in particular was after him. I struggled to remember the name, show Sean that I was right. 'Miller, I think it was, or Hilton maybe.'

Sean shook his head the whole time I was speaking and then stepped towards me and said it wouldn't make any difference. He tapped the side of his head with one finger. 'Think about it, Jack. Fuckin' think about it.' He stopped tapping and started making that right-handed cutting motion again, but this time he slapped it into his left. 'Two guys, two guns, one dead woman, one bloke bleeding to death. At *MacFarlane's*, for fuck's sake.' He held both hands out. 'You think they'll want to do anything other than lock us up so we don't see daylight again?'

'*Us*? I haven't done anything. You fuckin' shot her.'

He raised his eyes and touched his forehead. 'Oh yeah right, Jack, you're home free.' He paused for a beat, like he was pretending to think hard. 'Or how about kidnapping? Theft? Assault? Accessory to murder? You thought about that?' He dropped the act and lowered his voice. 'Don't be so stupid, Jack.'

'Doesn't matter. None of it matters. I don't care. What matters is that they'll go after *him*. Montoya. Mandy'll be safe.'

'No she won't. They might go after him, but what've they got? Nothing. But they'll have *us, Jack. They'll... have ...us*. And I'm telling you, Jack, you don't want to see inside the place I've just been. For me it's bad - but for you?' He shook his head. 'Jesus, Jack, you don't want to end up like one of those guys.'

I wanted to sit down, but there was nowhere to sit other than in the snow. Instead, I rubbed my face with both hands and closed my eyes. There had to be a way around it, I had to make things right, I wasn't going to run and leave Mandy.

Sean gave me a look that told me he thought I'd lost my mind and that he wasn't going to stop until I saw it his way. 'Oh yeah,' he said. 'And you should know that guys like Montoya have people everywhere, even in prison, so don't think we'll be safe there. *Either* of us.'

I sat down.

'Stand up, Jack.'

I felt something hard under me and reached into the snow to pull out Magda's tiny silver gun. The metal was wet and cold against my skin. I turned it and watched the way the headlights from the car played on the engraved surface of the barrel. It fit neatly in the palm of my hand, an accessory for a woman, designed to fit in a handbag. I took the gun by the handle, so small that only three of my fingers actually made contact with the pearled grips.

'Jack, we gotta go. It's the only way.'

I looked across at Hornrim. The shape of one leg was too big, the blood shadowing the snow around it. To one side of him, Magda's suitcase lay open; beyond him, and about him, her clothes and her belongings lay pooled where he had thrown them; here, at my feet, their owner lay dead; and here, in my hands, was her protection.

No, there had to be another way, something that was just out of view. Like when you know a name and it's on the tip of your tongue, begging to be remembered. I tried to see it, make it come, but it wouldn't. All I could see was red on white; all I could feel was the stickiness of my fingers.

My brother grabbed the shoulder material of my jacket and pulled me to my feet. 'Put it down. We have to go. We *have* to run.'

And that's when I saw it. The hotel, the packed suitcase, the gun, the fear, the running. Magda had been running. 'Wait a minute,' I said looking up from the weapon. 'I think there *is* another way.'

'*What*? No. No, Jack.' Sean's fist tightened around my jacket. 'No way.'

'Listen to me.'

'We've wasted enough time, Jack.'

'But maybe Montoya doesn't even have to know.'

'Doesn't have to know?' Sean relaxed his grip on my shoulder and narrowed his eyes. 'How we gonna do that?'

I stared past my brother and nodded to myself. It didn't cover everything, but it might be enough. 'We make it all go away, Sean. It's the only way to be sure.'

*

We hooked our arms underneath Magda's armpits and dragged her over to the car. Her heels left tramlines in the snow and there was a dark stain where she'd been lying. I opened the boot and we hefted her up. Sean took her feet and said, 'So what you gonna tell Sawn-off?' His voice was distorted with the effort of lifting.

I turned away from her face and lifted her head and shoulders so that they were resting on the lip of the boot. Once Sean tucked her feet into the dark space, I gave her a push and let her tumble in like she wasn't a person. Like she was just a bag of body parts.

I took a deep breath. 'I never saw her. I went to the hotel, she didn't turn up.' There wasn't much room in the boot, so we had to shift her around a bit, like a piece of luggage that doesn't quite fit in the space. 'He won't know any different.' Touching her hands and her face was the worst. 'He'll have to believe me.' The exposed skin was still a little warm. 'Fuck you for this Sean. Fuck you.'

Despite the cold, I was sweating by the time Magda was squeezed into the boot. When we were done, I stepped back and tried not to think about the mess on my clothes and my hands and my face and my hair. I picked up the suitcase and threw it in after her, along with the handbag that had been over her shoulder. After that, I got to my knees and felt for stray pieces of jewellery, perfume bottles, anything that might be left. 'This is bad, Sean. This is really fuckin' bad.'

Sean grabbed a handful of her clothes 'Yeah, you already said that.' He stuffed them on top of her. 'It won't work you know. He won't believe you.'

From where I was kneeling, I threw a pair of shoes into the boot saying, 'She already checked out of the hotel. She was running away from him. He'll think she got away.'

'He won't.'

I stood up and closed the boot firmly, shutting Magdalena away forever. 'Have you got a better idea?'

'Yeah, we fuck off. Get away.'

'No.' I turned around and went to Hornrim who was lying on the ground, still clutching his left thigh. 'This way is better.' The material of Hornrim's trouser leg was dark with blood. 'This way it all disappears.'

We yanked him to his feet and took him to the car. I opened the rear door and we pushed him onto the backseat where he lay down on his side and curled into a ball, probably wishing he hadn't come along for the ride. Then I leaned in the front and chucked Magda's gun into the glove compartment.

I held out my hand. 'Yours, too, Sean.'

He reached one hand around behind him and then hesitated, his body tense.

'*Now*, Sean.'

He loosened a little, freed the gun from his belt, and reluctantly slapped the warm metal into my palm. I put it beside Magda's, thinking about what Sean had said yesterday. No gloves in there now, just guns.

The last thing we did was cover the bloodstains on the ground with fresh snow and dump a pile of soggy pallets right on top of it. I reckoned there'd be no reason for anyone to move them – not for a while, anyway - and when they did, the blood would have faded and all traces would be gone.

I cast my eyes across the scene. 'What have we forgotten?' I hoped that the snowfall which was still coming down would be heavy enough to cover the tyre tracks once we'd driven away.

Already getting into the car, Sean raised his voice. 'Nothing. Let's go.'

I looked around one more time before I climbed behind the wheel and shifted the car into reverse. I took it back a few yards so that the lights were shining on the whole area and got out of the car again.

From inside, Sean shouted, 'What you doing?'

I looked around and nodded, 'Yeah. I think that's everything,' climbed back in, reversed a few more yards and did the same thing, ignoring Sean shouting, 'What the fuck are you doing, Jack?'

Under my breath. 'Just to be sure. Can't miss anything.'

I did it three more times before I finally turned the car and drove down the low incline which had led us up to MacFarlane's. At the bottom of the hill my stomach tightened and my throat constricted. I threw open the door and leaned out to vomit, but nothing came up. I dry retched for a while before my body finally began to settle. Feeling more relaxed, I leaned back on the headrest and breathed deeply before pulling the door shut and restarting the stalled engine.

I lit a cigarette to get rid of the taste in my mouth and turned to look at Sean who was staring straight ahead with a calm look on his face.

I shifted the car into gear and drove away.

ized*

RUBENO 'SAWN-OFF' MONTOYA

Feeling a little light headed from the vodka, I finally settled in the living room at the front of the house. It was as good a place as any and there was no point in just pacing. Carpetto was coming, unstoppable now, and it didn't make any difference if I was pacing or sitting or fucking hanging upside down like a bat. As it was, I was lying on the sofa, remote in hand, television on 'mute'. It was some kind of chat show, the low kind, the caption at the bottom of the screen telling me *'I'm a man and my boyfriend doesn't know it'*. Big TV security guys with friendly faces were holding two people apart, a man and a woman I think, but it was hard to be sure. The camera panning across to the audience, standing now and shouting, punching the air with their fists when I heard tyres spraying the gravel outside.

The car was traveling quickly and by the time I reached the window, the noise had stopped and the engine was cut. The heavy curtains were closed against the night, so I pulled them to one side and saw the car door open. Carpetto stepped out into the flurry and came towards the house, head down, shoulders hunched against the weather. The security lights were on and I watched the figure approach, never looking hurried.

When Carpetto reached out and pressed the bell, I was expecting the sound, but the ringing still made me jump. Carpetto *always* made me jump. I pulled my tie straight and slipped my shoes back on, not wanting to meet Carpetto in just my socks - that would have been weak and homely. This was not a social call and it wouldn't have felt right, not wearing any shoes when I invited a killer into my home.

I went to the door, unbolted it and opened it.

Carpetto stepped into the hallway without a word. She walked straight past me and went directly across to my study. I closed the front door and followed her. Our shoes click-clacked, out of beat on the marble, but once we were in the study, the carpet dampened the noise. Her perfume was subtle, feminine, and left a trail for me to chase.

Carpetto removed her beige Macintosh, laid it across the arm of one of the chairs and sat down. She crossed her ankles neatly in front of her, and leaned forward slightly, smoothing the line of her skirt and pulling it over her knees. She shifted, cleared her throat and then clasped her hands lightly on her lap and waited. She looked like a church rep.

I took my seat on the other side of the desk. Behind me the wall was lined, floor to ceiling, with leather-bound books which had never been read. A narrow wedge of brightness crept into the study through the slightly open door but other than that, the only light came from the lamp on my desk – the type with the green shade over the top.

I didn't offer Carpetto a drink. I already knew that she wasn't a drinker.

She held my gaze for just a fraction too long, like she was making a point of it, trying not to look away, and I waited for her to speak, knowing that she normally liked to lead the conversation. But this time she stayed quiet. I did the same, watching her face, thinking how her skin was washed-out. Carpetto always looked like she stayed indoors, like she wasn't used to daylight, but today she seemed strangely pale and drawn. Her dark brown eyes were dull where usually there was a kind of sparkle. Not the kind of sparkle you'd *want* your woman to have in her eyes, mind you. Hers was the kind of sparkle that a kid might have when he's pulling the legs off a fly.

What she was wearing didn't look like cold weather gear for a hardened hit man. Excuse me, hit *woman*. A knee length skirt, black, and a thin red polo-necked sweater. The neckline was furled gently underneath her chin and the deep colour contrasted with her pale skin. Black tights, black heels, strong calves. She was almost human. Her hair was so black it was blue and it fell in curls about her face. It was the only thing about her that looked bright and alive. Her features were hard - not masculine, just hard. Her jaw was clenched, her brow was taught, her neck tense.

'You look good,' I said. 'Different, but good.' I'd never seen her dressed up. She might've been going out, maybe on a date, but I couldn't think what kind of person would want to date someone like Carpetto.

'Come to the point, Mr. Montoya. As you well know, I am not in the business of small talk.' She had no accent; she pronounced her words just right. 'If there is something you wish to discuss with me, then I suggest you speak up and have done with it.' Her tone was business-like, final, no fucking about. 'I have important things to do.'

I don't know who it was that said, 'if you want a job done properly, get a woman to do it', but I reckon they must have known Antonia Carpetto. 'Point taken,' I said leaning forward and resting my elbows on the desk in front of me. 'I have some work for you.'

Her hands stayed in her lap. 'So I understand. You said it had something to do with Magdalena,' she cleared her throat. 'Mrs. Montoya.' Her eyes narrowed, just for a second, flicking away, and then she was looking right at me again. 'Your wife.' She cleared her throat again, it was a habit she'd had since I'd known her, but it seemed worse today. It was a high-pitched, two-tone sound that lasted just a fraction of a second. I used to wonder how she'd ever creep up on anyone in the dark.

I stood up. 'Magda's...' Talking about her was hard, and I knew that Carpetto had a way of seeing right through a person. I turned away and pretended to look up at the shelf of books but my eyes were closed. 'Magda's...'

'What? In trouble? Missing? Dead?' Her voice was hoarse.

'All of those things.'

She paused before she spoke again. 'You've seen this for yourself?'

'No.'

She said okay, took a few seconds and then asked me to tell her everything. Told me that she needed all the details if she was going to do this right for me, so I gave her the edited highlights, starting out by telling her that I kicked Magda out of the house.

She asked 'Why?'

'It's not important.'

'It could be.'

'Okay,' I said. 'I found out she was screwing around.'

'So?'

Now I turned around and gave her a hard look. ' So I didn't like it. She's my fuckin' wife.'

Carpetto didn't flinch, didn't even blink. 'All right, ' she said. 'You know who with?'

I rubbed my forehead. 'No.'

She nodded, took a deep breath and let her head bow for a second before looking up. 'And then what happened?'

I told her that Magda had packed her bags and left the house. I told her how I went to my safe that evening, like I always do. I told her how I felt when I saw that Magda had stolen something from me; something very valuable.

Carpetto looked at me, her face like it was cut from fucking stone, and said '*The* box? The one with the St Francis inside?'

I sat down. 'Jesus, Carpetto. How did you know that?'

'I know everything, Mr. Montoya,' she blinked, closing her eyes for longer than she needed to. 'Everything.'

I thought about asking her if she knew who my wife had been screwing.

'So you arranged for someone to retrieve the box for you,' she said.

'That's right. Sledgehammer. You know them. I gave them instructions to bring the box back. *Nicely*. I didn't want her harmed, but it didn't work out that way.' I glanced at the clock on my desk, the green digits telling me that it was nearly an hour since Deeks had called. 'Look, do we have time for this? Surely you...'

'Your bouncers got heavy with her?' She was sitting up straighter now; every part of her on full alert. Christ, she thought I was sending her out after my own people.

I held up a hand. 'No, something happened to them. There was trouble at the club. One dead.'

She looked surprised. She obviously didn't know *that*.

'Some kid,' I said, shaking my head. 'At least that's the way it looked, but when I worked him over, things looked different.'

'In what way?'

'I think he was covering for someone. A friend maybe.'

'Did you kill him?'

'No, I gave him a second chance. I made a mistake.'

'That's not like you,' she said, but I let it pass. She was getting into her flow and I wanted her out of my house as soon as possible. 'So you made a deal with him?' She asked.

I nodded. 'Kind of. I thought he could get the box back for me. I wanted someone who could get close enough to Magda to tell her that I didn't want to hurt her, that I just wanted the box to come back. I told him I'd kill him and everyone he knows if he fucked up. He has a girlfriend, it was easy enough to find her.'

'And you trusted him?'

I sat forward and said, 'What do you think?' but she just stared at me so I relaxed and went on. 'No. No, of course I didn't trust him, but he was perfect for the job.' Like I had to explain myself to this woman. 'Magda wouldn't know him, he was soft, he was scared. He was honest, you know, like a regular person. He'd treat her right and he wouldn't harm her, didn't have it in him.' I sighed. 'At least, that's the way it looked.'

'How many are there?' she asked.

'Three. Deeks said he's never seen them before.'

'Just three in total.' Pause. Her eyes rolled up and to the right. I don't know, maybe she was working out how many bullets she was going to need. How much money she'd get per shot. 'Okay, then what happened?'

'From what Deeks said, they took her up to Macfarlane's on...'

'I know where it is.'

I forgot – she knows *every*thing. 'Right,' I said. 'So they roughed her up, guns came out and...'

'And Deeks stood and watched.' She interrupted me again.

'Looks that way.'

Her expression tightened. 'I will want to speak with him,' she said. 'What else did he see?'

The whole conversation was just like that, backwards and forwards like a fucking ping-pong game. The words just came at me one after another, bang, bang, bang. And all the time she sat stone still, never once moving. Like a cat watching its prey. Cold and mean.

When she had it all she nodded and took a deep breath. 'There's a chance she may still be alive,' she said, the pitch of her voice a little higher, and for the first time since sitting down, she moved. She pushed up her sleeve and looked at her watch.

'I don't think so.' I stood up and went into the shadow, pacing the darkness at the far end of the room. 'He saw her shot. Saw her go down.'

She didn't turn to watch me, she kept on looking straight ahead. 'If he didn't feel her pulse or look into her eyes, then he can't be sure.' Talking a little faster now, some of that composure starting to melt. 'She might still be alive.' She might've been trying to make me feel better, but she'd never struck me as the caring type.

I shook my head. 'I don't think...'

'It's possible,' she said. 'People don't just fall over and die when you shoot them. Trust me, I know.'

She was forgetting I'd done a few myself, but I nodded 'Yeah,' even though I didn't think there was much chance of finding Magda alive.

I came back from the shadow and sat down behind the desk as Carpetto was saying, 'I need to get to her as quickly as possible.' Hurrying now, her voice almost a whisper. 'Let's not waste any more time,' she stood up. 'Deeks is still on them? He knows where they are?'

'He was when I last spoke to him.'

'How long ago was that?'

'An hour, maybe more.'

'Right,' she said, 'I'll need Deeks's number and a second mobile. Yours will do.' She pursed her lips. 'And this Jack Presley and his friends? What about them?'

'Do what you do best.' I lifted the two briefcases that were on the floor by my feet. I put them on the desktop. I had plenty of cash in the safe and it had only taken a few seconds to fill the briefcases after I'd called her. I opened one and turned it around so that she could see the money inside.

Carpetto looked at it with a cool expression. Nodded once. She didn't need to count it. She knew it would be right. Each briefcase would contain a hundred and fifty grand - not a penny more, not a penny less. That's the way we did it.

I closed the briefcase and pushed it across the desk to her. 'There will be others, too.'

She nodded, and that was that. Carpetto was unleashed.

CARPETTO

Ignoring the bitter weather, I folded my Macintosh and placed it on the back seat of my BMW. I opened a black, military style kit bag and removed from it a long dark overcoat, a pair of trousers, a pair of boots and a small, flat carry case. I closed it back up, placed the two briefcases of cash in the passenger footwell and, without turning to look at Montoya's house, I climbed into the car and immediately removed my shoes and skirt. There was plenty of space for me to pull on the trousers and lace up the boots. Once dressed, I threw my skirt and heels onto the backseat and started the engine.

As I waited for the windscreen to de-mist, I put the flat canvas carry case on my knee and unzipped it. I took out the Hardballer, its custom made dry suppressor, and a magazine. They were ice cold. I tested the action on the slide, checked the clip and then palmed it in and racked it. I placed a spare magazine in the pocket of my trousers, attached the suppressor, engaged the slide lock and stowed the gun in the door compartment beside me.

I was annoyed to see that my hands were shaking.

I closed my eyes and breathed deeply ten times, counting the exhalations. I did the same thing again, this time counting the inhalations, then I opened my eyes and held out my hands. I spread my fingers, clenched them and then held them relaxed. Now they were steady.

JACK

After we left MacFarlane's, Sean didn't move, didn't make a sound. He just stared straight ahead, and everything was quiet. Hornrim occasionally moaned, but other than that he was as silent as Sean was. I wondered if maybe he was bleeding to death, dying in the back of my car while I drove away from the nearest hospital, his smell lifting from the back seat like a mixture of changing rooms and butcher's shops. I thought about how I'd feel if Hornrim died, playing it out in my head, seeing him stone cold, eyes dry, and thinking I already had one body to deal with, so maybe another one wouldn't make too much difference.

I drove us away from town and hit the motorway. What I really wanted to do was get to Mandy, make sure she was safe. I wanted to take her as far away from Montoya as possible, go to her right there and then, no messing about, and whisk her away. But I knew I couldn't. It wouldn't look good if I turned up as I was. Me and Sean splashed in someone else's blood, Hornrim bleeding to death and a corpse in the boot. No, that wouldn't be any good at all. Besides, Mandy should be okay for a while. By my reckoning, Montoya might be getting a little agitated by now, wondering where his box was, but he'd wait. He should stay off at least until the morning; that was when I was supposed to show up.

And before I could see Montoya, I needed to lose the car and the body. I needed to clean us all up and deal with Hornrim. Leave no traces. No comebacks. And I'd already decided what to do. It always looked easy in the films. The gangsters would have a scrap yard lined up so that some big bloke with hairy arms and coveralls, who understood the situation could crush the car. They'd have one of those machines that would turn it into nothing more than a box of steel with a body all squashed up inside it. No clues, no comebacks, just what I needed. But I didn't know any scrap dealers - didn't even know any scrap yards - so I was going to do the other thing. I was going to ditch it. The quarry wasn't far out of town, only a couple of miles from Mandy's, and no one ever went down there except tear-away kids who were looking to drink cheap cider, and dump stolen cars. And this wasn't the weather for either of those things.

'You going to tell me your plan then?' Sean's voice made me jump, coming out of the quiet like that.

'Shit, you gave me a shock.'

'Yeah? Good.' He lit a cigarette and exhaled hard. 'So you going to tell me your plan, then? You going to tell me how this is going to work or you going to leave me to fuckin' guess?'

I told him what we were going to do, what had come to me when I was sitting on my arse over at MacFarlane's. I told him we'd drive down into the quarry, get out of the car and push it into the lake. I told him that as soon as we got back to the flat I'd report the car stolen. I'd meet Montoya first thing and tell him that his wife never showed.

'And Hornrim?' he asked.

'What d'you mean?'

'I mean what do we do with him?' Sean turned and looked into the stinking darkness in the back seat. 'It looks like he's still alive. *You* want to do him or you want me to?'

My stomach tightened. '*Do* him?'

'Yeah, what else?' Still looking at his quiet friend. 'Maybe you should give it a go. Or maybe you reckon we should just send him down with the car as he is?'

'What? No...'

Turning around now. 'What then? How do we deal with it? What's your plan? Fuckin' hell, Jack, you got to think about this.'

'I have. I thought...'

'We going to pull him out? Drag him all the way back to town, is that it? What we do with him *then*?' Sean settled back into his seat. 'You thought this through, Jack? You sure you know what you're doing?' He folded his arms.

I sat up a little and looked at Hornrim in the rear-view mirror, seeing the car filling up with water. Seeing him coughing and panicking, his face turning red and then blue.

I shook my head and looked back at the road. 'Yes.'

'Yes? Yes what?'

'Yes we pull him out. Yes we drag him all the way back to town. We're going to dump him at the General.' It would be tough, it would take a while, but the two of us could do it. 'You got a problem with that?'

'Well, it's a fuckin' long way to drag the guy if he's dying and bleeding all over the shop and can't even keep his fuckin' eyes open, isn't it? Could take hours.'

'It won't take that long.' I mumbled it.

My brother shrugged. 'Be easier if he just died.'

'Fuck, Sean. He's supposed to be your friend.' I said the words, but part of me was thinking that no one liked him much, no one would miss him. It would be like drowning a Christmas puppy. From what I could tell he was unconscious, had lost a lot of blood all over the back seat of my car. Slide him into the cold water, he probably wouldn't even know it had happened.

Sean watched me from the corner of his eyes. 'And what if he can't keep his mouth shut, Jack?' He lowered his voice like he was letting me in on something special. 'You want to make *all* of this go away, right?'

'Yeah.'

'*All* of it?' 'The only way to be sure', you said.' Like he was testing me.

I took my eyes off the road and looked at my brother. 'Right,' I said. 'All of it. The only way to be sure.'

The flakes came down and curved towards me, hitting the screen and piling up until the wipers took them away to the corners. The glass was smeared and it was difficult to see the road.

I pressed the washer but it just whined.

The wipers kept on chugging.

We sat in silence for a while, and I thought about what we'd said. I listened to the engine, to the road, to the sound of my brother smoking and grinding his teeth, and I thought about what we had or hadn't just agreed. I thought about what I might have missed. I thought about Sean. And I thought about loose ends.

Then Sean was talking again, saying, 'What if it's frozen, Jack? You thought about that?' his voice demanding, accusing, sounding like it was never going to stop. 'The lake, I mean. What if it's frozen, Jack?'

He was right. There wouldn't be much point in rolling the car out across the lake if it was solid. There was a chance it might crack and go under, but then again, it might not. It wasn't worth taking the risk. 'Okay,' I said. 'We'll burn it. We'll take it down to the quarry and burn it. It'll be just one more burnt out wreck in a dumping ground full of them.' There was plenty of other rubbish there, it might be years before someone opened the boot and found what was left of the bodies. *Body*. Maybe never.

'We'll stop at the petrol station,' I said. 'Buy a couple of those cans.' It would be easy enough to douse the car and torch it, and in my mind I saw myself down by the lake, watching the orange glow cast by the flames. The heat would be intense. The car would sear and pop. I wondered if the smell would be like it is when you catch the tip of your finger with a match. Like pork scratchings.

'Good plan, Jack. I like it. Burn up the car. Burn the evidence, get the fuck out of Dodge. I like it.'

'Except we won't be going anywhere, Sean. I have to get cleaned up, face Montoya, remember. Go to him empty-handed and tell him that I didn't see his wife. We're not there yet, there's still a long way to go.'

'Yeah, course.' Sean reached over and switched the CD Player on. 'How long 'til we get to the petrol station?' 'The Clash' came between us. Loud.

'Five minutes; maybe ten,' I said, switching it onto the radio and turning it down.

'Time for a joke then.'

'No, Sean, no jokes.'

'Go on, Jack, just one.' He drummed his fingers on the dashboard. 'Just one,' he said again. 'It'll pass the time.'

I wasn't in the mood for jokes but I didn't want Sean any more agitated than he already was. I was going to need him calm. 'All right,' I said holding up a finger. '*One*.'

'Excellent,' he said. 'Make it a good one.'

The air in the car was thick with the stink of smoke and sweat and blood and fear.

I thought for a while and said 'Okay. So, this guy walks into a bar, right...'

CARPETTO

As I drove, I placed my mobile phone in the hands-free cradle and twisted it towards me so that I could see the dial clearly. It beeped and lit up for a few seconds before the screen and keypad went dull. I wanted to keep that phone available and unused, just in case Magdalena called. It was a long shot but I had to keep all of my options open.

Once I'd seen to my own phone, I took Sawn-off's from the dashboard and scrolled through the menu looking for Deeks's number. I put in the earpiece, dropped the phone on the seat next to me and pressed 'ok'.

Deeks answered almost immediately. 'Yeah?'

'Deeks?'

'Who wants to know?' he asked.

'Don't pretend not to recognise my voice you greasy little toad. Where are you? Are you still following them?'

'Oh, it's you.'

'Tell me where you are,' I said. '*Exactly*.' He told me and I tapped it into the GPS. 'And they're all still in the car?' I said.

'Unless one of them vaporised.'

'Don't waste my time. Are they all still in the car? Yes or no will do.'

'Yes,' he said.

'Good. Keep on them. I'm not too far away; I'll be there as soon as I can. If anything changes, I want you to call me on Mr Montoya's number; I have his phone.'

'Y...'

'Keep *yours* switched on,' I said.

'Okay.'

'If you lose them, I'll kill you.'

'Oh, for f...'

'Do you understand everything I've said?'

He paused.

'Do you understand?' I asked again.

'Yes.'

'Repeat it back.'

He sighed. 'You'll be here soon. Keep my mobile switched on. You're on Sawn-off's number if I need to call.'

'What else?' I said.

'Don't lose them.'

'Or else...?'

'Yeah, yeah, or else you'll kill me.'

'Good.' I hung up. I pressed my foot harder on the accelerator and the car responded immediately.

JACK

Sean stopped nodding to the beat from the radio and a smile cracked his sunken features. Chirpy music continued to waft into the car and surround us. 'It'll look good won't it?' he said.

'What will?'

'When it all goes up. The fire, I mean. When we burn her up. Course, when they find her, it'll be your car she's in.' He's staring at me now. '*Yours.*'

I was still for a moment, feeling his eyes on me. 'Doesn't matter,' I said. 'They'll have it down as stolen. Probably never find it, anyway.'

'But if they do, they'll tell him. You hadn't thought of that, had you? They'll tell Montoya.'

I searched my brothers eyes, my mind starting to work hard again, and said, 'Yeah, but no one'll know it's my car,' I was thinking of all the things that might lead to me. 'Everything'll burn up – the plates, the chassis number, everything. There'll be no way of knowing. No prints, no fibres, no nothing. It'll just be another burnt out Ford, that's all.' I wondered if there were other ways of identifying a car.

His voice rose, like he was asking a question. 'Just another burnt out Ford that you've reported stolen. It wouldn't take them long to put the two things together.'

'Okay, so I won't report it.'

'And if they don't tell him, he'll find out another way,' he crossed his arms and tilted his head. 'He's like that, this guy Montoya; he finds stuff out.'

'I said I won't report it.'

'We should steal another one,' he smiled. 'Burn that out. Use yours to get home.'

I turned to my brother and let my hands drop lower on the wheel. 'That what this is about? You can't be arsed to walk home? You'd rather drive back in a car that's full of blood and fibres and fuck knows what? And this is from the guy who wanted to run.' I glanced at the road and then back at Sean. 'No. This car is evidence. It's what says we've done what we've done. It's got to go.'

Sean shrugged. 'Then we burn yours too. That way, when they find it, it'll be clean. No bones in the back. Two cars, eh? It'll be some bonfire.'

I shook my head and held up a hand. 'We're not making this any worse. No more cars.' I felt the tyres lose their grip on the road, so I grabbed the wheel to steady us and said, 'We make this one clean, Sean. We clean it, we burn it, we walk away.' My fingers tightening, feeling like they were going to become part of the steering wheel. 'I don't want to talk about it anymore.'

Sean shrugged again and watched me for a while. Then he leaned back and slid down in the seat. After a few minutes, he closed his eyes and then I was on my own. I watched the road and thought about burning cars.

Five, maybe ten minutes later, I saw it. The green sign over the forecourt was like a beacon. Underneath, four pumps stood idle. Two rows of two. Some kind of wagon was pulling away from the exit, the sound of its engine like a thunderstorm rumbling far away, but other than that the petrol station was quiet.

I stopped beside the row of pumps that was furthest away from the entrance and turned off the engine. After the darkness of the road and the effect of the snow on the windscreen, the lights under the garage canopy were crisp and intense. I squinted and waited for my eyes to become accustomed to it.

Sean just kept his closed.

'Don't pretend to be asleep,' I said.

'Not pretending. I *am* asleep.'

I took off my jacket and the sweater I was wearing underneath. I'd be cold in just a shirt but it wouldn't do for someone to see the bloodstains. I checked myself in the mirror to make sure I looked okay. 'Just get out and fill up,' I said. 'I'll go in and pay.'

'It's too cold out there,' he said, eyes still closed. 'Anyway, I'm asleep.'

I didn't want to get into it right here, so I climbed out and slammed the door. I took the nozzle from the pump, yanking it hard when it didn't come out immediately, and stuck it in the tank. I had to pull the trigger a few times before the assistant inside pressed whatever it is they have to press to make it all work. She was putting stock on one of the shelves and I watched her come running over looking harassed, like she was having a bad night or something. She had no idea.

I stood at the back of the car, filling the tank and trying to ignore the chill from the metal pump handle. I turned away from the camera which was mounted at the back of the forecourt and kept my head down as much as I could. I didn't want to give anybody a reason to check the tapes.

I tried not to look at the boot either, I didn't want to think about what was in there, so I peered down into the back seat instead. The window was dirty and it was dark inside but I could see Hornrim, lying on his side with his legs tucked right up, like a child sleeping safely in the back of his parent's car. He didn't look too bad, not in this light anyway, but I knew that there was nothing peaceful about what I was seeing. Just a nobody bleeding to death in the back of a used car. He was still breathing, his body rising and falling, but it was slow and shallow like an old dog that's on his last legs.

I sighed and glanced over at the main building, where the shop was and the lady had come running. The window was rimmed with multicoloured lights and there was a two-foot glowing Santa standing in one corner. Snowflakes and snowmen had been sprayed onto the glass with fake snow. I looked past and through them to check out the rows of brightly coloured wrappers on the shelves. I spotted a microwave beside the drinks cooler and suddenly felt hungry. Maybe I'd get us all something to eat, God knows we needed it.

I waited until the pump clicked off, telling me the tank was full - it would be more expensive but the car would burn better that way - then I went to the display at the far end of the forecourt. Cans of anti-freeze and screen wash were stacked alongside motor oil and small blue bottles of some kind of gas, butane maybe. Beside those, red and green plastic petrol canisters were piled four or five high and three deep. I took a couple of green ones from the top and went back to the pump. I filled them to the brim and placed them in the foot-space behind the driver's seat. Something to get us started.

As I walked to the shop, I opened my wallet and checked my money. Not too bad. I had more than enough to pay for the petrol and buy something to eat, so before going to the counter, I took a boxed cheeseburger from the rack and put it in the microwave. I blasted it for a few seconds while I grabbed packets of stuff from the line of shelves. When it pinged, I took out the steaming package with the picture of a burger on it and opened it. It wasn't quite the same on the inside as it said it was on the outside but, then, nothing ever is. I nuked two more.

At the counter I asked for cigarettes and handed my money over to the assistant who was wearing a red hat with white fur trim and a white bobble on the end. She was plump and old, with purple veined cheeks and a double chin. She smiled a big smile full of Christmas cheer. 'Merry Christmas,' she said as I left. 'And have a safe journey.'

I went back to the car and opened the door. The first part of the plan was done and it was no more challenging than buying petrol

'Did you get cigarettes?' was the first thing Sean said.

'Yeah. Thanks for your help, by the way.'

He opened his eyes and turned his head. 'And food?'

I leaned in towards him. 'Yeah, and food. Here,' I said dumping an armful of stuff on my brother's lap. Cheeseburgers, crisps, chocolate.

'Don't know if I can eat all that, Jack,' Sean held out his arms.

'You don't have to, it's not all for you.' I climbed in and pulled my jacket on. The car smelled a little fresher now, the air and the petrol chasing out the sweat and the stale cigarettes.

'Well who, then?' he said, but I didn't bother to reply.

'Enough food here to feed a fuckin' army,' Sean was rummaging through it now. 'Mind you, it's gonna be a long walk home. We'll probably need it.'

I opened one of the burger boxes and held it by Hornrim's face. I wondered if maybe the smell of the food would bring him round long enough to eat something. He looked crap. White as a sheet. There was a smear of dried blood across his forehead and his clothes looked damp from all the bleeding.

'Don't get too excited,' I said. 'It's just junk.' Hornrim opened his eyes, just a flash of the whites, and then they were closed again, so I pushed the burger closer to his mouth. 'You want this? You want a bite?'

Hornrim nodded his head, almost impossible to see it, then he opened his mouth a little. I held the burger and let him take a bite. He chewed for a moment and then opened his eyes again. 'Don't burn me, Jack.' Just a whisper as he struggled to push himself up into a sitting position and tried to grab my hand. 'Don't let him burn me.' His movements were slow and heavy.

I dropped the burger beside him and pulled away, making him fall back onto his side. 'We need to go.' I started the car and took us back out onto the road.

After a couple of minutes, I shifted in my seat so that I could see Hornrim in the rear view mirror. He was lying down again, burger in hand. 'Check he's all right,' I said to Sean.

Sean took the last bite of his own burger, crushed the box and dropped it on the floor by his feet. 'You fucking check him.'

'Sean.'

'What?' He looked at me.

'I'm driving. Anyway, you're supposed to be his friend.'

'Yeah?'

'Yeah, so check him.'

Sean glanced over his shoulder and said, 'He's fine. He'll be fine. Don't worry about him.'

'Check him properly.'

'Hey, what makes you such a fucking saint all of a sudden? Since when did you care about Hornrim?'

'Since he was about to die in the back of my car,' I said. 'Just check him will you.'

Sean rolled his eyes at me, then turned around. Hornrim was lying in his curled up position again. Sean grabbed his shoulder and shook it but Hornrim didn't respond, so Sean took the burger from his hand and settled back into his seat. I could see that Hornrim had taken a few bites.

'Mustn't want it,' Sean took out the pickle and dropped it on the floor. 'Looks like he's asleep.'

'Asleep or dead?' I asked.

Sean bit into the burger, spilling ketchup on his chin, and spoke round the cooked meat. 'What the fuck do I care?'

JACK

I drove a few more miles, don't know how many, before I took the slip road and left the last of the overhead lights behind us. The road narrowed and the night closed in, and then there was just the lane and the darkness. Real country darkness.

There was no traffic, just the occasional light in the distance behind me, winking in the mirror, and on either side, tall hedges bundled past as if they'd go on forever. Trees crept towards us and then whipped away, nothing more than shapes beyond the reach of the headlights. The car jumped and rattled in potholes, the snow fell. Sean smoked and drummed his fingers on the dash. I strained my eyes. Hornrim was quiet.

The air coming in from outside, creeping through the vents, smelled like shit and puke and rotten cheese all mixed up together. I heard Sean take a deep breath, sucking the stink right down and saying, 'Fuckin' banjo country, this.'

'Uh-huh.' I was leaning forward now, closer to the windscreen.

'Marry their cousins and stuff,' he said.

'Uh-huh.' Everything was black and white out there, snow coming at me, my whole head was aching.

He looked at me. 'We eat that you know.'

I wasn't watching him, but I could feel his eyes on me. 'Eat what?'

'That stuff that smells like shit,' he said. 'It's on our food. They put it on the fields.'

'Do they?' I said, easing off the gas. 'I thought they gave it to animals. You know, to eat when the grass is gone.'

He straightened his whole body. 'To *eat*? You mean they put it in their mouths and chew it up?'

'Yeah, I think so.' I was squeezing the steering wheel now, trying to keep the car straight.

'They *chew it up*? Smelling like that? No fuckin' way.'

The car dropped into a pothole and we both lifted a couple of inches from our seats. 'Well, maybe not, then,' I said.

'How d'you know that anyway?'

'Dunno. Just do. One of those things, I suppose.' I was watching for the sign now, leaning even closer to the windscreen, knowing it would be hard to spot.

'One of those things? Since when were you a fuckin' bumpkin?'

'I'm not,' I said.

I could hear the grin in his voice when he changed his tone and said, 'I am. Well, I *could* be. You know me, I love the country.' Then he imitated a redneck accent, 'Can I shoot him now, Pa?'

I tried not to smile. It wasn't a time for laughing.

'C'mon Cletus,' he said and started to twang 'Dueling Banjos' while pretending to play one, high up on his chest. Eventually, not getting the response he wanted, he sank down into his seat and went back to his drumming, nodding his head and lighting another cigarette. I slowed the car right down and kept my eyes peeled. The turning wouldn't be too far away, but it was cut into the hedge somewhere on the right so it might be hard to spot. I squinted against the black and white.

'It's around here somewhere,' Sean said, his fingers coming to rest on the dashboard. 'Just a bit further.'

My stomach was beginning to turn. Round and round like a tumble dryer.

'It's close,' he said. 'It's gotta be.'

I nodded slowly. I was going to have to read the situation carefully when we got there. I needed to play it cool, couldn't let Sean get too worked up. The way he was now, he was liable to flip out and do anything.

'There it is!' he said. 'Stop. Look. It's right there.' He leaned across me and pointed. 'There.'

Ahead and to the right, I could just about see the old sign which said 'Site Entrance', but only when the headlights were right on it. Another couple of summers and it would disappear into the hedge altogether. I slammed the brakes on hard, forgetting about the snow under the tyres, and the car skidded forwards for a second before the back end stepped out and overtook us. I did what I could, but once you're going, you're going, so we rode it out, and when we came to a stand still, the blue Ford was directly in line with the path to the quarry.

'Nice one, Cletus,' said Sean. 'Just like the old General Lee.'

My knuckles were white around the steering wheel but I looked at him and grinned. 'Cheers, Enus. Enus the...'

'Yeah, yeah,' he said. 'Enus the penis, I know.'

'Suits you.'

'Yeah, yeah.'

'So, you gonna open the gate then, Enus?'

I was surprised that I didn't need to ask him twice. Maybe he was starting to chill out a bit. He climbed out of the car and went to the gate which barred the track leading down to the quarry. He brushed off the thick snow and unwound the chain which was supposed to secure the entrance. He fought with the rusted catch and pushed the gate inwards to leave a wide arc in the snow. Sean didn't bother waiting to close it, he just climbed back into the car and slammed the door. Once he was in, I crawled along the track, down towards the quarry.

Hadlebridge quarry was a dump, just like Macfarlane's was. You can trust the Presley boys to take you to all the nice places. I'd been down there a few times as a kid, but it wasn't really my thing. Sean, on the other hand, had been a regular Hadlebridge partygoer. It was a good place for him to lead people astray. Steal a car, do a few donuts, then down to the quarry for a bit of drinking, smoking and inhaling whatever they'd managed to nick.

A bit of sunshine and some care and attention would've probably turned Hadlebridge into a nice place to visit, but instead it had been left and forgotten. The track from the road came down between piles of rocks and dirt, ending up in a flat area of mud which acted as a kind of dirty beach for the water which lapped at it. The far side lifted away like a cliff, up to where the land had been cut away when it was a quarry. There were still trees up there and I remembered that in daylight you could see where the roots grew out of the soil and around the rocks on the face of the cliff. They just stood there and swayed, curling their toes, hanging on to the brink.

The mud beach looked a lot better under the snow but it was still littered with burned cars, ice glittering on the brown and silver husks when our headlights swept over them. I didn't want ours to stand out, so I stopped between two of the wrecks and switched off the engine.

Sean looked at me and smiled. 'Right,' he said opening the door and jumping out. 'Let's get to it. Where's the juice?'

'Don't get carried away, Sean. Just wait a minute.' We weren't Cletus and Enus anymore. We were Jack and Sean now. Or maybe Jack and Enus.

'Where d'you put it?' he said. 'The juice. Where d'you put it?'

'Maybe you should just stay there,' I said climbing out. 'I'll get the petrol. You just stay over there...' I pointed to a pile of rubble a few yards away, '... and don't smoke.'

'Why can't I do it?'

'Because it's better if I do it,' I could see him over the top of the car, and I watched his face screw up as he thought about that.

'You don't trust me, do you?' he said.

I opened the rear door and reached in to take out a petrol can. 'Well, you've messed everything else up so far.'

Sean shrugged and put his hands in his pockets. 'Okay. I'll stand over here, then, shall I?'

'Good idea.'

'Just let me get some cigarettes first,' he said. 'These are finished.' He held the packet upside down for me to see.

'All right, just don't smoke anywhere near *me*. Or this car.' I patted the roof.

'Yeah, yeah, chill out, Jack.'

My plan was to open the boot, cover Magda over in petrol, and then douse the plates and the chassis number on the instrument panel, but standing at the open door, looking in at Hornrim lying there, I thought I'd better check him first. If he was alive I'd drag him out, we'd take him to the General and dump him, just like I told Sean. If he was dead, I'd burn him with the car.

I put the petrol can down and climbed further onto the back seat, lowering my ear to his chest and listening. His breathing was shallow, he was definitely still alive, so I grabbed his shoulders and tried to pull him out but he wouldn't budge. I moved to a better position and tried again, but still no luck. A dead weight like that - like Magda had been - Hornrim was too heavy for me. 'Hey!' I shouted. 'Why don't you give me a hand here?'

I heard Sean say, 'Fuck him. Leave him where he is.'

'Sean. Get round here and help me.' I tried to work my hands under Hornrim's arms. 'We're not going to burn him alive.' The edge of the doorframe was cutting into my knees.

'Why not? He's probably gonna die anyway.'

'Sean, we can't just...' I stopped when I heard the sound of liquid hitting the roof. I pulled back out and looked around, catching the smell straight away.

Sean was on the other side of the car, holding the green can in one hand. Petrol was splashed across the roof. It was running down the windscreen and across the bonnet. Now he was pouring it across the dash and onto the front seat.

'For fuck's sake Sean, what're you doing?'

'What does it look like, Jack, I'm juicing the car up.'

'Not yet. Jesus!'

He pulled his hand back and stood there, the black nozzle on the can staring up into the sky. 'What? What's the matter?'

I gritted my teeth and held my hands out towards him. 'We've got stuff to do first.' Trying to keep my voice calm, like I was standing in front of a rabid dog saying, 'down boy.'

'What do you mean 'stuff'? What kind of stuff?'

I started to move slowly round the car, keeping my hands out in front of me, palms facing my brother. 'We need to get Hornrim out.'

'Oh, fuck Hornrim. Are we gonna torch this car or not?'

'Yes, but...'

'Then let's do it.' He started splashing petrol again, throwing it right over the car towards me now.

'Stop it Sean!' I ran round to him and tried to pull the container out of his hand but he pushed me away and I fell into the snow for the second time that night. 'Fuck.' I quickly regained my bearings and put my hands down, ready to push up. 'Sean, you ...' I saw something from the corner of my eye. The car's petrol flap was hanging open and there was a cloth stuffed into the tank.

I stood up. 'What is *wrong* with you? What are you doing?'

Sean threw the last of the petrol over the boot. 'What's wrong with *me*?' He tapped his chest with the can, the nozzle rubbing up under his chin. 'What's wrong with *you*, Jack?' Now the nozzle was pointed at me, Sean's arm outstretched. 'Can't you see I'm clearing up, Jack? Just like you wanted. I'm clearing it all up for you.'

'Well don't,' I snatched the can from his hand and threw it away from the car. 'I don't want you to do anything except stand over there.' I could smell petrol on us both. 'Just stand over there and do nothing.' I put my hand on his chest and pushed him away from me. 'Go on. Go.'

Sean glared at me and threw his fists down. He walked backwards a couple of steps like he was undecided, then he stopped, closed his eyes tight and turned around. He walked away, out towards the water, out of earshot, and then stopped, lacing his fingers behind his neck and looking down at his feet.

I wanted to follow him; to walk right up to him and bat him round the head with the can that was just a couple of feet away. I wanted to be like him, just for a short moment of release, but that's when I heard the banging.

It took me by surprise, just starting up like that. Bang. Bang. Bang. Slow and muffled at first but getting louder and quicker. And underneath the banging I could hear a voice. I looked round behind me, where the sound was coming from. The boot. Magda. Jesus Christ, Magda was alive. She was alive and we were going to burn her to death.

I glanced over at Sean, but he was still just standing there, looking down at the ground, so I kept one eye on him while I went round and felt for the button under the rim of the boot. My fingers were cold and they fumbled on the icy metal but I found the catch with my thumb. I popped it open and lifted it, obscuring Sean from my line of sight.

Magda stopped moving as soon as she saw me, her eyes wide and beautiful looking up at me, terrified. I froze, she froze, and for a moment we just stared. And then she spoke. 'Help me.'

I reached in to pull her out. 'I'm so sorry.' My throat was narrow, my back tingled, and my skin tightened around my skull. I felt like I'd been cured of a terminal disease. Magdalena Montoya was not dead. We hadn't killed her, and everything was going to be all right.

Using me for support, she moved herself into a sitting position. 'Thank you.' Her face was streaked with blood and her mascara was everywhere. Her hair was knotted, and she was shaking, unstable, her fingers tight around my hand. 'Thank you.' Her clothes were covered in a crust of dried blood. 'Thank you.' Like I was some kind of hero for saving her.

She began to cry, so we stayed like that for a while, holding onto each other, her in the boot, me out, until the crying passed and we heard Sean's voice.

'This looks nice,' he said.

DEEKS

He looked like he was drunk. He was all over the place, walking back up the quarry path like that. Swaying from side to side. Stupid sod probably had half his brains blown out when the car went up – that's assuming he had any brains in there to start with.

I'd followed them from MacFarlane's, stayed out of sight when they stopped off to fill up, and then trailed them all the way down to Hadlebridge quarry. It was pretty obvious what they were planning to do, so once we were there, I pulled off the road and stayed put. I had a clear view all the way down to where they were, amongst the other wrecks. They wouldn't have had a clue that I was watching them, but they put on a good show. I particularly liked the explosion; the way the car lit up for a few seconds when the petrol first caught and then the grand finale when the tank went up. It was like watching it in wide screen and Dolby sound surround, and I'd swear I could feel the heat from where I was. Other than the thing with Montoya's wife and Carpetto, it's probably one of the best things I've seen for a while. It wasn't exactly as I'd hoped - nor as *they* had expected, I reckon - but I was happy enough with the outcome, and I learned a few things that might be worth something.

There was nothing more than barbecued spare ribs down there now, at least from the smell that was coming up to where I was sitting, and I could still hear the hiss and spit of the fire. There was an orange dome of light over the centre of the quarry, and the shadows played off the other wrecks onto the face of the cliff. It was quite a torching that the Presleys had pulled off, and if it was intended to remove all the evidence, then it was probably more than enough to do the job.

And now here he was, tottering up towards me, looking like he'd drunk about ten pints of vodka, and my only dilemma was whether or not to kill him. I'd seen him pick up Carpetto's cannon but it would be easy enough to deal with that, given the state he was in. He looked like he could hardly stand up. I could do him from here, dump his body in the wreckage of the car and he'd be gone forever, but then I didn't know what that bitch Magda had told him. I'd seen her talking to him, and she might have given him something. It didn't look like the box, but it could've been something that would lead him to it.

Instead, I checked my weapon and made my way down towards the quarry on foot. Once I was on the path, though, my position was lower than it had been in the car and I couldn't make out anything past the point where the track curved around a large pile of rocks and headed further down into the pit. That meant Presley was out of sight now and I wouldn't be able to see him until he rounded the corner. On the other hand, it could work in my favour. If I decided to take him alive, then all I had to do was wait for him to pass and stick the gun in his ribs. He'd tell me what I wanted to know.

I walked as quickly as I could without slipping, reached the bend and ducked down behind the convenient pile of mud and stones. I was a little out of breath so I calmed it down. I didn't want him to hear me.

He took a long time.

I expected him to appear after just a few seconds, a minute tops, but he didn't come, so I thought about going to look. Maybe he'd taken a fall, turned up his toes and was lying flat on his back, breathing his last. Or maybe not. Maybe he wasn't as out of it as I thought.

I waited a while longer, checking the luminous dial on my watch and following the hand through five slow minutes before my legs started to ache. There still wasn't any sign of Presley approaching so I risked standing up. I stretched, counted off a couple more minutes, and then started back onto the road when I heard what sounded like a car door slamming. My breathing stopped. It couldn't be. The car was trashed, I saw it go up.

An engine started.

Damn.

Headlights appeared around the corner.

I ducked back off the road, tucked myself behind the snowy mound of debris and watched Carpetto's BMW come sailing past, the tyres skidding and sliding all over the shop.

Shit, damn, bollocks. Carpetto must've left her keys in the car, and now Presley was on the move again. On the move and heading straight for wherever it was the box was hidden. I didn't want to lose him. I was too close now.

JACK

Sean looked from me to Magda and then back again. 'This is nice,' he said.

I didn't look at him, couldn't take my eyes off Magda. 'Sean, give me a hand. Help me get her out.' I was supporting most of her weight, she was weak and having trouble making her legs work. 'Everything's going to be okay.'

'How d'you reckon on that?' Sean didn't make a move. Stayed right where he was, letting me struggle with Magda.

'What?' I took one of her legs and lifted it over.

'I mean why should I help her? How d'you reckon everything's going to be okay?'

I pulled her other leg over so that she was sitting on the rim of the boot, her weight still resting on me. I pushed against her, propping her up, and looked at him. 'What you talking about, Sean? She's alive.' I could feel my brow squeezed tight, not understanding how he couldn't see it as clearly as I could. 'We'll get the box and everything'll be okay.' She was completely out now, standing between us. 'Montoya will leave us alone now. Mandy will be safe.'

Sean lowered his voice, like Magda wasn't there, like he thought maybe she wouldn't hear if he didn't look at her. 'Sure we'll get the box, but I tried to kill her, Jack, don't you remember?' Speaking through his teeth. 'I thought I *had* killed her.'

'Well you didn't, Sean. Look at her. She's alive.'

Sean's eyes shifting off to one side, staring at nothing in particular, then he's looking back at me, head on one side. 'She'll tell him.'

I felt Magda go stiff, her grip tightening around my arms, her finger nails digging through my jacket. 'I won't tell anyone. I'll give you the box.' She was shaking her head from side to side, her body trembling. 'I'll give you anything.' Staring at me, only me. 'Please.'

I held her and told her not to worry. I told her she was going to be okay. I told her I wouldn't let anything happen to her. 'Sean, get Hornrim out of the car. It's time to go.' We'd have to walk, the car was covered in petrol.

Sean didn't move. His tone changed, lost all expression 'I want to know where that box is first.' His eyes right on hers now, like I wasn't there anymore.

'Sean. We're gonna go home and sort this out.' I wrapped Magda's left arm around my shoulder and started to move. 'We need to get away from here.'

Sean stayed still. 'First the box.' His words were flat, no emotion there at all.

'C'mon Sean. Get Hornrim.' My own voice feeling weak.

Sean raised his hand, pointing his gun at Magdalena's head, and he stepped forward so that the end of the barrel was no more than six inches from her face. 'I want that box...' he said stretching his arm out, pointing the gun right between her eyes.

'For god's sake, Sean, put it away.' I wished I hadn't put it in the glove box. I should've kept it on me. 'She already said she's going to give it to us.'

'...*then* we torch the car, Jack, *then* we go home. You and me, just the two of us. It all goes away. Like you wanted it, Jack, remember?' His look was drilling through her, as if he wasn't even seeing the person in front of him.

I kept Magda steady and reached out with my free arm, lifting my hand towards my brother. I wanted to touch him, make him see that it was okay.

'Yeah but it's all changed now, Sean. We can sort it out. Everybody gets what they want. Mandy's going to be all right.'

He twitched away from me. 'Fuck her, Jack; all I want now is that...'

I heard a noise I didn't recognise - one that sounded as if it should've been louder - and Sean's head snapped away from me like he'd been punched hard in the face. His back arched and the rest of his body went with it. I flinched away from him, losing my grip on Magda, and closing my eyes against whatever it was that touched my face. It might've been his finger tips brushing my cheek as he went back and down, or it might've been something else. Magda fell against the car and slid into a sitting position. Sean folded up and dropped flat on his arse, his legs twisting underneath him. His gun went up in the air and clattered against the wreck behind him.

I went to my knees beside my brother, seeing a dark, wet patch where his nose and mouth should have been. I touched my hand to his shoulder and shook him gently.

Footsteps somewhere behind me. A slide, a ping and a click of metal. A voice I didn't know. A woman's voice right beside me saying, 'He's dead,' but sounding like it was a lifetime away.

Then I was turning my head and looking up, everything out of focus except for the dark hole in the end of a shining barrel. The woman who held it was in shadow, blurred, but I didn't try to look at her. Instead, I closed my eyes and waited, wondering if I'd feel it go in.

DEEKS

As soon as Carpetto's car was past, I ran back to my own. I started the engine and followed Presley, but not too close - just like before. The boss would want to know what had happened and if I played it just so, gave him the right story, it might work in my favour. If that bitch had given Presley something, then I wanted him to have a clean run all the way to the box. I didn't want anyone near him but me. I'd have to persuade Sawn-off to go in another direction altogether.

Once we were back out on the country road, I calmed myself down and tried to ignore the drag down the side of my face. I let my cheek dance as much as it wanted to and grabbed my phone. I dialed Sawn-off at home.

'What's going on?' he said. 'Why haven't I heard anything?' He was talking faster than usual. He'd lost control of the situation and it was pissing him off. I wondered if it was worth telling him about Carpetto and his wife, it might push him that little bit further, but then it's always good to keep something back.

Instead, I told him, 'Carpetto's dead.'

'What?' I could picture his face, everything slipping through his fingers.

'Yeah, I know,' I said. 'Hard to believe, isn't it? She managed to do two of them. Sneaked up on them and they never saw her coming. It's good to see her in action. Pop, pop, real Carpetto class...'

'Get on with it, Deeks.'

'She got distracted, though. Your wife she...well, she wasn't dead.' I'd let him think she was alive. Just for a moment. Wind him up and let him go in the opposite direction.

'And now?' he said.

'Well, they had her in the boot, see. I dunno, maybe they thought she was a gonner at MacFarlane's, I know I did, but then she started yelling and banging, just as Carpetto came down.' I was making it up on the fly. Lift his spirits and then dash them on the rocks.

He started to reply but the car slipped, skewing to one side and I had to grab the wheel with both hands, taking the phone away from my ear. When I was under control again, I went back to it, hearing him mouthing off, saying something about, '...listening to me Deeks?'

'Yeah, just lost you for a second there. What d'you say?'

'I said 'Is my wife still alive'?'

I tried to remember what I'd told him. Oh yeah. 'Well, Carpetto got distracted by all the noise, boss. She looked away for a second, I mean just a *second*, and that Jack Presley guy jumped her. He got the better of her and popped her a couple of good ones. He was like a fucking maniac, boss.'

'The kid shot her?' said Sawn-off. 'You sure? Shot Carpetto?'

'Chest and face.' I lied. ' She went straight down. All messed up, she was.'

'But my wife is alive? You stepped in, right? What about my wife?'

'No time, boss, I was too far away, and Presley just went mad, emptying the gun into the boot, blasting away like Bonnie and fucking Clyde and...'

'He didn't open it?'

'The boot? No, he put a rag in the petrol tank and turned it into a giant Molotov. Gave it a light, and it went up like a bomb. No one could've lived through that, boss.'

Sawn-off didn't say anything for a while. I could hear him breathing hard on the other end. He'd be walking around in that big stuffy, pompous office of his, wondering what to say next. Probably sucking on one of those cigars, waiting until he could speak without sounding like he cared. Me, I just kept my eyes on those two red lights shining up ahead. The ones that were leading me to seven figures.

'You sure about all this?' he said. 'How come you're okay?'

I was ready for that. I knew he'd ask. 'It was bad down there, what with all the shooting and the explosions and ... and then Mrs. Montoya, and by the time I got there ...' I was laying it on thick now. '...I tried to stop him, boss, I really tried to stop him but he had the gun and...and he got away.'

'And the box?' he said.

'I think he had it with him. He took something from your wife, forced it from...'

'Where?'

'From her hands...'

'I mean where did he go, pencil dick?'

I was thinking *I'm looking at his taillights right now you stupid northern monkey*, but said 'I don't know, boss. He took Carpetto's car.'

'Well go and fucking find him, then. Go to his place, anywhere he might be. Find him.'

'Anything you say.'

'Good. I know where *I'm* going,' he said and the phone went dead.

I knew too. He'd go after Presley's bit of gash, ready to dish out some punishment. I'd told him all about her. Mandy, she was called. Mandy, Mandy, Mandy. Sawn-off would go after her while Presley went running after the box. And I'd be right there behind him. I'd wait for my moment, slot him, take the box and...well, and Sawn-off would never see me again. Job done.

MANDY

I hadn't heard from Jack all night. I had work tomorrow and I needed to sleep but he usually rang before I went to bed. I called him at the flat but there was no answer. He hadn't even switched his machine on.

When we first started seeing each other, I tried to persuade him to buy a mobile, but he told me he couldn't afford one. I offered to get one for him, as a birthday present not as a freebie, but he told me he didn't want one. He didn't like the idea of always being at the other end of a phone, he said. I told him he could turn it off if he didn't want to be contacted, but he said he might as well not have one if it wasn't switched on.

I opened a book and tried to think about something else, my eyes flicking up every now and then to look at the clock on the mantelpiece, but it seemed to be stuck on half eleven. I kept having to re-read sections to get a proper grip of it , and ended up just fanning through the pages. It wasn't like Jack not to call. It wasn't like him at all.

I waited half an hour and tried ringing his flat again but there was still no answer. I poured a large glass of cold Chardonnay, taking one of the two wine glasses which I kept in the cupboard over the fridge, and at the same time I was thinking about Sean. I couldn't *help* thinking about him. I knew he'd be bad news for Jack, just like he'd been bad news for me all those years ago, but

I told myself that Jack was a grown man and that he could look after himself. He was fine; everything was fine.

I called the flat again but there was still no answer so I had another glass and sat down in the kitchen. The wall clock said twelve thirty-six, or maybe it was thirty-seven, so I went through to the living room and checked the one in there. It said the same thing. I picked up my book, put it down, and switched on the television. There was nothing on, so I switched it off again, staring at the blank screen and sipping my drink.

Eventually I fell asleep on the sofa with my book in one hand and a glass of wine in the other. I've no idea how long I slept - it was a while before I had the chance to look at the clock again - but I was awoken by the sound of the doorbell. I jumped up, splashing wine onto the carpet and the sofa. Jack.

I went to the door, slid the chain on and opened it to look. I didn't recognise the man but he was very well dressed. 'Hello Mandy,' he said. His face was turned down towards the doorstep, but his eyes looked up and straight at me. He smiled, showing me his teeth. 'I'm a friend of Jack's.' Then he kicked out so hard that the chain snapped off and the edge of the door smashed into my shoulder. He stepped into the house and pushed the door shut with one foot. He stood over me and looked down while he took off his coat.

'Oh fuck,' he said. 'Are you in some deep shit, or what?'

JACK

Magda tried to shout but her voice was weak and it came out as just a whisper. 'No more,' she said.

I waited and listened, seeing nothing but the colours behind my eyelids. I heard soft footsteps; the sound of cloth on cloth; skin on skin; quiet comforting; concerned whispering; the words 'how did you find me?' spoken through tears.

When I opened my eyes again, the gun was gone.

I didn't realise I'd been holding my breath, but it rushed out of me, used and hot, and I gulped to swallow more in. I turned around to look at Magda. She was half standing, half-leaning against the back of the car, just as she had been when I helped her out. But this time it was the woman who was holding her, not me. The woman who had her back to me and was whispering to Magda. One hand was touching Magda's face, stroking her hair; the other was out to one side, holding the gun away from them. She spoke quietly, moving down, taking Magda's jacket aside, lifting her shirt.

'Don't worry,' I heard her say. 'It's just a scrape.' Her voice was soft. She touched the wound, feeling where the blood had stiffened. 'You're lucky he was no marksman.' She was gentle, she cared, and yet her eyes were everywhere, seeing everything. 'You're in shock,' she said, but all the time she was being so attentive to Magda, her head was scanning left and right, watching the area around the car, constantly keeping me in the tail of her vision.

When she was content that Magda was okay, she stood up, kissed her forehead and then turned to me. Her face changed in an instant. The reassuring smile dropped away and everything went from sunshine to thunder. Three steps, four at most, and she was over me again, the barrel of her gun pressed hard into the place where my jaw meets my ear, the metal still warm from the shot that killed my brother. I moved to get away from it but she kept the pressure on like she was going to push that big gun right through my neck.

'Give me one good reason not to do this,' she used the same words Montoya had used two lifetimes ago. She sounded calm, like she was threatening to wash the dishes, but I wasn't really sure who she was talking to. Me or Magda. Maybe even herself. 'One good reason,' she said again.

I looked down at Sean. He didn't look like my brother anymore. His eyes were rolled high. No nose to speak of. The tail of his jacket was twisted and pulled up, his legs contorted beneath him. He was still wearing my shoes.

Now I wanted to see her. Magda's angel, the woman who was going to kill me. But the gun pressed harder still, turning my head away, and a sticky hand grasped the back of my neck. 'Don't look at me.'

'Please,' I said, closing my eyes so that I didn't have to see Sean, and although I knew that my life was about to wink out, all I could think about was Mandy. I thought about how she'd feel. 'Please,' I said. 'Please.'

From my left, 'Don't kill him.' It was Magda's voice.

'I've already been paid,' said the woman. The muzzle pressed harder. 'It's done.'

'Not him. It was the other one who...'

'He was going to burn you.' Harder still.

'He was trying to help me. He's...' Magda's voice was weak and sounded quieter each time she spoke. I hoped that she'd stay awake long enough to save my life.

'He was trying to help you?' The woman.

'I'd be dead if he hadn't.' Magda.

'You sure?' The tightness of the gun loosened.

'Please, Tony, leave him,' Magda said. 'No more shooting.' But when she used the name, the pressure increased again.

'Don't,' said Magda. 'You've already killed his friend, isn't that enough?'

'My *brother*,' I whispered.

Magda and Tony were silent. All I could hear was the water in the quarry lapping at the rocks.

The pressure loosened, hesitated, and then barrel of the gun eased away from my head and Tony stepped back. I waited for the shot, my brother's dry blood tight around my eyes when I squeezed them shut.

'All right, get up,' said Tony. 'But don't look at me.' The calmness in her voice never changed.

I did as I was told, keeping my back to Tony and Magda.

'Walk away from the car. Out towards the water. Lace your hands behind your head and don't turn around. Don't move too quickly. Don't look at me. Don't speak. Don't do *any*thing that will make me want to shoot you.'

I walked until the toes of my boots were touching the water. I looked out onto the lake and breathed deeply. The snow had stopped and the night was quiet. There was a wind skimming the top of the lake. I watched the ripples and thought about Mandy. If I was going to die, I wanted her in my head when it happened.

Movement behind me. Whispering, as if Tony and Magda were arguing in hushed voices and then footsteps, coming closer. I braced myself.

'I've been thinking,' Magda spoke to the back of my head. 'About what you said before.'

I continued to stare across the water. Wind and ripples on the lake.

'About it being the real thing?' She made it sound like a question. 'You and Mandy,' she said, remembering her name. 'It *is* Mandy isn't it?'

I didn't answer.

'If you hadn't tried to stop him - your brother I mean - then he would've killed me, wouldn't he? Just now. By the car. He would have killed me and I wouldn't be here for Tony.'

Above me, on the other side of the water, the trees shuffled like a thousand pieces of tissue paper.

'So maybe that means I owe you,' she said.

I took a deep breath and closed my eyes.

'I have something you need.' She mumbled the words, her mouth working hard to make them come out. 'I can help you. I can help Mandy.' She moved alongside me and I turned to face her. She looked rough; not the same woman I'd seen back at the Monterez. She was pale now, her make-up streaked. 'Here,' she said. 'This will help.'

She reached out and took my hand in one of hers, and with the other, she pressed something into it. The object was warm, as if it had been kept close to her, hidden. 'It's a key,' she said holding my look. 'For a safety box at the hotel. Room two-eleven. You'll find what you want in there.' She closed my fingers around the key. 'And this is someone who can help you.' She let go of my hand and took a card from her pocket, holding it out for me. 'A policeman. A policeman who's looking for the box.' Magda gazed out across the lake. 'He asked me to help him find it, but I was greedy. I wanted it for myself.' She shivered. 'Or maybe I wanted to punish Rubeno, but the truth is, I never would've been able to sell it. No one could.'

I took the card without reading it, and slipped it into my jacket along with the key.

'Funny thing is, your brother thought it was the box. Some valuable little box that would fit in my bag, but it's not small. And it's what's inside that matters.'

I didn't say anything, didn't ask.

'It's a painting,' she said. 'All folded up and faded. They say it's worth tens of millions, but it's not worth anything like that because you could never sell it. It would stand out too much; be noticed. No, it's worth *favours*. You pass it on to the next guy and he does a big favour for you, then he passes it on to someone else and it goes round and round like that. It was stolen from some place in Sicily back in the sixties and it's been jumping from one connection to the next since then. Mafia connections mostly, that's why it means so much to my husband. It's about the history, you see, not the money.' Magda put one hand inside her jacket and pulled out her mobile phone. 'Maybe it's time to cut the connection. If this policeman were to find that box, it would make him very happy. He would help you.' She switched the phone on and handed it to me. 'Especially if he found my husband in the same place.'

I let her put the phone in my hand.

'Give him a call,' she said wrapping her arms around herself and hunching her shoulders. 'Do the right thing,' and she walked away without another word.

I turned to watch her, the way she stooped her body to one side now, and as she reached the blue Ford, Tony took her into her arms and the two women stood for a moment, holding each other. They looked like the real thing. When they broke their embrace, Tony supported Magda with one hand and they turned towards the path. Everyone was going home.

Except for Sean.

I looked over at my brother's body and noticed a shadow through the rear window of my car. I'd forgotten about Hornrim. I could see that he was sitting up and I wondered how long he'd been like that, how much he'd seen or heard. Not that it really mattered anymore, not now, not after I made the call; not after I did what I should've done already. Hornrim's silhouette was turning and leaning as if he was searching for something, and then he was still, like he'd found whatever it was. A blurry hand rose towards a blurry mouth. I tried to think what he would've been looking for, he wouldn't have seen me put the gun in the glove compartment, so it wouldn't be that. Could be he wanted something to eat. Maybe a drink or a cigarette. A *cigarette*.

When I shouted, Tony turned towards me, swinging her right hand up in an arc. She was still holding the big steel gun. Magdalena looked over at me with an expression of surprise, then Hornrim snicked Sean's Zippo and they were all gone. Just like that. The car sucked away the air in the quarry, swallowing it up, heating it to melting point and then belching it back out at us. Tony and Magda were whipped away like dust in a storm and their bodies disappeared in an orange eruption of fire. I was engulfed in a searing cloud of burning air and thrown out into the icy water.

I remember lying on my back thinking that it wasn't very deep, and how it was a good thing I'd decided not to push the car out into it. After that it was dark for a while.

When I finally dragged myself from the water, my hair was singed, my face felt raw and my left ear was bleeding. For the rest of my life, I'd be stone deaf in that ear, but I guess I was lucky. Luckier than the other three, anyway.

I didn't bother with Hornrim - there probably wasn't that much to bother with - so I went straight over to Magda and Tony. The way they were lying was unnatural, all twisted and broken like that. The flames which curled around the car, crackling and hissing, were vomiting black smoke into the night, casting moving shadows across the bodies, but I could still see that most of their clothes were gone. What was left was smouldering, its edges glowing.

Carpetto's gun lay a few feet away from them so I picked it up and stumbled away. I don't know why I took it, I suppose I just thought I might need it. Even if I didn't know how to use it.

Dazed, deafened and shell-shocked, I blundered along the path, away from the lake; away from the quarry; away from the stink of death and burning. I had a key; I had a card; I had a gun. And I didn't know what I was going to do with any of them.

MONDAY 20TH DECEMBER
A.M. EARLY

BURN OUT

JACK

Tony's car was crouching just off the path, the door open, the keys hanging in the ignition like she was expecting a quick getaway. She obviously hadn't reckoned on Hornrim. As soon as I started the engine, the CD player came on, nice and gentle, Celine Dion singing over the buzz in my ear, sounding like nothing had happened. I recognised the song straight away – The Power of Love – and found myself hoping that it was the whole album in there. It made me think about Mandy, and how she played it for me when we first started going out, sitting in the dark, drinking wine. I told her I didn't want to hear it, it wasn't my thing, but she played it anyway and we sat there and listened while we got to know each other. It was the first CD she bought me, her sounding like a kid telling me I should put it on if I needed something to remind me of her, but we hardly played it at all anymore. Didn't need to.

Now I turned it up loud, taking the road as fast as I dared. On the seat beside me, Tony's gun was bouncing around on the soft leather, me having no idea if it was loaded or not - not even knowing how to check. My face was hot and raw from the fire and my ear was dead. My hair was burned and the car was full of its stink, all mixed up with leather and pine air freshener.

I wasn't sure how Tony fitted into the whole thing – whether she'd come after Magda on her own or whether someone had sent her. I remembered she said, 'I've already been paid', or something like that, so maybe Montoya sent her after us, I don't know. I thought about it for a while, wondering how the hell she'd found us out there at Hadlebridge, and then I gave up. There were too many questions and it didn't really matter anyway. What mattered was that Montoya was expecting to see me in a few hours, bringing him his property and telling him that his wife was okay. There was no way I could give him everything he wanted, though, so I had to make sure that Mandy was safe before I went after the box. He knew about her, probably knew where she lived, so I wanted to get her out of the house before he found out what had happened. She had to be priority number one.

Celine was looking back through the years, getting into 'Only One Road' when I came towards the village and slowed the car right down to avoid the camera. They'd put it there last year to stop the boy racers testing out their two litre engines on the long straight road. First time I came down there, Mandy sitting beside me, she said that the Roman's had built it straight like that to stop the locals from ambushing them. All the locals do now, she said, is race their cars up and down it.

I turned down Mandy's street and stopped right across the entrance to her garage, hitting the brakes so hard that I lurched forward and the belt snapped me back, cutting tight across my chest. I hardly noticed, though, loosening it off, grabbing Tony's gun and jumping out, not thinking how Mandy might react seeing me like that.

I reached the front door at a sprint and held one hand out to stop myself from bumping into it. I banged with my fist until I heard the catch loosen, then took a step back as it opened. I saw Mandy's face, smelled her smell, and thanked God she was safe, but I was too excited to see what her eyes were telling me.

I stepped into the hallway and wrapped my arms around her, the gun heavy in my hand. She reached out and pushed the door closed behind me. 'Oh Jack,' she whispered.

And then there he was, the man who'd wanted to put a nail through my knee. He was stepping out of Mandy's living room saying, 'Hello fuck-face. Remember me?'

DEEKS

I pulled up a few yards behind Presley and watched him jump from the car and dash over to the house. He banged on the door until it opened, and then he was gone.

Of course, I knew where we were going. I realised that the moment he hit the old road, but I can't say I wasn't disappointed. I thought the kid might've had more fire in him than that. If it was me, I would've gone straight for the box - he and Magda must've talked about *some*thing down there by the lake before the barbecue started up, so he must've known what it was worth - but now we were here, all of us together. Sawn-off, Presley and me. One two three. All in the same place, all wanting the same thing.

I could see Sawn-off's car parked with all the others a bit further up. That meant he was in the house with the girl and Presley, and the way he'd sounded on the phone, it wouldn't take him long to kill them both. That was the only thing I was sure of right now – well, that and the fact that the box had drifted well out of my reach.

I wondered if I should go now, while the going was good. Sawn-off was probably thinking I could've stopped his wife from being hurt, so he might want to see me in a closed coffin along with the rest of them. And once the kid was gone, there was no telling where the box might be, which meant there probably wasn't much point in hanging around. I could head south for a while, look for some work down there. It wouldn't take me long to re-hook the kind of connections I needed. There'd be other employers, other boxes, other retirement funds. So, thinking that running was the best option, I reached down to change gear and that's when seven figures popped into my head.

Seven figures.

Shit, that's a lot of money, and you never know what's going to happen. Maybe the kid might give it all up to Sawn-off; try to save his life by telling him where the box is. It could be worth me sticking around, after all. The opportunity might present itself again, set me up for life. If I could ease my way around Sawn-off, tell him what he wanted to hear, then I'd be able to stick with him, keep the box in my sights and wait for my chance. I reckon I could do that. Worth a try.

I tucked my hands into my pockets and slipped down in my seat, letting the engine tick over, the fans blowing hot air onto my face. There was nothing for me to do now but sit and wait.

BURN OUT

RUBENO 'SAWN-OFF' MONTOYA

When I came out of the living room, the kid looked like he was going to prolapse. Poor little fuck probably couldn't believe how bad his luck was. He'd come all this way, waded through all that shit, jumped through all those hoops, and this was how it was going to end. Shot to death in his girlfriend's house, poor bastard.

He looked worse now than he did when I'd finished with him yesterday. His hair was singed and he smelled like roast pork. His face was bright red, like someone had held him over a steaming kettle and I almost felt sorry for him, holding onto his girlfriend like that. I was still going to kill him, though, so I raised my gun and pointed it straight at him. He looked over his girlfriend's shoulder and pushed her away. Not hard but gentle. He was moving her out of my way, not his, as if it would've made any difference. I mean, just one barrel from my sawn-off would've taken both of them along with most of the plasterwork. She stepped back and pressed herself against the wall, frightened even though I hadn't touched her yet, but probably knowing what was coming her way. Roughing up young talent isn't really my thing, but she was going to have to go, right before I saw to him.

I thought I'd keep it light to start off, though. Light but with an edge, so the kid would know I meant business. He'd killed my wife, I was going to kill him, but I'd let him wait a while, let him sweat. I wanted him to see it coming like a bad storm. Like on one of those cheap satellite home video shows when you're watching a tornado spinning closer and closer towards a building, and there's nothing anyone can do other than wait for it to finish its business and move on. I wanted the kid to have that prolapse and I wanted to be there when it happened. 'Jack Presley,' I said. 'I think you'd better hand that over to me.'

He held it out, arm stretched.

'You sure that's your real name?' I said taking the weapon. 'I never met anyone called Presley before. I once heard of a bloke from over the water but I never met him. I suppose there was that guy from the Troggs, too, but you wouldn't remember him. Before your time.'

Presley just stared, his hand dropping back down to his side.

'And you didn't change it yourself?'

He shook his head, not more than a few millimetres each way, his eyes staying dead centre, his chest up and down like he'd run all the way here.

'Your folks fuckin' comedians or something?'

He still didn't answer.

'Or maybe they're just hot for The King?'

'I don't know,' he said, sounding like his voice didn't want to come out.

'You don't know? What d'you mean you don't know? You don't know your own folks?'

'They died.'

'Runs in the family.' I looked at my weapon and smiled, thinking it was pretty fast wit under the circumstances. Not razor sharp, but then nobody'd had much sleep here and none of us were thinking happy thoughts.

I laid my shotgun down on the stairs and inspected the piece he'd given me. It was a professional tool, not some cheap homemade zip gun. 'Carpetto's Hardballer,' I said. 'Custom job.' It was all steel with blacked out grips and its name etched down the side. The can on the end was about a mile long. 'Sounds mean that, doesn't it?' I said turning it over in my hands. '*Hardballer*. Like it would turn your fuckin' knees to pulp.' I waved the gun towards his knees and he winced like I'd stuck a hot pin in his eye. I suppose he didn't like me talking about his knees. I let it linger there for a second, then pointed it straight at the door and squeezed the trigger. I wanted to remind the kid what it could do, how quiet it would be. It kicked, popped, and smoke guffed into the air carrying the tight smell of cordite. The sound of the bullet ripping through the door was louder than any noise the gun made. 'Not bad,' I said nodding at him. 'Not much louder than a morning fart. I like that. I could shoot you as many times as I fuckin' want and no one would ever know. Until they find you all bled out with a lot of new holes, that is.'

While he thought about that, I went over to his girlfriend, Mandy, and pressed the barrel of the forty-five against her lips. Her eyes closed tight and she tried to disappear into the cracks in the wall but she didn't make a sound. She was tougher than she looked.

'Leave her alone,' he took a step towards me but I cut him off, telling him to stay right where he was. The girl and I had already had words; we came to an agreement while we were waiting for him to show up. Her only job was to keep her mouth shut. The minute she started freaking out, going all girly on me, I'd put a bullet through her boyfriend's head. Mind you, she'd probably worked out I was going to do that anyway. The only thing she was buying him now was time.

'So, you got a favourite?' I looked at Jack.

'What?'

'I said have - you - got - a - favourite?'

His eyebrows twitched and came together like he didn't understand so I said, '*Elvis Presley song*. Have you got a favourite Elvis Presley song?'

He shook his head.

'My wife did. You remember *her*, don't you? We talked about her when we last met. When you were on the chair, remember?'

His eyes were wide and bloodshot, like his mind was going to overload any minute.

'I was going to shoot you in the face but decided to give you a way out. I said I was getting too old for this shit and you promised to do something for me. You do remember that don't you?'

Presley nodded.

'What's the matter? Cat got your tongue?'

'No.'

'Then fuckin' answer the question pencil-dick. Do you remember our meeting or don't you?'

'Yes, I do.' He shifted his eyes and looked at his girl.

I pressed the gun harder against her mouth, feeling her soft lips moving over hard teeth. 'Just you concentrate on me,' I said to him. 'Look at me, and only at me, but keep her pretty little face in your mind, 'cause it won't stay that way for long.' He looked back at me and when I was sure I had his attention, I continued. 'You promised me two things,' I said. 'Do you remember that?'

'Yes.'

'What were they? Maybe I made a mistake. Maybe I need you to remind me.'

'I promised to bring the box for you...'

'And what else?'

'And not to hurt your wife,' he said.

'That's what I thought. That's exactly it. And not to hurt my wife.' I looked away, pursed my lips and breathed deeply. Magdalena was gone. She had her faults, god knows, but she was my wife for fuck's sake. Affair or not. When I turned back to Jack, setting my face like concrete, I said, 'Guitar Man.'

'What?' His eyebrows came together again, giving me the look that said 'what the fuck are you talking about?'

'Guitar Man,' I said watching him start to shake his head and move his mouth. 'My wife's favourite Elvis song. Knew all the words if you can believe that, the way he sings it so fast, but she won't be listening to it again, will she?' I said. 'Because you fucked her up, didn't you?' I was just about ready to let the air out of his head now.

'No...I....'

'You fucked her up and then you burned her.'

I expected fear, the guilty look of a man who's been caught with his pants round his ankles and his dick in the wrong woman's mouth, but that's not what I got. I got confusion and doubt. I've stood over a lot of different people at a lot of different times and they've all tried to fool me no matter how guilty they were, but none of them ever looked as confused as he did. You can tell a lot from the way a guy begs for his life, and with him, it was like he was hearing all this for the first time. It was the same look he'd given me in his flat when I mentioned the Sledgehammer.

'Don't look so surprised, Jack. You were there,' I said, wanting to see if the reaction was the same. 'You pulled the trigger, blasting away into the boot where you put my wife after your fuck up at MacFarlane's. You'll be telling me you didn't kill Carpetto next.'

'Who? No. No, I didn't. I...' If he was faking it, then he was good.

'And let me guess; you don't have my box either?'

'No but...'

'And what the *fuck* did you think you were going to do with this?' I shouted, taking the gun away from the girl's lips and pointing it at him. 'You planning on killing *me* now, is that it? Take my property for yourself?' The fact that he'd brought the gun said something, but not much. Anybody in his position would've done the same thing. You're going to see your girlfriend and there might be some fucked up psycho gangster in her house, what would you do? Pack some heat or rely on fierce looks and harsh language? 'You thought you were gonna pop me? That you would somehow get away with this?' I came close to him and grabbed the collar of his jacket, ignoring the smell of his burnt hair.

'No. No. I didn't touch your wife,' he said leaning away, his voice starting to come back a little. 'I swear it. I promise.' Its pitch getting higher now that everything was starting to sink in. 'It was an accident. It was a fuckin' stupid accident.' He was more animated with each word, every inch of his face was pleading me not to pop him.

'It was no accident,' I pressed the gun to his head. 'You shot her. I know you did. I had a man on you, keeping me up to date. He said you shot my wife and you shot Carpetto, and then you burned them up.'

His eyebrows nearly crossed over, switched sides and jumped off his face this time. 'What? No. He's wrong,' he said. 'She was still alive, then some woman came. Tony. She killed my brother...'

It had a kind of justice.

'...she shot him before he could do anything. She was gonna kill me too but your wife stopped her. She stopped her...'

Everything was coming loose now, the kid looking like he didn't know what the hell I was talking about, his mouth running away with him, and I tried to remember what Deeks said happened down there at Hadlebridge. About Carpetto getting wasted and about the kid blasting away like Bonnie and Clyde and now I was thinking that he must've reloaded the gun if he'd emptied it into the back of the car and I was wondering how he would've done that. He would've had to get the better of Carpetto, shoot her – twice, Deeks said – and then empty the gun into the boot - I'm pretty sure Deeks said he *emptied* it into the boot – then find some rounds, reload, and torch the car. And from the look and smell of him, Presley must've got caught in that fire himself. And then there was the third guy. I mean, what the hell happened to the *third* guy?

No, what Deeks told me was close to what Presley was saying, but it wasn't the same. It was obvious the kid wasn't a stone cold killer, it was all over his face, but I couldn't think why Deeks would've lied about what happened.

'...and she told me where the box is,' he was still babbling.

Unless Deeks was hiding something, like how he could've stepped in; like how he could've stopped this from happening.

'*Then* you killed her?' I said, pushing him hard, thinking that either way it didn't really matter. Presley and the girl were going to die whatever happened; I'd deal with Deeks later.

'No. Then the car blew up,' he was coming back down now, all his energy used up. 'There was petrol everywhere, all over the car and then Hornrim lit up and... no one killed her. It was an accident. A stupid accident. I swear it.' He hung his head and his tone changed. He wasn't pleading anymore, he just sounded tired, like he'd had enough. 'I didn't kill your wife.' He looked at me. 'But I do know where your box is.'

I closed my eyes and breathed hard, pinching the bridge of my nose with my free hand. The box. Of course. It was all about the box. Maybe the kid's brother knew about it. Magda *definitely* knew about it. Carpetto, too. In fact, Poppy the fucking cat probably knew about it, so why not Deeks? Why not him? It would've been a good reason to lie, and I'd given him the perfect opportunity to watch what happened to it.

Maybe my first instincts about the kid had been right. Jack Presley was the one person who *hadn't* lied to me in all this. The only one.

DAN SMITH

JACK

'I didn't kill your wife.' I looked up at Montoya and saw that his eyes were different. When I came in they'd been burning, like he was going to finish it all right there, but now he looked calmer, his eyes flicking away to the picture on the wall by the stairs. It was some kind of Chinese symbol, a black character on a red background with a green surround. Mandy had bought it from a shop in town last year and told me what the symbol meant – something deep and meaningful – but I couldn't ever remember what it was. 'But I do know where your box is,' I said.

It was all I could give him to take his mind off his wife and what he thought I'd done to her; the only thing I had to bargain with and it seemed to do the trick. His jaw relaxed just enough to show me his diamond tooth. His eyes winked alight, his brain turned over in his skull and his shoulders relaxed, lowering the gun a few inches so that it was pointing at my chin instead of my nose. 'Tell me.'

Things were calming down now. They'd dropped a notch and we'd come back down from eleven. Montoya's rage had gone, and I think he knew I hadn't killed his wife so I took a risk and said, 'Why don't I get it for you?'

'Don't fuck around, kid, Just tell me where it is.'

I had to say something so I told him, 'It's at the hotel.'

'The Monterez? Where? Some kind of safety deposit?'

'If I tell you, you'll kill us.'

'You can bet I'll kill you if you don't,' he said.

I hesitated.

'Okay.' Montoya stepped back and waved us into the room at the end of the hallway. 'In the kitchen.'

It was cosy in there, the lights were on and the colours were warm. There was a white mug, upside down beside the chrome sink. A cartoon girl was painted on the side and she was surrounded by the words 'Sex Goddess'. I imagined Mandy drinking tea from it.

'Sit down.'

We sat down at the table, side by side, and I reached out to hold Mandy's hand. God knows what she was thinking; what must have been going through her mind after having Montoya in her house and then me turning up looking like I did. With my eyes, I started to tell her I was sorry, but then Montoya sat opposite us and said, 'Hands on the table.'

We did as we were told, palms down, fingers spread. The table felt cool.

He leaned forward and touched the barrel of the gun to Mandy's lips again. 'Now,' he said looking at me. 'We had an agreement. Two things. One of them you've fucked up already...'

'I didn't touch her. I already told you that. I didn't touch her.'

He sighed and lowered his arm so that it was resting on the table, elbow to forearm. The gun was still in his fist and the butt clunked against the wood. 'Just tell me where the fuckin' box is.'

'Will you let us go?'

'Would you believe me if I said yes?' He didn't wait for an answer. 'Look kid, no bargains, no deals, no nothing, all right? Maybe you didn't hear me right the first time so I'll say it again. I want that box. *Then* I'll decide what we're going to do. You don't tell me right away, maybe I'll start getting interested in knees and elbows. Hands and feet, too.'

Since I arrived at the house, Mandy had been silent. Not a word until that moment. She looked at me, then she looked at Montoya and said 'Please,' her voice soft but firm and loud, not quiet so you could hardly hear it. 'Please.' And that's when I knew I had no choice. I had to give him what he wanted.

'Okay,' I said standing up. 'I have a key. She told me where the box is.' I looked at him, asking without words if it was okay to show him. He nodded okay, so I slid a hand into my trouser pocket and removed the key. I held it up for him to see. 'It opens a safety deposit box in the hotel. Box two-eleven.'

'That's what she told you?'

'That's what she told me.'

'Put the key on the table and sit down.'

I placed the small silver key in the centre of the table and slowly lowered myself back into the seat. Montoya palmed the key and reached across to push Mandy's head down onto the table.

Mandy didn't resist and he didn't use a lot of force. When her left cheek was flat against the wood, Montoya touched the gun to the top of her head and looked at me. 'You did the right thing, kid, I'll make it quick for both of you.'

MANDY

When the man pressed my face to the table and put the gun against my head, I closed my eyes, thought about Jack, and waited for him to kill me. There wasn't anything else I could do. Except say 'Don't lie to him, Jack.'

'What?' They said it together, the same surprise in both voices, but they each knew what I meant.

The man stood up and took the gun away from my head, so I opened my eyes and watched him looking at me, his mind running through what I'd just said. The way it seemed to me was that I might not know the detail, but I could see what was going on. He wanted something to which only Jack could lead him. And if Jack were lying about the Monterez, then maybe the man would never see this box that he was after. Especially if he killed us both. What I just said was the only reason for him to keep us alive, and he knew it right away.

He shook his head at me. 'You're bluffing right? Trying to save yourself?'

I sat up and looked at Jack, but he didn't know how to react so I looked at the man with the gun. He raised it to my face again, wavered, then turned away and walked the length of the kitchen. It's not a big kitchen, so it didn't take long and he was back with us in seconds. He ran a hand across his slick-backed hair and sighed. Then he flattened his palm on the table and hunched his shoulders so that his overcoat hitched up and made it look as if he'd left the hanger in. 'Shit,' he said and did the walk again. When he arrived back in front of us, I could tell that he'd made up his mind what he was going to do. It didn't come as any great surprise, though, it was the obvious choice. 'All right,' he said. 'Have you got any rope?'

'No,' I said to him.

'How about tights, stockings, that kind of thing? You must have something like that.'

'Upstairs,' I said. 'In the bedroom.' My lips burned where he had pressed the gun against them and they felt tight when I spoke.

'Go get 'em,' he said.

I stood up slowly and looked at him.

He pulled Jack's chair away from the table and pointed the gun at Jack's knee. 'Well go on then, sweetheart, don't dilly dally.'

I went straight upstairs to the bedroom and opened my underwear drawer. I had a few pairs of tights and stockings, nothing too kinky, so I grabbed them in one hand and closed the drawer.

I looked at myself in the mirror that was above the dressing table. I was tired and pale with dark, saggy half-moons under my eyes and hair like a bag lady, but I didn't look half as bad as Jack did. My poor Jack. I knew Sean would cause trouble. I took a small pot from my dresser and rubbed on some mango lip balm while leaning closer to the mirror to see the damage. Bloody thug, burning my lips like that.

I stared into my own eyes. Green and white and black and bloodshot. I was more scared than I'd ever been in my life, but I wasn't going to die, and this was my chance, right now, upstairs where the thug couldn't see me. There wasn't a lot that I could do, not while he was holding a gun to Jack, but I had a pretty good idea of what he was up to so I should be able to do *something*.

I was sure I'd put enough doubt in his mind that he wasn't going to kill us right now. He'd come back and do that once he had his box. If the box wasn't at the Monterez, then maybe he'd come back and kill me to make Jack talk.

He'd be saving me for that one. But the only way he could make sure we'd still be here when he came back was by tying us up somehow, and that meant he was going to leave us alone. And I was buggered if I was going to be there when he came back.

*

Within a few minutes of going back into the kitchen, Jack and I were facing each other, attached to our seats, hands tied behind our backs and feet bound to the chair legs. Once he had us secured, the thug ran the crotch of a pair of tights around Jack's forehead, pulling his neck backwards, and tied the legs down to his wrists behind him. Jack's head was held right back, face to the ceiling, and the gusset of my tights was flopping in his face - which was bizarre. If it hadn't been so frightening it would have been funny.

Then the thug rummaged in the kitchen drawers, the sound of metal clattering on metal, and came to stand behind Jack. He flipped my gusset back out of his face so that it was lying over his head like a prayer hat and he looked down. 'Open wide,' he said.

Jack opened his mouth and the thug slipped a large kitchen knife into it. He pushed it down until the point touched the roof of his mouth.

'Bite,' he said. When Jack bit the knife, the thug let go of it. 'Try to talk and...well, you work it out, you're a smart guy.'

He did the same thing to me.

'Don't go anywhere, will you?' he said when he was done. 'I'll be back as soon as I can. And you'd better fuckin' pray that I get what I want. If you're lying about that box, then I'm gonna drop in on the hardware shop on the way back. Buy me a nice big hammer and a bag of nails.'

He left the kitchen and I listened to his footsteps in the hall. I heard the front door open, then he was gone.

No time to waste, I immediately went for the scissors. It wasn't easy because my wrists were bound tightly and my head was in an uncomfortable position. I could also feel the point of the knife just where the roof of my mouth is soft and fleshy and I was worried that the chair would topple backwards making it slip down my throat.

I moved my hands around as much as I dared, trying to stretch the nylon that was binding my wrists. Once they were a little looser, I wriggled my fingers down towards my bum. I felt the thick lip of my back pocket, pushed inside it and then I was touching the handle of the nail-scissors I'd taken from my dresser. I hooked my finger into the ring and tried to pull. The position was awkward and the chair wobbled backwards. I shifted my weight forwards, preventing myself from going right over and held the position, working my stomach muscles hard. From there I tried again. Being further forward helped, the blades of the scissors were no longer stuck underneath my bum, and they easily slipped out of my pocket. After that it was simply a case of cutting through my tights. I'd make Jack buy me some more when this was over.

JACK

Mandy was amazing, so strong, I couldn't have asked for more. No crying, no complaining, no whining, no tears, no nothing. She thought fast and acted even faster, standing up beside me like a jack-in-the-box.

She held up the scissors for me to see, snipped them once in the air, then cut me loose and threw them onto the table where the key had been. 'What the *hell* is going on?' she asked.

I was so proud of her, I hugged her and kissed the top of her head before saying, 'Wait here.'

I went to the kitchen door and looked into the hallway to check that it was clear.

'What's going on?' she asked again when I came back. She was holding a bottle of vodka in one hand and a mug in the other. It was the ' Sex Goddess' mug from beside the sink.

'It's complicated,' I said.

'*Complicated?*' She drained the mug.

'Yeah. I'm not sure I really know myself.'

She sploshed some vodka into the mug and gave it to me saying, 'Try me.'

'Not now, it'll take too long. And there's something we have to do.'

'Like what?' she said. 'We can't stay here.'

I knocked back the vodka, feeling it burn hot and cold on its way down. 'No, not for long anyway. If he doesn't find what he's looking for, he'll come back. Probably come back anyway.'

'And *will* he find what he's looking for?' she asked.

'I don't know.'

'And did you do what he said? To his wife, I mean?' She looked right through me.

'No. I didn't.'

'I didn't think so,' she said and moved back to perch her bum on the edge of the table, putting her hands behind her for support. 'It was Sean?'

I nodded.

'And is he...?'

I nodded again and Mandy left it at that, waiting a while before saying, 'So what's this box he's after?' I couldn't believe how calm she was but I was glad for it, it made things a lot easier.

'Don't know,' I said. 'She told me it was some kind of painting.' As I spoke, I felt in my pocket for the business card which Magda had given me a lifetime ago. 'Doesn't really matter, anyway. Whatever it is, it's worth a lot of money, and it's supposed to be in that safety deposit box.' When I pulled it out, it was soft and crumpled, and felt a little damp. Like both its carriers, it had been through a lot.

White card, black print, colourful logo in the corner. A name, an address and a telephone number. Harry Milton was the name and it rang a few distant bells.

'Don't drink any more of that,' I said to Mandy. 'We'll have to take your car.'

I went into the hallway and lifted the phone. 'Do the right thing', Magda had said. I dialed the number on the card and then paused with my finger over the send button. It was the right thing to do. I pressed the button and the number dialed through. It rang a few times and I wondered if anyone would come.

'Yes?' The voice sounded tired.

'I want to talk to Harry Milton,' I said.

'Who's calling?'

'I want to talk to Harry Milton, is he there?'

'I'm sorry, sir, but unless you tell me your name, I can't process the call.' The voice was direct, matter of fact. Can't do that, sir; more than my job's worth, sir; you'll have to do as I say, sir; fuck you, sir.

'Presley,' I said, knowing what the reply would be. 'My name is Jack Presley.'

'This some kind of joke?'

Yep, I was right. 'Oh for fuck's sake, I don't have time for this,' I said. 'Just put him on the phone.' I told him that if I got to speak to Harry Milton sometime in the next five seconds, then there was a strong chance that I could give him what he wanted on some guy called Montoya. If not, I was going to put the phone down and he could go f...

'*Sawn-off* Montoya? One moment,' said the voice and the line went quiet.

Several seconds later, someone else came on. 'Yes?' It was a voice that didn't take any shit.

'Harry Milton?'

'Yes.'

'I'm a friend of Magda's. She asked me to give you something.'

'Magda? Is she okay.' His words were guarded.

'Not really, no.'

'What's happened?'

'She wanted me to give you something. A stolen box.'

'The St. Francis? Where is it? Has she got it?'

I told him the hotel name, the safety box number. 'Montoya's gone to pick it up,' I said.

'*Sawn-off* Montoya? You sure about that?'

'One hundred percent.'

'How long before he's there?' he sounded excited like a teenager about to have sex the first time. No more Mr. I Don't Take Any Shit.

'Not long,' I said. 'If you go now you'll catch him.'

'And what about Magda? Is she...'

I hung up the phone and leaned back against the wall, breathing hard. If Milton wanted Montoya bad enough, he'd go to the hotel whether he thought it was a crank call or not. I didn't have time to give him the whole story and he'd find out soon enough anyway.

'Now we go to the police,' I said to Mandy. 'Magda said Milton would help us if he gets what he wants.'

'And will he?'

'I don't know. Hope so,' I said and kissed her cheek. 'Come on. We'll go in your car.'

I left Mandy to collect her keys and coat while I went outside to move Carpetto's car away from the garage.

Outside, it was a new day but it was still dark and it felt like the same one. I climbed into the BMW, fired the engine and moved the car enough to give Mandy the room to drive out. Then I switched it off and sat in silence and watched the house. It wasn't long before Mandy appeared. She closed the front door, locked it and walked to the garage. She was beautiful. She had to stretch to open the garage door and her figure looked good the way her clothes tightened around it. I wasn't ever going to let her go.

I bowed my head and rubbed my eyes with both hands, ignoring the sting from the burns. It was over. No more guns, no more fires, no more threats, no more pain. No one wins, everybody loses, but at least it was over.

Then, from the corner of my eye, a glimpse of something in the foot well of the passenger seat. Black and silver, hiding in the night.

Mandy pulled her car onto the drive, flicked on the headlights and waited for me. I leaned over and lifted one of the briefcases from the footwell. I placed it on the seat, popped the two catches and opened the top. I stared at all that cash. There was thousands in there. *Thousands*.

Huh. You had to love the irony.

BURN OUT

Buy this book at:

www.lulu.com/dansmith

www.amazon.com